1

MaskerAde

"Call me . . . *Captain Commanding*!" I shouted as I launched myself into the air.

"Whatever, *Evan*." Glen rolled his eyes, but I pretended not to notice.

"That's just my secret identity," I replied, returning to the ground where Glen was having his wire rig connections double-checked. "It's not the real me."

Well, actually it was. Evan Quick, mild-mannered and utterly ordinary kid, that's me. But not today. Today was my thirteenth birthday, and for the next two hours, with the help of the game room at MaskerAde Pizzeria I was about to become Captain Commanding, the world's greatest hero.

The MaskerAde game technician moved on from Glen to check Jamal's rig, and I jumped into the air again, using the movie-style flying rig to do a double backflip before I landed. On the big curved screen in front of us my Captain Commanding avatar did the same—pretty awesome!

"You're really good at that," said Maria, the fourth member of our little group and my neighbor from across the alley.

I grinned. "I practice a lot. The home rig doesn't let you jump as high, or do more than a single flip, but that one gets you a killer knockout kick in Masks Versus Hoods if you can manage it."

"I wish my parents would buy me the fly rig for my Game-Device," said Jamal. "But we live in an apartment, and they say management won't let them mount it to the rafters. *Weak.*"

The technician finished up with Maria. "You kids are good to go." She looked at me. "Your parents paid for two hours. I'll hit the buzzer and give you a ten-minute warning when your time's almost up. Till then, have fun."

Glen grinned. "Start with Masks Versus Hoods, me and Jamal against you two?"

"Sure." I nodded and stepped back into my quadrant.

Unlike a home GameDevice setup, MaskerAde had a full circle green screen that allowed them to really put you inside the experience. They also had their flight rigs hooked up to pivoting overhead arms that let you move around a lot more than the fixed home version. Add in a fancier version of the regular 3-D goggles and earpiece set and you were pretty much inside the world of the game.

I did a quick run-through of some of the Captain's best moves, and watched my avatar do the same. After that I slammed back a MaskerAde energy drink—MaskerAde was nearly as big a franchise as Captain Commanding. Then, I dropped the can in the hamper. I was ready to rumble. I clenched my fists and bowed to the center of the circle. In response, the avatar moved over and settled around me. For the next two hours, I was going to be Captain Commanding!

Then I heard Jamal whisper, "Why does *he* get to be Captain Commanding?"

Glen hissed back, "Because it's his birthday party, knucklehead."

That brought me down a little, mostly because it reminded me Jamal wasn't really my friend. I mean, we were on the same track team and all, but I just wasn't one of the jocks. Not in the way Glen and Jamal were. Sure, I worked my butt off in track and with the weights. But that was because I wanted—more than anything in the world—to be a real Mask, with powers and everything—not because I liked working out.

Actually, none of the others were *real* friends. Glen was the one track jock who went beyond tolerating me into something almost like being friends—when we were at meets or if my parents were buying MaskerAde pizza and the game room, anyway. Jamal was just part of the package if you invited Glen anywhere. And Maria, well, she was my neighbor—just kind of there—and you needed four players to get the most out of renting the game room.

I pushed all that aside. Not having friends wasn't the worst thing in the world. No, that was Spartanicus—the Captain's archenemy. That, and not having my own powers. Well, not normally anyway. But now the game activated, and Glen turned into Spartanicus, and right here, right now, I was going to kick his butt! Beside me, Maria turned into Flareup and we charged Spartanicus and Jamal—who was playing as SteamPunk.

After a couple of bouts of free-for-all, we paused and slammed another round of MaskerAde, then switched to scenario play—my favorite.

We started with the very first appearance of Spartanicus. I was flying over Heropolis alone—Maria would come in later with this one, after I got tagged out. I saw a green flash below as the back wall of the City Mutual Bank exploded outward. I pivoted in the air and blinked left-right-left-left to order the flying rig to let me land.

As I dropped toward the pavement, I tried to really *be* the Captain, experiencing this scene for the first time, pretending that I hadn't seen the historical vids a hundred times. Of course, in the real world, the Captain had arrived in the Commanding Car, but that wasn't nearly as cool as flying in—*and stop thinking so much, Evan! Just enjoy the moment!*

"What's happening, citizen?" I asked one of the civilians knocked over by the blast. "Can I help?"

There was another green flash, and my wire rig yanked me sideways to simulate being hit by the beam. I landed hard on my butt, but turned it into a backward roll, jumping high into the air when I got my feet back under me. I got my first look at Spartanicus then. A big man, he had scars on his face and wore a sort of leather gladiator's outfit. He stood in the hole in the bank's wall with a sword in one hand and a small round shield in the other.

I blinked three times and lasers shot from my eyes. Spartanicus moved with impossible speed, interposing his shield and redirecting the beams so they hit my feet. That tipped me forward, and I balled up both fists, flying straight at Spartanicus. The scar in the center of his forehead ripped open, exposing a green jewel and a blast of energy hit me full in the face.

The indicator in the corner of my goggles blinked a red warning to tell me I'd taken a big hit, but I ignored it, just as Captain Commanding had all those years ago. I had to protect the civilians injured by the original blast, whatever the cost. Spartanicus put up his shield again, and I flipped over in the air so that I slammed into it feet first. The game stuttered a bit as I changed what had happened. I actually knocked Glen out of his avatar for a moment. But it caught up a second later as the image blinked over to cover him up again.

He bounced back to his feet a moment later and came at me, but I did the double-backflip-kick move, smashing him into the shattered bank vault door. I pretty much cleaned the floor with him for a little while after that. Which isn't how it went in real life. But, while I'm not much of a jock, I know everything there is to know about the Captain and how to make the best use of his powers in Masks Versus Hoods.

In fact, I was pretty much on my way to rewriting Mask history by taking down Spartanicus for good, when a deadly ninja throwing-gear hit me square in the face, and my rig dragged me backward into the bank teller's desk. The display told me I was KO'd and had a five-second timeout.

I wanted to shout *Unfair!* SteamPunk hadn't even gotten his powers yet when this fight happened. But it was a four-player game, and they had to bring the others in somehow. *Fine.* I gritted my teeth and held still while Spartanicus and SteamPunk did a completely out-of-character victory chest bump. They were just turning to come at me again, when a gigantic blast of blue energy tumbled them both sideways.

That was mostly accurate. Foxman *had* saved Captain Commanding at the bank that day, but Maria insisted on playing the girl version of the Foxman armor, and that messed with my head. The helmet and mask were right, with the classic Foxman grin, and so was the metal tail that still somehow contrived to look fluffy, but the rest was plain wrong. Not that anyone cared much about a has-been like Foxman anymore.

But, I was a giant Mask nerd, and the girl armor made my inner purist itch almost as much as the arrival of SteamPunk with his throwing-gears and aether rays. I'm not sure if it was better or worse that she'd chosen to crossplay Foxman—who at least had been there—than if it would have been if she'd played one of the many girl Masks that hadn't. But then my time-out was done, and I forgot about everything but being Captain Commanding and beating the heck out of Spartanicus.

We took a five-minute break to catch our breaths after that round, and to have another MaskerAde each—the stuff was awesome! Then we moved to another scenario. This one played out at the Colonel Cuddlebear factory where they make all those custom Masked-animal plushies. Of course, Colonel Cuddlebear isn't a *real* Mask. Sure, she's got some seriously buff powers, but she hardly ever uses them for anything but marketing. She *had* messed up the Fluffinator pretty good when he tried to animate the Cuddlebear plushies to take over Heropolis, but that hardly counted. It was mostly in defense of her brand. And seriously, "Cuddlebear?" *Please*.

Jamal played the Fluffinator and Maria switched to Cuddlebear while Glen and I stayed the same. Captain Commanding hadn't really been there, and neither had Spartanicus, but there was something about punching a six-foot stuffed bunny into a cloud of white fluff that made me forget to be grumpy about the inaccuracy.

One fist directly on the button nose, and, *POOF!* The world's biggest dandelion-down explosion. It was so much fun that we all forgot about hitting each other for a while as we went after the army of plushies. Flip, kick, *POOF!* Jump, spin, laser eyes, and *FIZZ!* Flaming, exploding dandelion. Pure, joyous destruction, and we unlocked Cuddlebear for full play, so Maria stayed in that role when we moved back to straight up Masks Versus Hoods for our last couple rounds.

Mom and Dad were waiting for us at the table with the pizza already ordered when we got out.

"And another round of MaskerAde," said my mother, "because I'm a saint and I don't want the sugar crash to hit till you're all home."

There wasn't much to do after that except eat and take everyone home. We didn't really have a lot to talk about outside of the game. I mentioned that none of them were what you'd call real friends, right? Maybe I'd better explain.

I'm smart enough to do well in my classes without busting my butt, but I'm not that into academics, and I don't hang around with the brains and the grinds. The athletes tolerate me because I do bust my butt there, but they're not my natural crowd either. The geeks are probably closest to being my people, because a lot of them are pretty Mask crazy, too. But my—by their standards—wholly unnatural association with the jocks makes me a little too suspect.

It's weird, really. All the books and vids about school paint everyone as being *in* or *out*. Either you're popular and everyone loves you even if you're mostly a jerk. Or, you're not popular and you get shoved into lockers. Nobody tells stories about kids like me who slide through school with no real connections and no real enemies. Kids who are just *there*.

Sometimes it makes me feel like I don't exist, like I'm a ghost. That's how my teachers treat me, too, like furniture. Mom says it's because I don't cause enough trouble for them to worry about me, and I don't brain it up enough to be a pet. Whatever the reason, I'm not really close to any of the other kids, and I'm okay with that.

Really.

2

Camp Commanding

My alarm went off at nine, like it does every day in summer—my mom doesn't want me to get too out of touch with getting up in the morning. I stared at the little beeping devil and willed it to turn off like I did every day ever. Nothing. So I willed it to blow up, catch fire, fly out my window, and turn into a frog, each in turn.

It just kept beeping.

So, no mental powers. Also, I felt like I'd been run over by a bus. I decided to blame it on drinking most of a case of MaskerAde the day before. I smacked my alarm to make it shut up, and moved on to the next big test—rolling out of bed . . . and not catching myself.

It's tougher than you might think.

I hit the floor hard and banged my nose. It hurt.

So, no flight and no invulnerability.

Grabbing the leg of my bed, I lifted. No superstrength either. Also, no laser eyes, no power jewels sliding around under my skin, no hurricane breath, and no stretching my arms and legs like taffy.

All around, a disappointing morning. Oh, and did I mention that I felt like burned toast? Because I really, really did. Still, I had things I was supposed to do, so I dragged myself off to the bathroom for a shower and all the other stupid morning things that people without powers had to do. Maybe my mom would let me go back to bed afterward if I fell asleep in my oatmeal.

Whatever happened next, I was going to have another superboring entry in my hero's log. Superboring appears to be my only real power.

~~~ ~~~

"Evan Quick, Hero's log, May the 25th, and . . . no. I just can't do this. I'm not twelve anymore, and I am *never* going to be a Mask. Get over yourself, Evan."

With a sigh I flicked off the camera on my phone and reached for the button to trash the video. It was always kind of a stupid dream, and my thirteenth birthday was as good a reason to admit that as any. No one knew what gave people superpowers. Not these days, and there was never going to be another Hero Bomb. I was out of luck.

When my phone offered me the option to "select all" of the videos in my hero's log folder, I stabbed the button with my thumb. It really was time to give up. Past time.

"Delete?"

No real Mask could possibly feel as wrecked as I did right then. If a sugar crash could take me out like this, what hope did I really have? I clicked yes and there was a dream dead. Thirteen for twenty-four whole hours and a complete failure already. Nothing to look forward to except high school, a boring degree in college, and years of drudgery afterward. I might as well plan on majoring in accounting like my dad and get it over with.

I fell back on the bed and stared at the poster of Captain Commanding on the wall above. It was life-size. The big man wore a red, white, and blue uniform and had one arm out like it was resting on your shoulders. I'd always done my hero's log sitting in front of it so it would look like we were friends or something. Kind of pathetic, no?

"Evan, honey, are you ready?" My mother called up the stairs. "We need to leave for Camp Commanding soon."

"I'll be down in a minute, Mom."

Awkward. Here I was giving up my Mask dream on the same day Mom took me to get a season pass to Camp Commanding—the promised land for Mask nerds. This was the first year I was going to be allowed to go by myself. I should probably have told her to forget it, since all I really wanted to do was go back to sleep, but I didn't want to let her down.

She and my dad had been indulging my Mask fantasies for ages. I'd never exhibited the tiniest sign of any kind of powers, but they were always willing to drive me to see the latest hero movies in megamax 3-D, or buy me tickets to Camp Commanding, or pick up a fresh box of Commanding Grahams for breakfast. Whatever, they were supersupportive—always telling me I could grow up to be anything I wanted, no matter how ridiculous.

Seriously? Both of *them* had supersupportive parents, too, and look where they ended up. Dad's an actuary, kind of the nerd king of accountants. Mom's a professor at a big university where she teaches and does mathematical modeling of adhesives. That's what they wanted to be when they grew up? I don't think so.

Not when my grandparents include Dad's moms, the ballerina-turned-choreographer and her wife, the painter. My other grandmother is a chef, and her husband writes comics. They met when *their* parents' communes had a joint event. With that much cool in the generation before my parents, what happened? Some kind of zombie math ray? Or maybe every generation of my family was less awesome than the last. If so, I was utterly doomed.

"Honey, we need to go now!"

"Be right there!" I sat up, flipped my worn old Captain Commanding bedspread into a rough semblance of a made bed and stumbled down the stairs. I was totally beat. Maybe I could catch a nap on one of the slower rides.

⚡︎ ⚡︎

The parking lot had already soaked up a ton of sunlight, and opening the car door felt like opening an oven. Instant sweat monster. I paused before getting out, staring up at the fifty-foot fiberglass statue of the Captain that towered over the entrance to Camp Commanding. Today, he looked like he was judging me for giving up on my Mask dream . . .

My mom poked me in the arm and said, "That's it, no more MaskerAde for you, kiddo. You crash too hard the next day."

I sighed and rolled my eyes, but she might have a point. I was tired and I felt weird.

"Honey, are you all right?" My mother was giving me the strangest look, and I realized I still hadn't gotten out of the car.

"Mm-fine." I started shuffling toward the entrance to the park.

My mother fell in beside me. "Oh my, have we hit the grunting phase of teen communication already? That came on rather suddenly." She laughed. "I can roll with that. For the next—what, four years or so—grunt once for yes and twice for no, and I'll slide all your meals under the door of your room." She tilted her head to one side. "Or maybe you could learn to grunt in Morse code. That'd be adorable."

I stuck my hands deep in my pockets and hunched my shoulders. It really wasn't fair to have parents who were so intent on *understanding* and *supporting* you. I couldn't remember the last time I'd gotten yelled at. Not even when I yelled at them first—*do you know how frustrating that is?*

When I was three, they applauded when I had a giant grocery store meltdown, then rated it like an Olympic event. When I was ten, I had a fit about having to give them all my online passwords "for emergencies." Afterward, they produced a plastic replica of an Academy Award with my name on it. Well, really, it was a Captain Commanding action figure spray painted gold, but how do a couple of math nerds even think of that? Seriously, it drives me crazy sometimes how cool they try to be.

Most of the other kids at school had normal parents—there, but kind of vaguely in the background. Mine kept forcing me to pay attention to them by giving my every word serious thought and *listening* all the time. Sure, they mocked me, but only when I was being ridiculous. Infuriating at the time, if only aggravating in retrospect.

I sighed and rolled my eyes again—this time at myself. One

completely unfair side effect of having parents like mine is that it's really hard to sustain a sulk. You get to thinking about what you're doing, and then pretty soon you can't help but laugh. Not that I would ever admit that to Mom.

"Honey?"

"Yeah, Mom." I glanced up. "What is it?"

"Have a good day." She leaned in and gave me a quick peck on the cheek—*gross*.

"What?" We were only about a third of the way to the park's entrance, and here she was half turned around to head back to the car already. Had she figured out I wasn't really interested anymore? That would be a big relief, but . . . "Wait, aren't you supposed to be buying me a ticket?" *So confused.*

She laughed and waved her phone at me. "Already did, online, last night. New feature this year." She pressed a button on the screen. A half second later my phone binged at me. "Pass is on your phone now, wave it over the reader at the gate and you're in. I only wanted to walk up with you for old time's sake. But you look like you need some alone time, so I'm going to leave you here. Call if you need me to pick you up before the park closes."

"I . . . what about dinner?" Or lunch, for that matter?

"Online pass comes with meals. Wave your phone over the reader. It'll bill me." She looked over the top of her glasses. "But don't think that means you're going to eat garbage. I picked the healthy meals option, and the system won't let you buy anything that doesn't have a green sticker on it. So, no MaskerAde, no chips, no candy. Not on my dime anyway. Love you." Then she was walking away.

"Mom?"

She glanced over her shoulder. "Yes."

"Thanks . . . for giving me some space."

She snorted. "You're thirteen, you're going to need a lot of it."

Before I could think of anything sarcastic to say, she started walking again. Okay, they might drive me crazy, but my folks *were* kind of cool. As I got closer to the gates, I saw Glen and Jamal lining up ahead of me and ducked behind a handy adult so they wouldn't see me. They played basketball, too, and were with some of the guys from the team—not my people at all.

They spotted me anyway, and Manny, their semiofficial leader—team captain—called out, "Hey, Quick, where's your Dorkman suit?"

I winced inwardly, but knew better than to let it show. "It's in the Dorkmobile, of course."

My Dorkman suit was an acid-green spandex running shirt and matching tights my parents had bought me for winter track. Most of the other runners on my track team went in for loose running pants and baggy shirts. The one time I wore spandex to a practice, they'd called me out for wearing a Dorkman suit. It had taken me three months and a couple of fights to get the track guys to stop ribbing me about it. Unfortunately, the basketball team hadn't given up yet.

Manny made a big show of surprise. "What, you're not going to wear it into the park? I'd think this is the perfect place for it."

I shook my head sadly. "Dude, secret identity, duh!"

He smiled. "Good answer, Quick. You're not so bad. A little

15

weird, but all right. You thinking about trying out for basketball this year?"

"I might." You couldn't pay me enough, but I wasn't about to say that to the team captain. "But you guys are really good, and the competition's tough." No harm in buttering him up a bit if it'd get me out of the hot seat.

It seemed to work, because they went back to joking among themselves and left me alone after that. That was all to the good. I'm actually pretty bad at athletics, especially for someone on the track team. I do it anyway because, well . . . I looked up at the giant sculpture of Captain Commanding—because of that.

Have you ever really wanted something? I mean really, deep down in your bones? So bad you would do practically anything to get it? That's how I felt about being a Mask. I get picked last in any team sport, and I trip over my own feet if I'm not careful. But I'm still on track, and I lift weights with the real jocks every day of the school year.

It's not because I like running or weightlifting. I *hate* running. Every single second that I'm out there putting one foot in front of the other I'm thinking, *I hate this, I want to quit, I hate this, I want to quit, I hate . . . etc.* Lifting weights is even worse. You've got all the work and none of the changing scenery to keep you from being bored out of your skull. But I still do it. Do you know why? Because the Captain works out every day, and because I have spent every day of the last ten years wanting to become a Mask so I could be just like Captain Commanding.

My dream would be utterly and completely pathetic if he didn't make such a difference. He's the most important Mask in the whole world. Sure, he can come off as a little full of himself, but the dude's earned the right. He's saved tens of thousands of lives. Personally.

That's really what being a Mask is all about, at least for the true heroes—helping people. I *hate* how corny I sound when I think this kind of stuff, but it's true. If I had superpowers, I could be so much more than plain old me. I could do the kinds of things that would make the world a better place. I could make a difference!

But then I got up to the ticket reader—a life-size fiberglass Captain Commanding—and I needed to head into the park. I waved my phone between his extended left hand and his face and his laser eyes scanned the code.

The Captain's recorded voice boomed out, "Welcome to Camp Commanding! Do you have what it takes to be a hero, . . . *Evan* . . . *Quick*?" My name came out in a stilted computer voice. That was new, a special feature for electronic season pass holders maybe. *Creepy.* I was about to move on when the voice spoke again. "Please follow in the Captain's footsteps for your chance to prove yourself worthy, . . . *Evan* . . . *Quick*."

What on earth? I looked around and saw a series of footprints projected onto the sidewalk behind the fiberglass figure. The prints went in sequence, red print, white print, blue print, repeat. They led off to the left and around the spinning, twisting, blinking bulk of the Sparktopus. Most of the rides at Camp Commanding were themed around Hoods and their battles with the Captain. The Sparktopus had eight lightning-throwing mechanical arms—a real monster.

I stood there half looking at the prints for a long time, trying to decide whether to follow them. But then I finally figured, what else did I have to do?

They ended at a little building I didn't remember ever seeing before. It was mostly masked by a hedge, so no real surprise there, I guess. A big glass door slid aside and a disembodied voice spoke from the ceiling, "Welcome, . . . *Evan . . . Quick.* This is your lucky day. Our records show that you turned thirteen yesterday. Is that correct?"

"Yeah."

"Did you mean 'yes,' . . . *Evan . . . Quick?*"

"Yes."

"Thank you. Your recent birthday makes you eligible for a special Camp Commanding gift *and* a chance to win your very own Mask uniform. Please place your hand on the scanner."

Say what you will about my chance of ever developing any powers, having my own uniform still sounded pretty cool to me. When a big arrow lit up on the wall and pointed to a small green screen with the outline of a right hand printed on it, I slapped my hand down. The screen hummed, and a line of light slowly slid from bottom to top. As it touched my hand, I felt a scratchy-tingly sensation, like someone was running an electrified metal scraper gently down my fingers and palm.

It didn't quite hurt, but it was pretty uncomfortable. I wanted to jerk my hand away, but I couldn't make my arm move at all. Before I had time to get too worked up about it though, the sensation stopped and I lifted my hand. My palm was bright pink.

A moment later, I heard a sharp clunk and then a sound like

one of those giant gumball machines operating behind the wall in front of me. I noticed a tiny door with a basket underneath the hand scanner just as a clear plastic capsule dropped out of it.

"Please take your prize, . . . *Evan* . . . *Quick*, and wait while we process your entry." This was followed by the sort of stereotypical computer-processing sounds you might hear in a cheap Mask movie.

I picked up the capsule, finding it surprisingly heavy. Inside was a ring with the golden ankh logo of the Office of Strategic Intelligence and Research, International Section inset into the red stone in the bezel. OSIRIS was the agency in charge of metahuman affairs. That was kind of a letdown, actually, since I already had an OSIRIS decoder ring. But I opened the capsule anyway—mostly because of the weight. I was quite surprised when the heavy metal loop fell into my hand—this wasn't a cereal box extra. This felt every bit as substantial as my dad's college ring.

I slipped it onto my ring finger, where it fit perfectly. Okay, *that* was pretty awesome, and it made me feel better about the creepy hand scanner. The computer-processing noises suddenly stopped with a gentle chime.

"Congratulations . . . *Evan* . . . *Quick*, you have been randomly selected to win your very own Mask uniform made from real hero-grade materials. Please enter the booth for the full body measuring scan."

A section of wall sank in and slid aside with a sharp hiss, revealing a round closetlike room lined with small red disks that reminded me of bicycle reflectors. It was more than a little intimidating. But I looked at my new ring and thought about how cool it would be to have a real Mask uniform even if I never got any powers. The Halloween opportunities alone would justify taking the chance. Still, as I passed through the door, I couldn't help noticing how very thick and heavy it looked.

There were a pair of footprints printed on the floor. When I stepped into the prints, the door slid closed behind me. I was committed now. I heard the gumball machine noise again and looked around for another basket. This time, a little door popped open, spitting out a set of dark swim-meet style goggles.

"Please put on the goggles, . . . *Evan . . . Quick.*"

They were so dark I could barely see, but I dutifully put them on. A few seconds later, I was glad I had. Every single disk in the room lit up like a steroidal sun lamp, bathing me in red light. Even *with* the goggles on I found my eyes watering. Before I had time to get too freaked out over that, I found something much better to freak out about.

Remember the tingly itchy sensation the hand scanner had given me? That! Everywhere, and stronger, and not only on the surface either. It felt as if someone had wired a little tiny battery to every single cell in my body. Not painful, but not the least bit comfortable either.

It went on and on and on until I thought I was going to come apart. I wanted to curl into a ball or scream or . . . well, anything! But I couldn't. I couldn't move at all. The beams coming from the disks had me pinned as tight as any Hood who ever lost a battle to the Wrestleosaurus.

3

Breaking News

After a long, burning time the force holding me in place released me and the door opened. I staggered out into the little lobby area and would have left right then if the outer door hadn't refused to open. I was pretty panicky and I pulled out my cell phone to call my mom and have her come get me, but there was no reception. Probably for the best, since my lying phone's clock said it was less than fifteen minutes since I'd come through the front gate. I'd feel pretty stupid about calling her before she even got home.

I was still a little wobbly at that point, but the very familiar act of checking my phone settled me down enough to think. The first thing I noticed was that the stupid electronic voice was blathering away again.

". . . work for you?"

"What?" I asked.

"Do you want me to repeat the message, . . . *Evan . . . Quick*?"

"Yeah, uh, yes."

"Your measurements are complete, . . . *Evan . . . Quick*. Due to the difficulty of working with fabrics like Armex and Invulycra, it will take some hours to complete your custom Mask uniform. It will be ready at this building after 3:00 p.m. Will that time work for you?"

"Yes." Anything to get out of there.

"Please come back after three, . . . *Evan . . . Quick.*" The big glass door opened and I bolted out into the park.

How to describe Camp Commanding? It's big. Not Disneyland big, but big enough for two separate roller coasters and a whole pile of smaller rides. It smells like new plastic and cotton candy. Everything is oversize and shiny and—as much as I hated to admit it—a little desperate looking, like it's trying too hard to be awesome. Or maybe that was just me after the booth.

I felt really, really strange, like Jell-O with weird fruit in it, all bouncy-squishy-shiny with odd bits floating around my innards. That gave the whole place the feeling of walking through a nightmare, and I had the strangest impression that the endless hordes of fiberglass Captain Commanding figures were judging me.

"Shut up," I grumbled at a particularly concerned-looking statue, making a passing gaggle of nine-year-olds look at me strangely. *Wow, did I feel funky.*

I noticed a hot dog cart then, and dug out enough cash for a can of Metamorphosis—MaskerAde's main competitor. *I know, I know, but I really needed a pick-me-up, and technically I wasn't violating my mom's orders, since she hadn't mentioned* Metamorphosis, *just MaskerAde.* For the first time ever, I didn't get an immediate jolt of energy.

I rode the smaller of the two roller coasters next—the Commanderiat, followed by the Shocktopus—and my favorite ride in the park, the SuperCollider. It's basically a giant pinball machine where you get to ride inside the ball. Picture a big hamster ball with a pilot's chair hanging from a three-way swivel in the middle, and you've got the idea. The swivels don't move as fast as the ball, so when one of the big paddles hits the ball, you go rolling along head over heels for a while until you slow down enough for the chair to get back to hanging upright. That's usually when you run into another paddle or a bumper.

It's awesome! But I just couldn't shake off the weird feeling I'd gotten from the booth, no matter how much I tumbled around or spun in circles. So the rides started to wear after a while. I finally ended up at the Captain's Bunker. Supposedly it was an exact replica of the armored fortress-penthouse he uses as a base, though I sometimes wonder if the real thing has quite so many posters of the Captain. The Captain's gym has always been a favorite of mine. It's full of exhibits that let you see how you measure up to the Captain, like a target range with a helmet that lets you pretend you have laser eyes.

There was also a set of electronic dumbbells that started out at five thousand pounds but stepped down every few seconds until a normal human could lift them. They didn't look like much, and without the positronic magnets in the stand, they barely weighed ten pounds. But the grips were real indestructibilium—because anything less tough might shatter in the Captain's grip—and the dynamo that drove the magnet was designed by Foxman back when he was still a real hero.

That part wasn't mentioned in the exhibit, but I'd read it in an old issue of *Commanding Quarterly* that my dad bought for me in an online auction at Hero's List. Foxman used to be the Captain's best friend, but no one talked about it anymore. Or Foxman for that matter. Not since the tilted tower incident in October of '99. After that, he basically folded up and slowly slid out of sight.

The basketball team guys came rolling in a few seconds after I did and went straight for the dumbbells. I tried to sneak out then, but Manny spotted me heading for the door.

"Hey, Dorkman, don't you want to try the weights?"

I shrugged. I really, really didn't. Not with an audience, but what was I going to say?

"Come on," he said. "You lift weights, and you're always on about Masks and Hoods. Don't you want to see how you stack up against a real hero? I'll even go first."

He reached for the weights then, and I knew I was stuck. At first, it was funny watching him take on the barbells. He puffed and panted at the beginning when they weighed five thousand pounds, but you could see he was really trying. He might not be all jerk, but I knew he wanted to show me up. Finally, they dropped down to something he could lift and I checked out the numbers as he did a couple of curls. Seventy-five pounds—I was going to have a terrible time matching that. I do lift, but I'm a skinny thing.

Manny stepped away from the machine and gestured me into his place. I resisted the urge to bolt. I'd been here before, lots. But not in front of an audience, not since the first time.

You see, the screen that shows how much you're lifting is

placed so it's really hard to see while you're actually trying out the weights. That lets you believe that you're doing better than you are, that maybe you're really lifting Mask-level iron. It's like it was *designed* to get your hopes up and then crush them. The first time I tried it, that's exactly what happened. I thought for one brief shining moment that I was finally getting powers. I was so excited I about burst a vein. But it was all just a cruel joke played by the guys who built the exhibit.

Every time I think about that, it makes me angry. What right did they have to give a kid hope like that and then snatch it away? Still, every single time I came to Camp Commanding, I had a go. I kept hoping that this time would be the one when my powers finally kicked in. *Stupid, huh?* Today, even though I had an audience and I was about to make a complete idiot out of myself in front of them, I felt that same burst of irrational hope. I couldn't help myself, and that made me even angrier.

I glared up at the banner above the machine. On one side, it had the Captain holding his barbells high, and on the other, King Arthur pulling Excalibur out of a stone. The way the artist had rendered him, Arthur looked an awful lot like the Captain. Below it said, "See how YOU measure up against CAPTAIN COMMANDING!"

Not very well, I thought.

But I didn't have any choice. Not with half the basketball team watching me. I reached for the dumbbells, then paused. Maybe if I watched the gauge while I was lifting I could at least avoid the trap of half believing I was getting powers. I was going to feel plenty humiliated without adding freshly shattered hope on top of everything else. It wasn't easy to get a look at the thing, but I twisted around and leaned forward until I got the gauge in sight.

I took the grips in my hands and pulled. Nothing. The meter read *5,000 lbs*. It felt like trying to lift a building. Still, I strained and heaved with everything I had. I threw my rage and disappointment into my back and shoulders and *lifted* with my whole body. Nothing. I pulled so hard my vision started to flash purple around the edges. *4,500 . . . 4,000 . . . 3,000 . . . 1,500 . . .* I felt something shift deep down inside me. Suddenly my whole body went tingly-itchy again like it had back in the booth. The meter blinked and repeated *1,500 lbs*. It had never done that before.

"What the . . . ," mumbled Manny.

I worked even harder, straining until I thought I was going to rip my own arms off . . . and the dumbbells moved. Just for a second, but I swear they moved—*3,000*. What the heck? This wasn't how it went! Something must have gone wrong with the display. Somehow, that made me even angrier—*4,000*. There was a distinct clunk, like I'd lifted the weights a tiny bit and they'd fallen back. The whole body-electric itch turned into something more like burning—as though my very cells were on fire—*5,000 lbs*.

"Impossible!" exclaimed Glen.

I pulled with everything I had then—*7,500 lbs*. I'd *never* seen that before. I knew Glen was right and it felt like the machine was mocking me. I yanked and twisted and . . . the dumbbells moved again. I could feel them lifting off the stand ever so slowly.

10,000 lbs . . . 000000000 . . . error . . . error . . . error . . . failure.

There was a tremendous zorching sound. Half the basketball team screamed. The glass plate in front of the meter cracked and smoke came billowing out of someplace in the floor. In that same moment, the dumbbells suddenly reverted to the ten or so pounds gravity made them. They came up away from the stand like they were rocket-propelled, and I went butt over brains—flying backward away from the machine.

I landed on the back of my head, hard! The whole world went pretty seriously wobbly for a bit. When it came back to normal, it felt like several seconds had vanished into elsewhere and taken me with them. Apparently, they'd also dragged me across the room, too.

That seemed like the only reasonable explanation for the fact that I was lying a good thirty feet from the machine. I couldn't think of *anything* to explain the way the dumbbells had somehow punched themselves deep into the concrete-block wall above me.

I blinked several times, looked at all the smoke and the sparks shooting out of what used to be Captain Commanding's very own weight system, and at the alarmed circle of jocks standing around it. All I could do was wonder how I was going to explain things to the park manager.

That's when the sprinklers went off.

4

UnMasked

Worst part of the worst day of my life? No one believed me. Not the firemen. Not the park manager. Not the lawyer who slipped me his card, "In case you need to sue . . ." Not my mom. No one. Not even with most of the basketball team as eyewitnesses.

Well, that's not entirely true. Pretty much everyone believed I'd been trying my luck with the dumbbells and something had gone horribly wrong. But they all just thought the equipment flaked out. That's sure what Manny was claiming, though he and the rest of the guys kept looking at me funny, and they all seemed awfully nervous about getting too close.

As for the rest, well: *Sure son, you were totally lifting ten thousand pounds and it broke the machine.*

I'm so sorry, young man, but what can you expect from something built by that awful Foxman?

Interesting story, kid, it'd sure build sympathy with a jury.

I'm sorry, honey, that must have been really awful—I know how much you've always wanted powers.

By the end of it, *I* almost didn't believe me. Especially since—when I had very quietly tried to lift the concrete bench the firemen had parked me on—I couldn't so much as budge it. If I *had* been superstrong for a few seconds—a big if—it hadn't lasted. Fifteen minutes later, I was plain old me again. Once the paramedics checked out the rest of the guys, they had all slipped off without a one of them even saying good-bye.

Why wouldn't anyone believe me?

I felt like shouting and punching things. Especially after the ride home with my mother in the car. When it became obvious that she didn't believe me either, I'd blown up at her. Apparently this was serious yelling, because there was no snark in her response. She just told me, "I'm listening, honey. I know this has been a hard day."

I hate that she can be so reasonable when I'm furious. And I hate that I hate it. And I really, really hate that knowing all that makes it almost impossible for me to sustain a good mad. Seriously, reasonable parents are a curse.

As soon as I was out of the car I stormed up to my room and slammed the door. Becoming a Mask was the most important thing in the world to me, no matter what I'd tried to tell myself when I deleted my hero's logs. Here I was, maybe on the brink of realizing that dream, and everybody kept "humoring" me about the whole thing. Didn't they understand what this could mean?

As incredibly corny as it sounded to say it—even silently in my head—Captain Commanding wasn't just *a* hero, he was and always had been *my* hero, the guy I wanted to *become*. I had the shirts. I had the breakfast cereal. I had the action figures. Heck, I had the underwear. If this whole episode with the dumbbells had even a shred of reality to it, maybe I was finally going to get my wish.

And there was a shred of reality . . . literally. A patch of something like a rubbery bit of cobweb, only thicker and really, really tough. It was slightly smaller than the palm of my hand, and I'd found it stuck in the hair on the back of my head in the minutes between the alarms going off and the firemen arriving.

When I first tugged on the thing, it felt weird, like it had roots going down through my scalp to the bone underneath. I think I screamed then, but my head was still ringing, and the whole memory is kind of fuzzy. A minute or so later, when I freaked out and yanked at it again, the thing came right off. It should have caught on my hair, but it didn't, and it had lots of little holes in it, like it had grown up around the hair without sticking to it.

I'm not sure why I hadn't wanted to share my strange little treasure with any of the dozen people I'd told my story to. Maybe because I was absolutely terrified someone would take it away from me—this tiny shred of hope for my hero dream. Whatever the reason, it was evidence that the weirdness of that moment wasn't all inside my head. Some of it had stuck to the back—in a sort of superscab.

I pulled it out of my pocket again now and looked at it for maybe the fiftieth time. It was stiffer and drier than it had been this afternoon, more like a bit of paper-wasp hive or a butterfly's empty cocoon. It smelled papery, too, and I wondered what it would look like in the morning, and how it would smell. Then I thought about the fact that it had come off my head—*out* of my head maybe—shivered briefly, and stuffed it into my nightstand . . . for a few minutes, before taking it right back out again and poking at it. It was so bizarre, like nothing I'd ever read about in all my years as a Mask nerd.

About an hour later, my mom checked in, tapping on the door and offering me a tray with a snack on it. I still hadn't finished staring at the cracks in the ceiling, so I grunted twice for no. Then I quickly tucked the bit of cobwebby stuff under my pillow, in case she decided to come in anyway. I still wasn't ready to share it with anyone, not even my mom. It was too creepy for that—and too precious—this symbol of my maybe-powers.

She stuck her head in briefly. "I'll get this in the morning, honey." Then she set the tray down and went away.

Without willing it, I pulled out the bit of superscab again, staring at it as I turned it over and over and over in my hands until I fell asleep. My alarm went off at nine, and after I failed to destroy the clock with my mind, I rolled out of bed, landing with a thud and verifying once again that I couldn't fly.

After I finished my powers check, I pulled out my little bit of superscab for another look. It felt harder now, with only the tiniest bit of flex, like the bits of plastic armor they wear in hockey or football. I wasn't willing to really push on it for fear I might break it, but I got a real impression of toughness.

Then I went down to the basement where my parents have a little home gym. I set the weight machine as high as it would go—a three hundred pound bench press—and, hoping so very hard that this would go like the Captain's weight machine, I threw my whole body into it. Nothing. It didn't budge.

Still, I had my superscab . . . so I set the machine to the best weight I could bench, eighty-five, and did a couple of reps. If I *did* manifest powers this summer, I needed to be ready.

~~~ ~~~

This is the part of my story where if I was in a movie they'd run a montage with inspirational theme music playing in the background and a clock on the wall with the numbers and dates blurring away two months. I'd keep working the weights and my runs, and by the end I'd be superbuff and those three-hundred-pound reps would go like nothing. Then, I would pick up my Mask suit at Camp Commanding and it would fit perfectly and I would go out and fight crime.

But my life is not a movie. The Mask uniform wasn't even there when I finally went back and checked a few days later. In fact, the whole inside of the building looked completely different now—restrooms—and I was too embarrassed to ask anyone about it. After what happened at the Captain's Bunker, *everyone* who worked at the park knew who I was. As the weeks went by I got more and more depressed.

What if the Captain's dumbbells had just malfunctioned and my only power was superscabs? That seemed ever more likely, since I never even broke one-twenty on my dad's weights. I tried but I'm simply too skinny. I'd like to blame it on my math-dork parents, but the reason we have a machine that even goes to three hundred is that Dad played football in high school—offensive line—and he *can* bench that much. Unfortunately, I take after my mom, who took ballet classes from Gran, which is how she met my dad.

Both Mom and Gran wanted me to take dance, because you can never get enough boys in the classes, but a moment of klutziness persuaded them to give up where my complete lack of enthusiasm had failed. You accidentally break one ballerina's stupid little toe, and suddenly it's no more dance for you, young man. If I'd known that at the start, I'd have been tempted to do it sooner.

The only thing about my summer that went even remotely like the Mask movie I wished I was starring in was that I collected another little shred of superscab.

I was mowing the lawn and I hit something with the blade. I still don't know what, but it shot out from under the mower, bounced off a tree and nailed my left eye. Things blurred out completely, and for a few seconds I thought I was going to end up with a head start on a career in piracy—black eye patch, don't ya know. But within a minute it stopped stinging, and when I blinked a couple times afterward, a bit of web dropped out of my eye.

I'm not sure "grows healing scabwebs" is the kind of power you can build a Mask career on, but combine it with the incident with the Captain's weights, and I really started to hope again. Enough so that I started secretly wearing a costume under my regular clothes on days where I thought I might encounter a crime.

I say *costume*, but it was really just my Dorkman running gear with a domino mask tucked away and some sneakers. All of which made me even more bummed about missing out on the uniform I had supposedly won that first day at Camp Commanding. I did wear the ring most days, but that was a poor substitute for custom-fit Armex and Invulycra.

Sigh.

～～ ～～

School. How did it get to be time for school to start again? I don't hate school like many of the other kids in my class, but I'm not a big fan either. I wasn't looking forward to getting back to my classes or seeing my fellow students. Especially not after the incident at Camp Commanding.

I'd bumped into guys from the basketball team a couple of times since then, and it wasn't much fun. The jocks used to tolerate me. But now they were treating me like I had some sort of weird disease that they were all afraid of catching if they got too close. That might have been easier to take if I had any *real* friends, but I don't.

I was feeling pretty alone and invisible by the third week back when my civics class climbed into a bus and headed for the Heropolis Museum of Masks for our first field trip. I ended up in the middle of the bus, sitting by myself and reading the latest issue of *Captain Commanding*, ignored or avoided by everybody. At least I was able to open the window and enjoy the crisp fall air—I love the dusty dry leaf smells of autumn.

When we got to the museum, Mr. Granger paired me up with one of the geek gang—Dave something—school policy insists we all have to have a buddy. But it took all of two minutes after the teacher took his eyes off us before we went our separate ways—Dave joined some of the other geeks at the front of the group when they herded us into the Hero Bomb exhibit and handed out headsets.

I ended up near the back of the line where most of the jocks were clustered. So, I waved at Glen and Jamal and asked, "How's it going?"

Glen waved back and looked like he was going to say something, but then Jamal elbowed him in the ribs and pointed at Manny, who stood in front of them in line. He wasn't turned our way, but Glen nodded and his eyes dropped to the floor. A moment later, Jamal turned to the front as he collected his headset. Glen caught my eye then and shrugged apologetically. Then he too turned away. I fell back to the very end of our group after I got my headset. There was no point in pushing in where I wasn't wanted.

I turned my audio tour on as we started moving. I'd been there a thousand times before and could practically recite it from memory, but at least it gave me the illusion that I had someone to talk to. Well that, and it drew me in every time I came to the museum. Maybe because this was how it all started, with a huge tragedy and a mystery we don't understand even now.

It began with "No one knows who set off the Hero Bomb or why. All we know are the results."

Up until December 15th, 1988, the Minneapolis–St. Paul metro area was mostly known for blizzards and exporting blondes to places where they don't have to shovel snow. The exhibit talks a lot about live theater and sports teams and all sorts of other stuff. But before Metamorphosis Day or, simply, M-Day, Minnesota was all about snow and blondes for the rest of the world.

Then, boom! Some kind of bizarre radiation bomb goes off under a bridge between the cities. Twenty-four hours later, half a million people are dead even though the only physical damage was to the bridge, which fell into the Mississippi.

The audio continued, "The explosion transformed several hundred of the survivors, giving them amazing powers—the first Masks and Hoods. Later on, Masks started popping up in other places around the world, but only in ones and twos, and often with much weaker powers than the Heropolis gang."

Heropolis. That's what the world rechristened Minneapolis and St. Paul after the bomb. Someone in the media started it within days, and it stuck tight.

The next exhibit after the one on the bomb is called A City of Heroes, and it profiles all the Masks that have come out of Heropolis, old and new. I fell farther and farther behind the group because I stopped and really looked at every exhibit. Glen waved at me to catch up once or twice when he thought the other basketball guys weren't looking, but I ignored him. I wanted to lose myself in one of my favorite places right then and I didn't really care if I got in trouble for wandering off.

I turned aside to look at the dusty old set of Foxman's mechanized battle armor, which sits under the stairs. It's not in the audio tour and most people miss it there. It's really crude, nothing like the streamlined gear Foxman developed in later years, which is almost ironic. His equipment has gotten so much better, but the hero inside seems to keep shrinking. It's hard to believe the reckless drunk who nearly destroyed the IDS Tower could be the same guy who used to be the Captain's best friend.

I spent a long moment staring at the bright red helmet with its long metal ears and pointed faceplate. Even in this roughly welded version there was something jaunty there, a touch of clever cool that none of the other early Masks had. Too bad the man inside turned out to be a total loser.

The next exhibit was a big poster with the heading: M-Day Mystery—Where Do They Go? One of the reasons Metamorphosis Day has become a thing is that metahuman activity pretty much goes to zero for twenty-four hours every December 15. Oh, sure there's the occasional petty Hood bank robbery or Mask fight, but mostly the Ides of December is a day where nothing meta happens. Most Masks and Hoods seem to disappear completely on M-Day. No one knows where they go, or why.

I looked up from the M-Day poster and realized that *my* school group had gone on to the next area, and the next group hadn't yet arrived, leaving the City of Heroes area almost empty. *Good.* I wouldn't have any competition for the best part, a big 3-D video screen at the exit from the City of Heroes exhibit.

It runs a slideshow of all the known Heropolis Masks, and it's interactive. If you stand in the right place, the machine will scan you into the show. I've spent hours staring into the vid, watching the endless loop of heroes and endlessly hoping that having my face show up there would somehow transform me into one of them.

But something odd caught my eye as I walked up to the screen this time, and I stopped to try to figure out what. It took me three long beats of staring at the casually dressed man standing in the interactive scan point to realize what. I'd seen him before. Here. In the vid. And *not* because he'd been scanned into it by the exhibit. I don't know if anyone less Mask-obsessed than me would have recognized him without his costume, but I did.

Spartanicus!

5

Enter the Captain

I desperately flailed for something to do when Spartanicus's eyes met mine. *Anything!*

He nodded very faintly. "You have a good eye, boy."

Here I was, face-to-face with the Captain's worst enemy, a man whose powers were only second to his own, and what did I do? Freeze up completely, like a total dip. That's what. *Utterly humiliating.*

Before I could unfreeze enough to yell for help or run away or even take a deep breath, the scar in the center of Spartanicus's forehead ripped open and a green beam shot out. It hit me full in the face.

Boom . . .

For one brief instant, my head felt as if it were coming apart. Then I fell out of the world.

The first thing I noticed when I started to come around was the industrial carpet and old concrete smell of the Mask Museum. When I opened my eyes, I found myself lying on my back on a padded bench only a few feet from where I'd fallen. I could tell because I could see the dented front left corner of the original Commanding Car overhead. It hangs in the entry gallery, and that view told me exactly where I was in the museum. I know, I know, I am a *giant* Mask nerd.

"There's more to you than meets the eye, boy." I turned my head and found Spartanicus standing on my other side, in full costume now. "If you scream or try anything funny, I'll have to kill you. I'd rather avoid that for the moment." His deep gravelly voice was surprisingly gentle for a man delivering a death threat.

"What's going on?" I croaked. I'd intended the words to come out bold and defiant, but a croak was the best I could manage. "Why are you here?"

"The future, boy. I'm here for the future." He turned and called over his shoulder. "HeartBurn, are we ready?"

"Whenever you are." I couldn't see the other villain, but I recognized her name—a Hood known for her incredibly destructive powers and ruthlessness. "The children are all tucked away snug in their beds."

"Then it's show time," said Spartanicus. "We have a Captain to kill."

"What about the boy?" asked HeartBurn.

"Bag him and bring him along."

"On it," said a third voice—female again.

"What!? Wait—"

A gentle, *fwumpf*ing sort of noise smothered my yelp of protest. My world went dark as something rough and faintly musty-smelling covered my face. I tried to move, but it felt like I'd been wrapped in heavy burlap.

"HeartBurn, bring him." Spartanicus's voice sounded muffled and oddly distant through the filter of cloth—this was no ordinary bag. "Mr. Implausible, Fluffinator, you know what to do."

I had only a moment to wonder at so many powerful Hoods being in one place before I felt a sharp jerk. The cloth covering my face suddenly tightened as someone grabbed it and yanked—dragging me up and off the bench. With no way to catch myself, my legs hit the floor hard enough to sting. I could feel myself being dragged along behind someone. Within minutes, I found myself bump-bump-bumping up what had to be the main staircase at the open center of the museum.

We took a sharp left at the top, heading toward the museum's megamax theater—a giant dome in the exact center of the building. I bumped over something flat and metallic—doors ripped from their hinges maybe. Then we took a right. Perhaps fifty feet later—the hall leading around into the front of the theater—we stopped. I could hear a loud yammering, like a flock of angry geese. My captor let go of the bag and my head hit the thinly carpeted concrete floor hard enough to send flashes of red and blue across my vision.

For what felt like a year and a day—but couldn't have been more than about ten minutes—they left me alone. I could hear occasional thuds and crashes rising over the continued yammering. I slowly came to realize the latter must be the sounds of many unhappy voices filtered through layers of reinforced fabric. I thrashed around a bit, but simply couldn't make any progress on getting out of the bag. I tried to reach my cell phone, but the bag was too tight. I should have been terrified if not utterly panic-stricken.

Instead, I felt a weird sort of calm, like some part of me knew everything would be fine. Another property of the bag? Mild oxygen deprivation? Too much *reasonable* drilled into me by my parents? I don't know, I was simply glad I could still think straight. I did jerk like a gaffed fish when a long fizzing sound ended in a tremendous, earth-shaking crash.

"What the heck was that?" I yelped, but I could barely hear my own voice over the sudden wild shrieking of the other prisoners.

Spartanicus must somehow have heard me, because my bag was suddenly yanked upright again—this time by a grip on the fabric between my shoulder blades. I heard his gravelly voice as my feet lifted free of the floor, "I've made a window, boy. Would you like to see it?" I felt myself being carried somewhere before he called, "Bagger, head!"

Fwumpf . . .

Bright light struck my dark-adjusted eyes and I could move my neck, though the rest of my body remained immobilized. I blinked at the brightness, looked down, and . . .

Vertigo!

My head spun and my stomach twisted as I found myself staring into a dust-filled abyss. I managed not to throw up long enough for my brain to adapt to the scene and let me sort things out. Again, the Commanding Car—this time seen through the roiling dust ahead of me—provided me the reference I needed to make sense of my position. I was hanging from Spartanicus's fist, twenty feet above the main lobby of the museum. The dust came from a huge section of concrete wall that used to separate the megamax theater from the open three-story atrium. It lay shattered on the floor below me as I dangled out the opening created by its removal.

I looked down again, this time to find out how I was being restrained. Seamless burlap—the work of Bagger—wrapped me tighter than a mummy. Bagger was a Hood more usually known for her long-running battle with Hotflash than any association with Spartanicus or Captain Commanding. She simply wasn't in the same league. What was going on here?

My view shifted wildly as Spartanicus twisted his grip, turning me back to face him. "What do you think? Have I improved the view, boy?"

"I liked it better the way it was . . . without your ugly mug taking up so much space, Spartanicus." I snapped my mouth shut.

I hadn't meant to say that, not a word of it. Heck, I'm not even sure what led me to *think* it—too many bantering Mask movies maybe. Whatever the reason, it was too late to take it back. I had been betrayed by my own mouth and there was nothing I could do about it. Spartanicus's expression clouded. I more than half expected him to shake me until my neck snapped. But he just raised one eyebrow and chuckled.

"Again, boy, there's more to you than meets the eye. What's your name?"

"Evan Quick." I'd intended to say it quietly, humbly, with an eye to calming down a man who could tear me in half. Instead, I found myself lifting my chin and speaking with pride. "But you can call me Mr. Quick."

What the heck!? My mouth was definitely trying to get me killed, and I crazily wondered what I had done to it lately. I'd have slapped it myself if I had a free hand to do so, but that was impulse not action.

"Should I fry his tongue out of his head?" HeartBurn stood behind Spartanicus, waist-length red hair clashing wildly with her skintight crimson costume.

"Not yet," he replied over his shoulder, "though I'll keep it in mind." He focused on me again. "I like you, young Master Quick. You've titanic brass, if no apparent brains to back it up. It's a rare man who can look me in the eye without half pissing himself, much less a boy. You'll do nicely."

He looked past me into the lobby, and my eyes followed his. "Final call," he said. "Mr. Implausible?"

A pair of lips appeared a few feet away from us. No face, no eyes, nothing but the lips. "Ready when you are."

He glanced back into the theater. "All fired up, HeartBurn?"

"You know it," she answered.

"Mempulse, you in place?"

An image from my last track meet flashed into my mind, a group of runners—me among them—all lined up on their starting blocks. The pistol sounded . . . and the vision faded away.

Spartanicus nodded. "Good. Bagger, you got this?"

The Hood called out from somewhere up near the rafters,

44

"With Mr. Implausible to back my play? Absolutely! Captain Overconfident won't know what hit him."

"What about the Fluffinator? Dolls and teddy bears all ready to roll?"

"Action figures and plush collectibles, thank you very much. And, yes, my army of toys is ready when you are."

"Then it's time to raise the curtain."

Moments later, I found myself dangling from a bent piece of rebar sticking out over the edge of the hole Spartanicus had cut in the theater wall. A disembodied hand holding a video camera hung in space a few yards in front of me.

Above and behind me Spartanicus began a countdown. "Three. Two. One. And go."

A bright flash drew my attention to the row of monitors above the ticket booth below. Every one had switched to a feed coming off the camera. I could see me hanging in front of Spartanicus's feet, with banks of theater seats rising behind him. Each of those seats held a person in a tight burlap bag. But where my entire head was sticking out the top of mine, their bags only exposed the occupants from the nose up, so that none of them could easily speak.

To move the scene from merely strange to bizarre beyond all reason, each seat in the theater had a large doll or stuffed animal standing on the arm of the chair holding a pair of scissors.

"Scissors?" I said. "Seriously?"

A set of lips appeared next to the camera. "The truck was supposed to be carrying straight razors. I voted for guns, but the Fluffinator says teddy bears are terrible with triggers."

A voice called out, "It's plush collectibles, all right? How many times do I have to tell you that!"

"Whatever," said the lips. "The main point is no fingers. Much easier to use something sharp and have them cut throats if they have to."

"Would you two shut up!" snapped Spartanicus. "And, please tell me we're not broadcasting yet."

"Sorry," said the lips. "You said 'go.' We're live."

In the monitors I could see Spartanicus shake his head sadly, then look into the camera. "Right, so toss the speech. Captain Commanding, I know you're watching this. That fancy scanner Foxman built you wouldn't miss the switchover in feeds. So, I'm going to cut to the chase. You. Here. Now. Take longer than fifteen minutes and we start killing peop—"

A crash and a rain of glass cut him off. Captain Commanding had arrived, courtesy of one of the skylights that supplied the bulk of the museum's daytime illumination. The Captain swooped down to hover in the air a few feet above and in front of me, facing Spartanicus. I felt a huge rush of relief. With Captain Commanding on the scene everything would come out fine.

"You've got my attention, evildoer! But you're not going to like the results!" The Captain always talked like that, all declarations and exclamation points.

A glance at the monitor told me Spartanicus wasn't impressed. He visibly rolled his eyes. Well, he was about to get his, so no worries there.

"Release the hostages unharmed and I might let you—guh!" The Captain curled into a gasping ball without falling out of the air. "Memories of Failure. Battering my Mind. Must. Fight. But So Strong. Too strong for Mempulse. What's happening!"

Spartanicus laughed. "That would be the combination of Mr. Implausible boosting Mempulse's powers and the oh-so-conveniently-placed Commanding Car serving as the perfect mnemonic amplifier for the scene I want you to relive in your last few moments on Earth. The day I beat you into a pulp."

The Captain balled up even tighter. "So humiliating. Saved by F-F-F-Foxman! Losing control. No!"

The Captain was losing? No, that couldn't be right. He'd come around in a moment or two. He had to.

Spartanicus snapped his fingers. "Bagger!"

A large brown lunch sack appeared around the Captain, its top neatly folded over. "Here's one bag he won't be able to punch his way out of."

"Scissors? And now a paper bag?" I was still sure everything was going to be all right. Maybe because of the ridiculousness of it all. "You've got to be kidding me." I didn't realize I'd spoken aloud until the lips appeared again.

"The bag's a very special design and a lot tougher than it looks," said the lips. "I've seen to the latter by boosting Bagger's powers, too. Besides, it doesn't have to hold Captain Overconfident for long, just until—"

A tremendous *fwooshing* came from behind me, cutting off Mr. Implausible, as a blast of blue flame suddenly engulfed the bag.

"That," finished the lips.

"Eat Heartfire, Captain Charcoal Briquette!" yelled the fiery villainess.

On the monitor I saw Spartanicus rolling his eyes and mouthing "Captain Charcoal Briquette? Really? Really?" I couldn't blame him. You didn't expect real Hoods to sound so much like their comic-book counterparts.

The bag was burning merrily now as HeartBurn kept pouring on the flames—though it didn't look like the fire was actually consuming the paper. That's when I really began to worry, but it seemed so unreal. This was Captain Commanding, after all. He couldn't lose. Not really.

The lips spoke again. "Surviving that should be soaking up most of the big boy's powers of invulnerability. Let's see how he likes what Spartanicus has to add to the party."

The big Hood stepped forward to the edge of the hole blasted in the wall and lifted his arms wide, palms out. I could see a thick scar on each hand, matching the one on his forehead. All three tore open, and for a brief moment I saw what looked like shining emeralds buried under his skin. They pulsed briefly and a triple blast of sizzling green energy burst forth, spiking the burning bag.

Without so much as a whimper, the bag holding Captain Commanding dropped out of the air, falling to the concrete below. It hit with a dull thud and lay still.

No! It wasn't possible.

"And, end scene." Spartanicus threw his head back and roared with laughter. "Let's strike the set. Bagger, loose the hostages. Fluffinator, see them out. Mempulse, you and HeartBurn keep an eye on the lunch bag with me. That won't have killed the big jerk. Not quite. If it so much as twitches, nuke it."

The monitors all went black as Spartanicus stepped to the

edge of the hole and jumped down to the lower level. He landed square on the bag holding Captain Commanding, but it didn't move. *It didn't move* . . . Spartanicus laughed again, then stepped to the floor, kicking the bag before moving a few feet away. Heart-Burn followed a moment later, riding a pillar of fire down like a reverse rocket ship.

"What about your boy Quick here?" asked the lips. "Cut him loose with the rest?"

"No, I want to hang on to him for a bit longer. Bring him down."

Bring him down. The fact that the Captain—my Captain—had lost the fight was starting to sink in. I felt a sort of sick helpless anger begin to burn in my chest.

"Can do." The lips had suddenly grown a head—thin and pinched, with pale cheeks and greasy brown hair.

It rotated in the air and slid past me toward the gap in the wall. The movement reminded me of a slow-motion video I'd seen of a frog's tongue being drawn back into its mouth with a fly on the end. I turned my neck as far as I could, following the head's progress. Next came a hand holding the camera. A moment later, another hand came down from the Commanding Car above. Both moved with that same elastic contraction. It made me queasy to watch—or maybe that was the rage that continued to build in my chest and stomach.

It was only as normal-length arms and a neck appeared when Mr. Implausible's body reassembled itself, that I noticed the rest of him already sitting in one of the front-row theater seats. I had a second to wonder whether most of him had been there all along, then he stood and walked toward me. Unlike the others, he was wearing street clothes instead of a fancy costume—a plain gray suit of the sort you might see on any corner in Heropolis.

Mr. Implausible leaned down and grabbed the back of my neck, casually lifting me and my bag free of the rebar hook. "Come on, boy, Spartanicus isn't done with you yet."

He extended one leg into the space beyond the hole in the wall, where his foot suddenly detached itself and slowly drifted down to the floor. He brought the other leg forward and that foot followed the first. When they were both firmly planted on the concrete below, we slid sinuously down after them. But I was barely aware of our motion.

From the second Mr. Implausible's hand touched the back of my neck I had been overwhelmed by the most intense sensation of cold—like someone was slowly coating my body with a layer of ice. It had started at the point of contact between the two of us, moving up to engulf my head before traveling down from there. It should have hurt. Instead, I felt increasingly strong, like one of those superconducting magnets that can only work at insanely cold temperatures. It was soothing somehow, too, though the cold didn't touch the hot fury that was filling the center of my chest.

"Where do you want the boy?" As Mr. Implausible dragged me around toward Spartanicus, his words sounded distant and spongy, like they were coming through deep water.

In response, I saw Spartanicus's lips moving, but couldn't make out what he was saying. It sounded like *mwah-mwah-mm-mwah-mwah*, only slower.

He also pointed at the giant paper bag. But I didn't think he was talking about me, because an instant later the bag vanished, leaving Captain Commanding exposed on the floor. The Captain was curled in a naked ball on his side. His costume had burned away, exposing angry red skin. Cracked bits here and there oozed blood.

HeartBurn kicked him in the shoulder, flipping him onto his back, where he uncurled. Bits of half-melted costume stuck to his stomach and thighs, providing a little bit of tattered modesty. His chest was rising and falling faintly, showing that he still lived. But that was the only way you could tell.

"Iiiiime . . . toooo . . . finnnnnish . . . thisssssss." I could understand Spartanicus again, though his voice sounded as though it had been slowed way down. "Parrrrrk the boyyyy, Mr. Implaaaaausible, Iiiii neeed aaaa boooooooost."

"Noooo neeed, Iiiii cannnn doooooo booooth." He extended an arm toward Spartanicus and his hand left his wrist, moving to touch the side of the larger Hood's neck.

Spartanicus raised both hands toward the Captain, though he was now moving with a weird slowness that matched his words. I glanced over my shoulder and saw Mr. Implausible close his eyes. Suddenly the icy cold that gripped me became a thousand times more intense. I felt like some kind of wintery god.

Without thinking, I lifted my arms away from my sides, ripping the thick fabric that held me like so much tissue paper. The shredded remains of the bag started to fall away, moving as though they were dropping through Jell-O instead of air. *Everything* had slowed down to match the voices.

Everything but me. I spun around, breaking Mr. Implausible's grip on my neck, and punched him with everything I had. He lifted off the ground and sailed away from me, seeming to pick up speed as he went. I turned again, and saw HeartBurn, a look of shock growing on her face, as she raised her fingers to point at me. Fire crawled forward out of the tips, but I easily ducked beneath the blast, grabbing up a thick piece of broken concrete as I did so. I flipped it at HeartBurn and it caught her square in the stomach, doubling her over and dropping her to the floor.

Things began moving more and more like they normally did. By the time I snatched up a piece of rebar and started toward Spartanicus, he was operating at two-thirds normal speed. Still, I was faster, and he didn't get his arms up in time to prevent my attack. I smacked him right between the eyes, and the iron bar bent into a half loop, wrapping itself over the top of his head. He stumbled backward, but he might have recovered if Captain Commanding's hand hadn't shot out and caught him by the ankle then, jerking him off his feet.

But even as he fell, his eyes caught mine, and for the second time in as many hours his forehead ripped open, unleashing a searing green beam that hit me full in the face. This time it was brighter and much more intense.

Boom!

I held on to consciousness for a few brief instants longer than I had the last time. I didn't much enjoy it, as it gave me the chance to fully experience what felt like a five-hundred-pound ball of molten lead smashing me backward off my feet. But it was only a brief agony, as the pain took me elsewhere before I could hit the ground.

6

Rise and Shine

. . .

. . .

. . . I felt like . . . butter melting into Mom's pancakes . . . or maybe lazy Sunday morning.

That moment when you know you're awake, but also know you don't have to get up, and realize that you can go back to sleep if you want? Yeah. That. Still, I had the nagging feeling there was something I really ought to care about.

I made an effort and opened my eyes, or thought I did anyway. All I could see was a hazy golden glow. Part of me wanted to be upset about that, but I felt too tired and mellow to care—like I had the world's heaviest and most comfortable blanket weighing me down.

"Is he going to be all right, Agent Brendan?" It was Captain Commanding's voice, clear and bold, but distant somehow, like I was hearing a video playing on a laptop in the other room.

Good, he must have won. I can go back to sleep.

"I hope so," a woman answered. "It's hard to tell. I've never seen anything quite like this." A hollow, thunking noise followed, but very close—like someone tapping on my skull.

"He's one of us, then?" The Captain again. "Metahuman?"

"No doubt of that," she continued. "Our boy Evan is well on his way to wearing a mask."

Me? They were talking about me? *Captain Commanding* was asking how I was doing? I was going to be a Mask? I should have been jumping up and down and cheering, but I still couldn't seem to move. Even staying awake took enormous effort.

"This has to have been very traumatic for him," the Captain said quietly, and there was a strange note in his voice that I'd never heard in any of his vids or interviews. "Do you think he *ought* to remember it all?"

"I'm not sure what you're asking," responded Agent Brendan.

"Well, I just got off the phone with his mother, and she said he's a *huge* Captain Commanding fan. I wonder if he won't be too traumatized by seeing his hero laid low like that . . ."

Agent Brendan snorted—it was an incredulous sound, not what I would have expected from anyone dealing with the Captain. "You mean the part where you were bleeding all over what was left of your uniform? Don't worry about it, I doubt he even noticed. He was kind of busy taking out Mr. Implausible and HeartBurn at the time."

"Don't mess around with me," said the Captain, his voice cold and dangerous. "You won't like the results."

"I didn't mean to . . ." Brendan's voice was weary but apologetic. "Look, Commanding, I'm sorry. It's been a long day and I

hate the idea of tampering with the memories of all those wit-
nesses. For a second there it sounded like you were suggesting that
we alter the boy's as well, and I spoke without thinking. I'm sure
that wasn't what you were asking, was it? That we alter a meta's
memories?"

"Absolutely not," the Captain said rather bombastically. "That
would go against the Commanding Code!"

"Not to mention being crazy dangerous," Agent Brendan
added cautiously. "And violating the daylights out of OSIRIS regulations regarding metahuman conduct."

The Office of Strategic Intelligence and Research, International
Section, had originally been tasked to deal with the aftermath of
M-Day and the Hero Bomb. These days OSIRIS was in charge of
pretty much everything related to Masks or Hoods, and it was
undoubtedly the agency Agent Brendan worked for.

"Right," said the Captain, "that, too. Anyway, I was only wor-
rying about the boy. He's had a rough day—going up against Spartanicus and all that. He helped me out and I wanted to make sure
he'd be all right."

"He'll be fine. OSIRIS plans on taking very good care of this
one. Good-bye, Captain."

"Good-bye," the Captain said, and his voice sounded stiff and
irritated.

"Interesting stuff you've wrapped yourself up with, Evan,"
Brendan said, and I heard the hollow thunking again. "The lab
techs are gonna love it."

Silence followed. At that point staying awake became too
much work.

A dull thump brought me suddenly and completely awake, and I jerked upright. Or, I tried to at least. My brain told my body to move, that's for sure. But nothing happened.

There was another thump. "Looks like some cracks are starting to form." It was a woman's voice with a distinct but completely unfamiliar accent. "Hopefully that means he's going to wake up soon, and not Contingency Beta."

A man answered her. "Contingency Beta? How likely is it that he's going to explode at this point, Backflash? The X-rays and ultrasounds all show that he's nearly healed."

"I don't expect a problem, Mike, but you never know. That's why we put him in a blast vault. If we do go Contingency Beta, the armor in the walls and floor should direct the force upward."

"And blow out the ceiling, venting the chamber."

"Not an ideal outcome," replied Backflash, "but infinitely better than having him go Contingency Beta in a populated zone, don't you think?"

Mike replied, "I don't like it. I suppose the whole chamber's rigged for jettison in case of Case Omega, too." He didn't sound at all happy.

"Of course. Case Omega is simply too dangerous to allow."

Where was I? And why couldn't I move?

Mike spoke again. "He's just a kid. They're all just kids these days. We shouldn't have to treat them like this."

"So, what would you have us do?" Backflash sounded more

weary than anything. "Take no precautions at all? Let meta events run and see what happens? That's how we got Spartanicus."

"I don't know. This just feels wrong."

I wanted out. Now. I pushed and twisted . . . and something gave with a crackling sound like a thousand people opening candy wrappers all at once.

"Something's happening." The woman's voice again. "I'm moving to the monitoring station and you are, too, Mike. Come on."

"I'm staying here. The techs all think the cocoon's nothing more than a healing mechanism. He shouldn't have to wake up alone. He's going to be disoriented enough as it is."

"Don't make me make this an order, Mike. You know the protocol."

"All right, but I'm doing this under protest." The man's voice was slowly receding.

"Noted."

A sharp metallic bang followed.

I jerked again, harder this time. That produced more crackling, and a flood of bright light as I forced myself into a sitting position.

I don't know what I expected to see at that moment—my bedroom back home . . . the museum lobby . . . a hospital room . . .

I got . . . well, none of those. I found myself sitting in a large room shaped like the inside of a Chinese takeaway box, with its walls sloping outward. The walls were thick and made of steel—obvious from the heavy rivets holding them together, like pictures I'd seen of armor on a battleship. The floor was the same construction, though;

there the rivets had been sunk in to provide a flat surface. The ceiling looked like it might be concrete, and everything was painted a dreary industrial gray.

What was going on?

I tried to move and discovered something was still keeping my legs from moving. A quick look showed me that from the hips down I was covered in what looked like spray-foam insulation stuff after it's been exposed to the weather for a year or two. More of it lay around me in lumps and shards. I picked up a piece and squeezed. It was much harder than it looked and I realized that it must be a thicker version of the scabweb I'd found on the back of my head at Camp Commanding.

Weird. Apparently *I* was what lay at the center of the candy coating.

I tried to move my legs again. Fractures spiderwebbed their way across the stuff, with more of that same candy-wrapper crackle I'd heard earlier. A moment later, the covering fell away and I was free. I turned and put my feet down on the floor—my cocoon had been sitting on a low steel table. I didn't stand up right away though since I felt a bit wobbly.

I poked at a chunk of scabweb. It fell to the floor with a soft crunch and I thought about the fact that the stuff had come from within me after Spartanicus nailed me with his death beam. It was surreal and kind of creepy. To distract myself, I looked around the room again. There was nothing but me, the table, and a heavy bank-vault-style door. The door had a small metal box welded to the center where I would have expected one of those big ship's wheel handles. I felt like I ought to have been frightened, but I was curious more than anything.

Where was I?

It was time to find out. I stood up, took two steps, staggered, and then face-planted on the steel floor. My left cheekbone made a horrendous cracking noise and then went numb. When I reached up to touch it, I could feel a thick and greasy liquid sludging its way out of my pores. Yay, more scabweb . . .

I was more cautious when I got up the second time, balancing carefully with outstretched arms as I made my way to the door. My legs felt like old sponge cake.

There was no handle, but the box in the middle looked like it might be some kind of electronic lock. It was about five inches square, with a shallow divot in the center the size of my fingertip. I poked at it, but nothing happened. Yeah, big surprise, there, Evan. If it *was* some kind of fingerprint scanner, it sure as snot wasn't going to be keyed to me. I sighed. It looked like I might as well get used to this room, because I wasn't going anywhere soon.

I half turned to go back to the table, then stopped as I felt a flash of that same rebellious spark that made me talk back to Spartanicus. Something crackled above me, like a speaker turning on, but no one said anything. I ignored it. I was *not* going to just sit here and wait for things to happen to me. Not if I could help it, anyway. I wanted to be a Mask, right? Masks rescued themselves; they didn't wait around for someone else to do it for them.

But really, what could I do? My arms felt almost as weak as my legs, and that door was thick enough that I couldn't have done much about it if I were as strong as I had been when I smacked Spartanicus with that piece of rebar. All I had on me were the clothes I was wearing when I went to the museum: sneakers, jeans, a long-sleeve tee, and underneath it all, my Dorkman uniform. Well, that and my OSIRIS ring. I looked at the box on the door again. What were the chances?

Zero.

Still . . . I pressed the emblem on my ring against the circle in the center of the lock.

Nothing.

"Wait, he's up already." It was the woman's voice from when I started to wake up—Backflash. "And, he's got his school ring, how'd he get that in with him?"

"I don't know," replied Mike's voice. "I suppose no one was really thinking about what he had with him in the cocoon."

I tried to pull my hand away from the door so I could turn to see the speakers—maybe there was a camera, too—but the ring was stuck tight to the reader.

"Well, it's too late to get back up there now," said Backflash. "Let's see how this plays out. Hey, is that microphone live? Shut it off."

"That's hardly—"

Backflash cut him off sharply. "It wasn't a suggestion, Mike." The overhead speaker crackled off.

At the same time the lock buzzed, and a metallic voice began to speak, "Signet verified. DNA sampling . . . Subject FLR871 verified. Student status verified. Authorization for all grade C and lower hatches verified. Updating user profile. Hello . . . Evan . . . Quick."

There was a sharp *click* followed by multiple deep *clunks* like metal bars moving. The door opened and I found myself facing a short hallway with an elevator-like door at the end. When I started toward it, I almost face-planted again. My legs were still really shaky, and I had to move slowly. It wasn't so much that I felt weak as that I felt weird, like I'd forgotten how to walk properly somehow.

When I got closer to the far door I saw there were no buttons. But there was another box. I pressed my ring to the circle in the middle. The process was faster this time.

"Door authorization verified. Summoning tram, . . . Evan . . . Quick."

The ride was really long. Long enough for my cheekbone to finish healing and for me to notice and peel off the scabweb. That was after I slid down to the floor because my legs didn't want to hold me up. Eventually, the trip ended, the doors opened, and I stood. I got off and moved slowly down another hall that opened into a much larger space.

I halted on the threshold, too stunned to do anything but gape for several long beats. I had entered alien territory—a huge globular room opened out in front of me. Big enough to play a football game inside, it arced both up and down, with a thick clear ramp of some glasslike material leading down to an equally transparent floor that seemed to have been poured into the lower half of the globe.

A brilliant point of light, like a tiny sun, hovered above the exact center of the dome. It was almost too bright to look at. That kept me from realizing what it really was for several long heartbeats—an actual miniature representation of Earth's sun, with even smaller planets hanging in the space around it.

Various bits of high-tech gadgetry were scattered around. Some of it pierced the matrix of the big transparent floor and extended into what I now recognized as a second open space below. But what really drew my eye was a huge and very alien-looking device? Sculpture? Growth? Whatever it was, it lay directly beneath the projected sun.

It looked like someone had crossbred a cactus with a whole school of jellyfish, dipped the results in a bright candy coating and then tried to build an orchestra's worth of musical instruments out of the results. Looking closer, it became clear that there were actually several dozen loosely interconnected whatever-they-were, with one particularly large pipe-organ-like device roughly in the center of the cluster.

7

Schooled

"Welcome to the AMO," a gentle voice said from just to my right, and I almost jumped out of my skin.

An older man was leaning against the wall beside the door. He wasn't trying to hide, and if it hadn't been for all the wild alien gadgetry I'd never have missed him. Mid-forties maybe. Fit, with a broad face and dark hair in a buzz cut. He was big and burly and kind of scary looking, but his eyes were a soft brown and strangely gentle.

He nodded when I looked at him. "Hello, Evan. I have to apologize for not being there to meet you when you woke up." His voice was quiet, and almost as gentle as his eyes. "I was . . . unavoidably called away, and by the time I got back here . . . well, you heard some of that over the intercom. This is a school for Masks and our Chancellor wanted to see how you'd do in strange circumstances." He smiled ruefully. "I am truly sorry that your first day at the new school started off with a test."

There was something about him that just made me want to

trust him, and I briefly considered telling him that I had heard him as I was waking up. But then I thought about the woman's harder voice and all that stuff about Contingency Beta and Case Omega—and somehow it didn't seem like a good idea to let *anyone* know I'd overheard any of that.

"Where am I?" I asked. "And who are you? And how long have I been asleep? And where are my parents? And did you say this was a school for *Masks*?" Somehow, once I started asking questions, I found that I couldn't stop, even though my voice was rising wildly.

The man held his hands up in a slow-down gesture and smiled a reassuring sort of smile. "First and probably most importantly, your parents. They should be on their way to OSIRIS headquarters right now. They've been waiting to hear from you, and I promise you can talk to them in a few minutes, once I've had a chance to answer a few questions you might have and given you a quick explanation of where you are and what's been happening since the attack at the museum."

He extended his hand. "I'm Professor Matheny, by the way, but you can call me Mike if you'd like. I teach music among other things. I'll be your advisor here at the AMO."

"Music? AMO? Advisor? I'm lost." And I was, though far less scared about the whole thing than I felt I ought to be.

"The AMO is the Academy of Metahuman Operatives. It's a school for people like you. It's run by OSIRIS and even its existence is classified."

"People like me? So this really *is* a Mask school?" That's when my legs gave out and I landed on the floor with a dull thump. I *was* going to be a Mask!

"I'm sorry." Mike squatted down and put a hand on my shoulder as I tried to get up. "Are you all right?"

"I think so, but my legs don't seem to want to work properly yet." My voice came out very small. It was more than a little bit embarrassing to collapse like that. Not very Mask-like at all.

"I'm sorry, I should have moved quicker to prevent that. The lab rats thought you might have some problems walking after you came out of the cocoon—electro-osmotic flow rates between the healing layers destabilizing the brain-body connection, or some other gobbledygook. They left a chair for you, and I should have had it ready at the door. Hang on while I get it." He started down the ramp.

"Lab rats?" *That didn't make any sense.*

"Sorry, the OSIRIS techs and scientists who study us." He collected a wheelchair from beside one of the alien machines at the base of the ramp and brought it back up to me. "That's why you were at the far end of nowhere." He jerked his chin toward the tram I'd ridden down in. "Quarantine is isolated from the rest of the facility."

After he helped me into the chair, he continued. "Now, back to the AMO. Here, you will learn how to control your powers . . . along with more mundane things like algebra and English composition."

"Wait, algebra, English comp? I thought kids who went to supersecret schools for people with magic or superpowers got to skip all that stuff. The Harry Potter books lied to me . . ." Okay, that was just plain babbling, but I couldn't seem to stop talking. I'd never even known there was a school for metas, and now I was going to be studying there. Me, plain old Evan Quick. Woohoo! "Wait, are you a Mask, too?"

"Slow down there, son. You've still got questions waiting for answers, and I still need to take you to talk to your parents." He began to wheel me down the ramp. "So, where to start? Let's go with the Mask questions. Yes, you are probably going to become one, and *everyone* at the AMO is metahuman."

I turned in the chair, taking another, closer look at Professor Matheny. "Then why don't I recognize you? I thought I knew every Mask there was."

"I didn't have all that much of a Mask career before coming to teach at the academy, and even when I was active, very few people got a good look at me. I was far too tiny for that." He smiled sadly and slowly started to shrink. "Some might even say minute," he added, in the tone of someone who doesn't expect you to get the joke. Then he returned to normal size.

"Oh my god, you're Minute Man! You fought the Shrinkster like three times back in '94." There was a great picture of the two of them duking it out on a dime like it was a boxing ring. "I always wondered what happened to you."

"Really?" His smile turned briefly into a grin. "It's nice to meet someone who's actually heard of Minute Man."

We were about halfway across the big room with its wild cacophony of weird gadgets at that point—nearly to the pipe organ thing. Most of the instrument-like devices had very uncomfortable-looking contoured seats associated with them. Imagine a chaise lounge built for something shaped more like a gigantic wasp than a human being.

A mesh lounger had been strapped over the top of the one under the organ, and it was occupied by a woman. I'd have guessed her to be somewhere in her late twenties by her features and the way she moved as she twisted around in her chair to face us as we rolled up. But there was something about the expression in her eyes that made me think she was older than that—much older. Her hair was a mixed green and gold—the exact shades of a circuit board. Reinforcing the effect, more gold ran down the right side of her face in precise angular lines, as though someone had tattooed an elaborate circuit on her skin.

"Hello, Evan. I'm so glad that you'll be joining us here at the AMO." I recognized her from her accent, so I wasn't surprised when she introduced herself. "I'm Backflash. I am the director of OSIRIS and Chancellor of the AMO, though the latter is mostly an honorary appointment."

That startled me, and I blurted, "I thought Orlando Mendez was the director of OSIRIS."

Backflash smiled. "Orlando is the political director—a four-year presidential appointment in consultation with the UN. I am the director of operations, which is a . . . quieter and less . . . impermanent role. Unfortunately, I am terribly busy at the moment." She looked at Mike, and he nodded.

"Come on, Evan, let's get you to your appointment with your parents."

Backflash smiled at me, a cold expression. "It's been lovely talking with you, Evan, and I look forward to seeing how your powers develop." Then she turned away and seemed to forget we were there.

The organ thing seemed to be responsible for projecting the solar system display above. At least, that's what it looked like from up close. You could see faint lines of light coming from various spiky pipes and extending out to the planets and other celestial features.

Too weird. I watched over my shoulder as Mike wheeled me away and saw a spiky blue-raspberry tentacle-thing suddenly curl down from the pipes above and touch its starfish-shaped tip to Backflash's forehead.

That was some superbizarre Mask technology!

Once we'd gotten out of easy earshot, Mike leaned down. "Sorry about the interruption in answering your questions there, but this is the only way to get from Quarantine to the school proper, and you can't just ignore the director. So, you've been asleep for a while—in some sort of regenerative cocoon."

We reached another huge vault-style door and he paused for a moment, placing his palm on a hand scanner, and leaning down to speak into a microphone and expose his eye to a retinal scanner. "Michael Matheny."

A mechanical voice said, "Handprint verified. Voice verified. Retina scan verified. Subject OHB113 verified. Bittersharp special-exception status verified. One-time passthrough/passback authorization for central core verified." The door swung open. "Reminder OHB113: passback closes special exception."

"Maximum-security level here." Mike stepped around behind

me again and we started rolling. "The central core is the only connection between the research side of the facility and the school proper, and Backflash is the only one with unlimited access. Kind of a design flaw in my opinion." A long, curved hallway lined with concrete opened out in front of us.

Mike's cell phone rang before he could continue. "Argh, sorry but I've got to take this and it's sensitive. Let me just put a sound damper on and I'll be back to answering your questions in five minutes, okay?"

"All right."

Mike suddenly went silent and I glanced over my shoulder. A shimmering bubble had appeared around his head, and though he was animatedly speaking into an earpiece he'd popped in, I couldn't hear a word. It was actually kind of a relief to not have to think for a few minutes. There was so much to try to take in.

As we were hitting our third hallway, I saw the first of my fellow students—two girls and a boy, maybe three or four years older than I was. They were playing some kind of game that involved flinging a handball at each other in the narrow corridor. It could have been as simple as some kind of tag, except for the way they were using their powers.

The taller of the girls had the ball when I first spotted them. She was Native American, with long dark hair and a bright smile. She pulled her arm back, snapped the ball at the wall, and . . . blinked out. One second she was in the center of the hall, the next, she was three feet to her left! And again and again—traveling fifteen feet in four quick snaps.

The ball bounced off the wall at an oblique angle, sailed straight through the chest of the second girl, a pretty Minnesota blonde, then bounced off another wall. When I say "through," I mean exactly that. In the instant before the ball would have hit her, she shimmered and went all misty and the ball went right on through her.

As the ball bounced a second time, it slapped straight into the hand of the blinking girl, who caught it, spun around and whipped it to the floor. It bounced up to the ceiling, down again and stopped dead in midair. The boy, a black kid with shoulder-length dreadlocks was making a catching motion, but he was a good five feet away from the ball. But then he turned quickly and made a throwing gesture, and the ball followed as though he had it, even though he didn't.

"What the heck . . ."

Mike must have been done with his phone call by then. "Delroy's a projector with a ten-foot range. Where he is and where it looks like he is are two different places."

The misting girl caught the ball this time, but paused and didn't throw it as she saw us. "Hey, Mike, new kid?"

"Evan," said Mike. "Evan, Gretchen, Delroy, and Selene. They're several years ahead of you, so you won't see much of them except maybe in the lunchroom."

"Hi," I said.

The trio made hellos and then went back to their game as we rolled away. This was going to be one coooool school.

"Sorry about all the interruptions, Evan. Normally, I don't have quite so crazy a day. Where was I? Oh, right, the cocoon. So, according to the OSIRIS agent who delivered you to our facilities last week, you were badly injured in your fight with Spartanicus, and your healing powers needed the time to put you to rights. If Mr. Implausible hadn't accidentally boosted your powers along with Spartanicus's you'd most likely be dead."

"Dead? Wait, last week? How long have I been out?"

"Almost ten days."

"What!? My parents must be frantic!" I was hurt they weren't waiting for me when I woke up, but I wasn't going to tell some stranger, no matter how trustworthy he seemed.

"Less so than they were a couple of days ago, if I'm any judge of people, though much angrier. I don't think they have a very high opinion of OSIRIS at the moment. Nor of their lawyer either."

"Lawyer?" What the heck . . . "I think I missed something. My parents don't have a lawyer."

"Didn't. Then kind of did. Now, don't again. After you went into your cocoon, an agent brought you to this OSIRIS facility for monitoring and potential emergency care—which you didn't need because your own powers were taking care of things. Your parents didn't like that and tried to hire a lawyer to sue OSIRIS to have you released back to them so they could take you to your local hospital. That was a horrible idea by the way. No regular doctor has anything like OSIRIS's experience with metahumans. Their lawyer explained the Franklin Act on metahuman activities to your parents, and what that meant in terms of their lawsuit. At which point . . ." He shrugged and lifted an eyebrow at me.

"Oh." I nodded.

It was another Mask nerd moment. The Franklin Act basically

created a bunch of special legal rules for activated metahumans like . . . well, me. The short version pretty much said OSIRIS didn't have to admit to my parents I even existed if they didn't want to. It also meant that, as a minor with metahuman powers, I had *very* limited rights at the moment.

"I see," I said after a few seconds.

"I think you actually do. That's unusual, and fortunate. After your parents talked to the lawyer, they stopped yelling at everyone and started asking questions in a much more polite way. As your advisor of record, I've been the one to deal with your parents since then. In that capacity, I'd like to ask you *my* first question. Do you want to talk to your parents?"

"What? Of course!"

"I'm glad to hear that, truly. Once we've sorted a few more things out, I'll be happy to arrange for you to see them."

"Why wouldn't I want to talk to my parents?"

"Any number of reasons. The most common one is that not every parent deals well with finding out their child is metahuman. It can get . . . ugly."

"Oh." I hadn't thought about that before, but as soon as Professor Matheny pointed it out . . . "I guess I can see how that might happen. My parents will be fine with it though. They've always supported me."

"Any more questions before we see them?"

"You said you're going to be my *advisor*?"

"Yes. Like a homeroom teacher, only much more so. AMO is a semi-residential school. Most of our students live here during the week, some even year-round, and that means teachers have a bigger than usual role in their students' lives. Every student is assigned to a faculty advisor when they start."

"Why you?" Then I realized how that sounded. "Not that I mean I'm not happy with you. It's just, well, you said you teach music, and I'm not a musician or anything and I wondered . . ." *Stop chewing on your foot, Evan.*

"Why me? It's a reasonable question. In this case, it's mostly because you arrived in a cocoon instead of on your feet. The school knew that you—and your parents for that matter—were likely to be freaked out at first. I'm pretty good at calming people down, and—"

Mike's phone chimed again and he pulled it out. "Hang on a second, this one might be about your parents." He answered. "Hello . . . Yes . . . Yep, we're almost there." He looked down at me. "Ready to talk to your parents?"

"Yeah, sure," I said, but my mouth felt dry and my head was still awhirl with all I'd just learned.

8

End Transmission

Mike wheeled me around another corner and through a door into a little half dome. Hanging from the center of the ceiling was another bit of cactus-candy tech like the stuff Backflash had been working with.

"Where are my parents?" I asked when I didn't see any more doors.

"They're at OSIRIS headquarters in Heropolis."

"But I thought . . ." I was *so* confused.

"Just hang on two ticks. I'm going to step out so you can talk to them alone. Whenever you're done, just say 'end transmission' and it'll shut the feed off."

Mike ducked out of the room. A moment later, the candy-apple-red cactus thingy on the roof pinged rather sharply, and my parents were just there, standing a few feet away like someone had teleported them in.

My mom spotted me first. "Evan! Where have you been?" She threw herself across the room and wrapped her arms . . . right through me. "What's going on!?! Why? What?" She half turned and spoke to someone I couldn't see. "Agent Brendan! What are you trying to pull?"

My dad had started toward me as well, but now he stopped and went to stand beside my mom.

A disembodied head appeared a few feet in front of my mom, a woman with short spiky red hair. "I'm sorry, Dr. Quick. Evan is in an undisclosed location. This holographic transmission is the best we can do for you today, though I'm sure you'll be allowed to see him in person soon. Now, we can't keep a line like this open for very long, so I suggest you focus your attention on your son."

The head vanished and both my parents turned back to me.

My dad asked, "Is that really you, Evan?"

"It's me, Dad. I'm sorry I didn't call sooner, but I've kind of been in a cocoon." Which sounded way stranger to say than it had in my head.

My mom walked over and went to one knee in front of my wheelchair. "Evan? It really is you."

"Yes, Mom."

Then she started crying. I didn't know what to do or say to that. My mom *never* cries. Well, except at weddings, but that's different. This was big gulping sobs, and it made me feel absolutely awful because I knew it was all my fault.

"I'm sorry, Mom. I didn't mean to scare you. I've just . . . it's . . . I . . . I'm really sorry."

But she didn't stop crying. After a couple more long seconds, my dad stepped forward. "Why are you using that chair?"

"I'm just a little wobbly after the cocoon," I replied. "But really,

I'm fine. See." I got out of the chair and reached out a hand to my dad. It passed right through him.

He winced. "We've been so worried, and OSIRIS . . . well, I never realized how much power the Franklin Act gives them." He looked at my mother, who hadn't stopped crying yet, but did seem to be getting it back together. "They pulled us both out of work and took us to their Heropolis headquarters without any explanations or even giving us a chance to call each other. Just 'come with me now,' and a flash of the badge. Then straight into a waiting helicopter and—"

My mother broke in, "I think they did it to frighten us. We've been very vocal about their taking you away, and they don't like being questioned. Where are you?"

"At the AMO," I said quickly. "It's a school for—"

"We know that much," my dad said, and there was a flash of exasperation in his tone. "This Mike person told us that much after he gave us a long spiel about classified information and the penalties for revealing it. But where are you?"

I was about to repeat myself when I realized he must mean where was the school. "I have no idea. I came in unconscious and I'm currently in a room with no windows." I could be at the center of the Earth for all I know, which would actually be cool in a scary way. "I suppose I can find out where the building is . . ."

"Do it." He looked really angry, a rarity for my dad.

"Now?"

"Of course now. We need to know where you are so we can come get you and bring you home."

"I don't think they're going to want to let you take me away like that—" I replied, thinking back to what Professor Matheny had said about the Franklin Act and my parents' recent experience with it.

"I couldn't care less what *they* want. We're coming to get you, and that's final. We're not going to have any more of this Mask nonsense afterward either. You're far too young. Go find out where you are. We'll wait."

I half turned toward the door, then stopped. I'd spent my whole life working toward this "Mask nonsense" as my dad put it. I really hated the way upsetting him and my mom made me feel, but I wasn't sure *I* wanted to let them take me away quite yet. I was still trying to sort things out. I had powers now. That was amazing and terrifying, and I needed to learn more about them.

"Evan James Quick," he said sternly. "Go find out where you are. Now!"

"I . . ." What did I want to say to that? "Dad, hang on for a second and listen to me. I need to think—"

"No!" my dad shouted. "There's nothing to think about. Do you have any idea how upset your mother is? How upset I am? You're coming home this instant, and that is final. We are not letting you follow this stupid Mask fantasy one second longer. We should never have been so indulgent in the first place. This ends now."

"Let me talk to him." My mother put her hand on my dad's shoulder and stepped past him. "Evan, honey, I know that you think you want this. But it's not reasonable." She spoke soothingly, but firmly. "You're only thirteen. Come home so we can talk about it. You don't really want to be a Mask. You have to know that. You're a good boy, a normal boy, a *human* boy."

I couldn't believe she'd said that. "Mom, even if I didn't want powers—and you *know* I've always wanted them—I have them now. Whether I *want* to be a Mask isn't the question anymore. I *am* a Mask." I couldn't believe I was arguing with my parents like this, but what I was telling them was true, and it was really important. "The only question is what kind I'm going to be."

"Don't be ridiculous," she said, her voice taking on an edge I'd only ever heard her use with university administrators. "You're a child, Evan. *My* child, not some freak who runs around in tights and a cape."

I felt myself starting to get genuinely angry. This was my *dream* she was talking about. "Freak? Is that what you really think of metas? Because you've never said anything like that before, and you've always known how much I wanted to be a Mask."

"That was different," she said, and I could hear her forcing herself to use her *reasonable* voice. "Every child wants to be a Mask when they're younger. I played Hoods and Masks like the other kids did. So did your dad. But that's *play*, Evan. It's not real. I never believed for a moment you were actually going to turn into some kind of . . . I mean really. The odds are astronomical. We've explained probability to you. You had to know it was a fantasy."

"Maybe," I said, "on some level. But it's not a fantasy *anymore*. It's my reality. Even if I came home right now, I'd still be metahuman. I'd still be a Mask, I just wouldn't be getting any of the training I need to become a hero."

"*If* you came home right now? *If?* There is no *if* about it, young man. You are coming home this instant. That is final. Your father and I have had plenty of time to talk this over, and we will not budge on this issue. This isn't a game of Masks and Hoods anymore, Evan. This is *real* and it's *dangerous*." There was a long silence, before she almost whispered, "You could have *died* at the museum. If Captain Commanding hadn't arrived when he did . . ."

Arrived? Woke up was more like it, but I didn't say anything because this was dangerous ground. If she ever learned how close I had come to checking out for good, she'd never agree to let me be a Mask. But that only made my own resolution firmer. I had to learn how to make the best of what I had become.

"I need to find out what I am," I said, my own voice shaky. "*Who* I am. I need to understand this."

"No. You don't." She crossed her arms and I could tell from the expression on her face that she wasn't going to actually *listen* to another word I said—that she hadn't really been listening for a while. "What you *need* to do is come home. If you don't find out where you are and let us come get you right now, there will be *serious consequences*."

That was it. Something snapped down deep in my chest. What possible consequences could my parents come up with that would be worse than getting hit by Spartanicus's death ray? Or spending a week and a half in a cocoon? I had already experienced some extremely *serious consequences* and survived them all right on my own, thank you very much. I was a Mask now. That was my truth, and I had to do this.

I took a deep, ragged breath and plunged over the edge. "Then I guess there will have to be serious consequences, because I *need* to learn more about the me I am now. Look, I'll talk to you again later—maybe tomorrow, once I've had a chance to—"

"Evan! You're not safe there. We are *done* talking about this, and you are coming home now!"

A movement behind my mother drew my eyes, as Agent Brendan stuck her face into the pickup field again. "Dr. Quick, I'm afraid that you don't have the right to make that decision anymore. If your son wants to enroll in Hero High, OSIRIS will make sure that happens." She looked at me. "Evan, do you want me to close this session down?"

"What!" yelled my dad. "Evan is our son. How dare you!"

Agent Brendan didn't even look at my dad. "Evan?"

"Yeah, I guess I do. I'm sorry, Mom, I have to do this. End transmission."

It was the hardest thing I'd ever said, but I had no choice. It had never for a second occurred to me that my parents wouldn't support me at least as far as finding out about what I was now, that they would, or even *could,* act so angry and irrational. There'd been something disturbing in my mother's voice when she called Masks . . . No, when she'd called *me* a freak.

I don't think she'd meant it that way, or thought through the fact that she was speaking about me. That was fear talking—fear for me, for my safety—but I didn't doubt for a second that was how she really felt about . . . well . . . us.

That day at Camp Commanding? The one where I broke the barbells? Not the worst day of my life.

Not even close.

9

Hero High?

Teeth, meet boot. Boot, teeth.

Not literally, maybe, but, man, if I didn't feel like someone had kicked me in the face. For as long as I could remember I had wanted to be a Mask. It was my dream. And my parents had supported me in it. Right up until it came true.

If you'd told me a year ago that I was finally going to get superpowers and that the first thing I did with them was rescue Captain Commanding, I would never have believed you. If somehow you'd convinced me it was true, I'd have been walking on air. If you'd then told me I was going to go to a super-secret school for Masks to learn how to use my powers? I can't even imagine how thrilled I'd have been.

If you'd also told me I was going to spend my first day at Mask school lying on an upper bunk in my dorm room, staring at the ceiling and wondering how my life had fallen apart instead of bouncing off the walls, I'd . . . I don't know. I just don't know.

I was living it now and I still couldn't make it come out right in my head.

"Hero High? Hero *High*." That's what Agent Brendan had called the place, but no matter how I said it or how often, I couldn't process it. "*Hero* High."

"That's not what we actually call the place." A boy's voice came from somewhere below me and I started—I hadn't realized I wasn't alone anymore.

I didn't know what to say, so I quietly closed my eyes and hoped he'd go away, whoever he was.

"Hey, you okay up there?" I felt the whole bunk shift, and a sudden weight on the mattress beside me.

Okay, he wasn't going away. I turned my head and met a pair of brown eyes only inches from my own. They belonged to a friendly face that was a slightly lighter shade of brown. He was standing on the lower bunk and leaning on mine.

"Uh, hi," I said.

"Yeah, I didn't think so. Hang on." The face blurred. The bunk shifted again, and without me having seen the intervening steps, I found a young man sitting cross-legged on the bunk by my feet. "Jeda Marquez," his hand was suddenly extended in an offer to shake. Again, I didn't see the motion that put it there. "You can call me Jeda. Or Speedslick, if you prefer."

He obviously wasn't going away, so I sat up and took his hand. "Evan Quick."

He shook it. "Is that your name, or your Mask handle?"

"Name, I guess. No one's given me a handle yet."

He laughed. "You guess that's your name? Man, you really are having a bad day. What happened?"

"I . . . I don't really want to talk about it." I did, but not with some stranger, and the people I normally took my problems to *were* the problem this time.

Jeda frowned. "You look like someone kicked you in the stomach there. Around here that usually means family problems. Folks throw you out?"

I found I couldn't stop blinking. His conversational leaps seemed even faster than the physical ones. "I'm sorry, what?"

"It's a pretty common story. Everyone is cool with having a Mask in the family right up until it happens. A lot of kids who go to school here aren't welcome at home anymore." He shrugged— a quick up-down movement that was almost too fast to see. "I know that stuff's hard to talk about, so I figured I'd blurt it out and give you the chance to talk about it if you needed to. Worst thing that happens is you take a swing at me. Best is I save you some grief."

"You know that's crazy, right?" I wanted to be angry at Jeda. Instead I found myself rather liking him. "This is a school for Masks. What if I was superstrong and punched your face out the back of your head?"

He laughed again, and suddenly he was sitting on the other top bunk, halfway across the room. "You'd never connect, you're not fast enough. I can tell because your pupils don't follow me. Besides, almost no one here has that kind of major power."

"No one at *Hero High* has major superpowers?" I raised an eyebrow skeptically.

"I didn't say nobody." He blurred off the other bunk and down to the main door—bouncing off it with a slight *thunk*, before assuming a casual pose as he leaned against it. The look on his face reminded me of a cat that had just fallen off a couch and was now pretending it meant to do that. "I said *almost* nobody. I also said we didn't call this place Hero High, though you might have missed that bit since you were sulking at the time."

"No, I heard you. I just kind of forgot about it till now." I didn't argue about the sulking bit, since there was no way to do so without sounding sulky or starting a fight, and I wanted more information. And a friend. I *really* wanted a friend. "So, what *do* you call this place? AMO seems like kind of a mouthful."

"School for Sidekicks, mostly. Nobody gets to be a Mask right out of the gate anymore. It's all training wheels, like five years of school, and age limits, and placement tests. Not to mention the internships."

"Wait, internships?"

"Uh-huh. Two evenings a week and weekends to start. More as you get older."

"That's ridiculous! You make it sound like we aren't even here to learn how to be heroes."

Jeda shrugged. "It's not so bad—once you get used to the idea." For the first time he sounded less than cheery and self-confident. "It kind of even makes sense."

"But how does that even work? Being a Mask isn't exactly like plumbing or teaching or some regular job." I saw Jeda's expression go a little sour and added, "Or is it?

"It's complicated. OSIRIS has gotten really powerful in the

years since M-Day and the Hero Bomb. Especially after the Franklin Act, which gave them legal authority to do pretty much whatever they wanted with us." He blurred back up onto the bed with me, moving more jerkily this time, like his powers were cutting in and out. "These days, they're really hard-nosed about letting new metas out on their own. If you try to hero it up without OSIRIS approval, they treat you like a Hood and take you down fast. Think instant stint in a metamax facility."

"So, what then? You're saying you need to intern with a full-on Mask before they let you do the hero thing?"

"If you don't want to get locked up, yeah, pretty much. Where else did you think teen sidekicks came from? Nobody *wants* to be Kid-Not-as-Awesome-as-His-Mentor." He blurred the words together so that they came out almost as one continuous name.

"I guess I really hadn't thought about it." Captain Commanding had never had a sidekick, and most of the Masks that did always struck me as second-stringers like Hotflash or Mixmax. "So, how do you get assigned to a Mask?"

"I know that look. You're thinking you want to sign up with one of the rock stars of the Mask world. Forget that."

"Why?" If I had to be a sidekick, maybe I could be the Captain's first. That'd be pretty cool actually—hanging out with Captain Commanding in his secret lair. I *had* saved his life. That had to count for something.

"Because the really big names either don't bother with sidekicks, or they already have giant waiting lists. Unless you're extra-major-super you're out of luck. Whoever OSIRIS finds for you, you'll take."

"We'll see about that." I had a plan again and that felt good.

Jeda shrugged. "If it makes you feel better, who am I to argue?"

I didn't like the sound of that, but I put it aside for the moment. "What else don't I know?" I figured I might as well get the bad news all out there at once. "What kind of school is this, if it's not one where we learn how to use our powers?"

"Well . . . most of us aren't all that super." Jeda rolled backward off the bunk, landing neatly on his feet—an effect made somewhat less awesome when they skidded out from under him and he had to do a sort of high-speed jig to stay upright. "Kind of like that." He laughed. "Not yet anyway. Since the Hero Bomb, new powers have gotten a lot weaker and more erratic. Sometimes they fade out completely. Sometimes they change or get stronger. You know about all that, right?"

I nodded. "Sure, some. They talk about that stuff in the magazines and vid programs, but not as much as they do the big-name Masks—it's not as interesting, I guess."

"Well, it's much more complicated than they say in public. We take classes on Mask history and biology here. Whatever is causing new metahuman activations is very different from the Hero Bomb. It's weaker and a lot gentler. Almost nobody dies anymore, but"—he paused and looked around like he wanted to make sure no one was listening—"look, some of this is stuff we get from other students or listening between the lines in lectures, so don't take it as gospel."

"All right."

"It seems like the new version partially activates a lot of people who would have died right away if they got hit by something like the Hero Bomb. They get really weak powers like changing the color of their eyes, or their powers come in okay but then fade out after a few weeks."

"So I might not have powers next week?" Wouldn't my fight with my parents look stupid then.

Jeda smiled again. "Don't worry about that. They wouldn't have sent you here if they didn't think it would take, or if you were too weak to make it as a Mask. All of the kids here at the AMO have at least some real powers. I'm fast, Erik goes transparent, Melody breaks things with her voice. It's just that almost none of us are in a class with someone like Captain Commanding or Sprintcess Speed or even Flareup. Add in that OSIRIS insists we all serve internships on top of our class time, and it gets kind of hard to think of ourselves as real Masks. You know?"

I could see that. Still, I had powers, I was at Mask school. Now I just had to get a good internship. Well, that and figure out a new school. I hadn't changed schools since I started junior high. At any other time I probably would have panicked about that, but when you compared it to nearly getting killed by Spartanicus and suddenly having superpowers, it didn't seem like that big a deal. I was finally on my way!

"Thanks, for being nice to the new kid," I said.

"No problemo. I—wait a second." He pulled his cell out and glanced at the screen. "Is that the time? Gottagobye!"

There was a blur and a bang as the door slammed shut, and then Jeda was gone. I smiled and shook my head. I liked him, but in some ways it was a relief to have him gone again. The talk with my parents had really knocked the wind out of me. Add in all the stuff Jeda had just told me, and . . . well, I definitely needed some time to think about what I wanted to do next. Well, besides asking Mike if he could set me up to intern with Captain Commanding, of course. I settled back on my bunk and tried to put together a good argument. That's where my mother said you should always start if you were going to be dealing with any kind of school administration.

~~~ ~~~

Professor Matheny's office was pretty big, and it had a couch, but aside from that it looked like every other professor's office I'd ever been in. The furniture was covered in that gray institutional fabric you only see when you get dragged along on some errand by your parents, and the rest of the room matched the couch—a saggy chair in that same gray, a big metal desk. The only things that gave the room any character at all were the Minute Man pictures and clippings and a number of instruments, including a fancy-looking guitar hanging on the wall right behind his chair.

It framed his face as he shook his head, now. "No, son, I'm afraid not. Even if it weren't awfully early for you to be looking at finding a Mask to intern with, there's simply no chance."

"But I've only just mentioned it to you," I told him. "How can you know the Captain will turn me down without actually asking him. I saved his life!"

"And that'd be enough all on its own," he replied wryly.

"What do you mean?" I demanded. Nobody disses the Captain when I'm around.

"Captain Commanding doesn't work with *anybody*. Not since the Foxman days." Matheny rubbed his forehead. "He . . . well, I've read your file. I know what Captain Commanding means to you, so let me put this as gently as possible. Our good Captain has a bit of an ego problem. He doesn't like to be upstaged. Heck, he doesn't even like to be downstaged. Or sidestaged. He really doesn't want anyone else on the stage with him at all."

"The Captain is a great man!" *How could he talk about Captain Commanding like that?*

"He is. One of the greatest. It's . . ." He sighed. "No. There's no way to sugarcoat this. Captain Commanding is a very great man, but he's not a *good* man."

"What?! How can you say that?"

"Because I know him, Evan—have for years." He held up a hand. "Hang on. I saved something because I thought we might be having this conversation at some point, though not quite so soon." He lifted the lid of the laptop on his desk and flipped through the tabs on his browser, stopping at one that showed me hanging from Spartanicus's fist at the museum. "Watch."

The scene played out as I remembered it, right up until Captain Commanding balled up in the air and started whimpering. At that point the audio fuzzed out and the edges of things developed rainbows so that it became very hard to see or understand anything. As the Captain dropped out of frame, it cut off completely and shifted to a shot of the Captain talking to a female reporter in the studio. He was wearing his full uniform, and his hair—he wore a half mask that was open on top and in back—was even more perfectly styled than the reporter's.

"It looked pretty bad for you there for a little while, Captain Commanding."

The Captain waved his hand dismissively. "Looked worse than it was by far. Much of that video was faked by Mr. Implausible. You know his powers change to fit the plot he's currently involved in, right?"

The reporter nodded vacantly.

"Well, this time his powers included the ability to make cameras see whatever he wanted them to. By running the feed through a power-removal filter, you can see where things departed from his script. That's the point where things went fuzzy on your clip. OSIRIS has taken the liberty of getting Mixmax to use his electromagnetic skills to re-create the real footage, and I've brought it along with me today."

The screen cut back to the museum. This time, as Captain Commanding burst in through the skylight, a dozen energy beams struck him from various directions. But the only damage they did was to open a couple of rips in his uniform, exposing his right biceps and about a third of his chest.

He laughed then. "Nice try, villains, but hardly enough to stop Captain Commanding! Prepare to be vanquished!"

In the vid my voice cried out, "Oh, Captain Commanding, thank god you've come to rescue me!" Then burst into sobs.

"That's not what happened," I whispered, but Professor Matheny just pointed at the screen, as if to say, "Keep watching."

The scene on the laptop showed the camera panning down to focus on Spartanicus as he fired a blast from his forehead. The camera whipped around to show it strike the Captain full in the chest before ricocheting off to blow up the old Commanding Car. As it fell, Mempulse tumbled out of the passenger seat and landed hard.

The Captain smiled, and you could almost see him thinking *Aha!* Another blast hit him, and this time he twisted to direct the ricochet into HeartBurn—standing on the stairs. She went down, too.

Showing no signs of learning, the Spartanicus of the video fired again, and again he took out one of his own henchmen. At that point, the Captain flew down and knocked him out with a single punch. Then he scooped me up and ripped away the imprisoning bag. Underneath I was wearing a Captain Commanding tee so garish and worshipful I'd have been too embarrassed to wear it at nine, much less thirteen.

"Oh, thank you, Captain Commanding!" I chirruped through my continuing tears. "You arrived just in the nick of time." Then I fainted into his arms.

After stroking my forehead and saying quietly, "Poor lad, the terror was just too much for him," he gently set me in one of the theater's chairs before moving on to release the other kids—many of whom were also wearing Captain Commanding gear.

"I don't even know what to say," I whispered. "That's nothing like how it went."

"No, it's not. But it is the official story as it's being reported now. Thanks to OSIRIS and this video, that's also the version all of the other kids who were there will remember."

I wanted to throw up. "Professor Matheny?" *How did I even ask this?*

"Call me Mike. Really."

That helped for some reason. "All right, Mike. Shortly after I went into my cocoon I thought I heard a conversation between Captain Commanding and an OSIRIS agent named Brendan. They were talking about altering people's memories. The Captain kind of implied mine should be fixed, too, but Agent Brendan was very firm about it. I thought it was a dream until you said that"— I pointed at the laptop—"was how the other kids would remember things."

"Now you want to know if OSIRIS is in the business of changing people's memories of metahuman events."

I nodded, feeling sicker by the moment. "That, and if what I heard could have been real. I was sort of in a coma at the time, so it seems impossible."

"The answer to the first question is, I am ashamed to say, yes. I wish I could deny it, but I can't. I won't make any defense of the practice because I think it's flat wrong. As for the latter? Who knows? Your cocoon seems to be a defensive measure as well as a healing one. Maybe something in you sensed a danger in that moment and it partially roused you. It's hard to say. People's powers vary wildly and we only ever really understand parts of them."

I looked at the ground between my feet. There was something else I wanted to ask but it was going to be even harder. I took several deep breaths and then rushed it out. "Is the Captain really like that? I mean would he really have them make me look like such a giant dork just to preserve his reputation?"

Mike's expression turned hard. "The Captain's reputation matters more to him than your life does. Don't ever doubt it." I think he saw the hesitation and confusion in my eyes because he added, "I can burn a copy of the video for you as a reminder, if you'd like."

"No thanks. Once was enough." Then something else hit me. "Wait, is this the story my parents have seen?"

"More or less, yes."

Well, that explained some of their flip out. "May I tell them the real story?"

"If you want to try, you're welcome to. You can even do it right now." He slid his office phone across the desk. "Here, you won't be able to use your cell until it's been added to our booster system."

I reached for it, then stopped. "I'm missing something, aren't I?"

"Maybe. It will depend on your parents. This is the official story and it's been repeated a lot. I can't say whether your parents will believe your version, but I *can* tell you that you will get no corroboration on it from anyone anywhere."

"Not even from you?" I felt like someone had punched me in the gut.

He looked deeply unhappy. "If I want to hang on to my job and keep taking care of my students, no. This is the OSIRIS-approved version of what happened that day. Any deviation from that line will be treated very harshly by the governmental face of the Mask community. If, on the other hand, I want to hang on to my integrity . . ." He sighed, then nodded. "But I'm not your parents' favorite person. Do you really think they'll believe me where they wouldn't believe you?"

"They're *not* going to believe me, are they?"

He shrugged, but I pushed the phone back to him. "I don't

think I want to do this right now, or talk to my parents." They were going to believe that terror-stricken idiot was me, no matter what I had to say, and I didn't want to talk to them with that in their head. Not right now anyway, it made me too angry. "This Mask stuff is a lot harder than it looks in the comics, isn't it?"

"Life is harder than it looks in the comics, or in books or movies for that matter. I'm sorry you're getting that lesson so early. Life is the hardest thing there is." And then he smiled his gentle smile again. "But that doesn't mean it's not worth it. I wouldn't trade it for anything."

I didn't know what to say to that, so I started to stand up, then paused.

"Is there anything else I can help you with, Evan?"

I thought of all the things I wanted to know and all the things I needed to do, but I didn't have energy for any of it. "I don't know, I feel so overwhelmed. I guess what I really need is time."

"Take tomorrow off. Unpack, read the school handbook, go over your schedule, put together a list of questions. Do whatever you need to do. School can wait for a day."

I nodded. Earlier—after my disastrous conversation with my parents—Mike had given me a big folder full of all kinds of stuff, including a two-inch-thick AMO handbook to help get me oriented. He'd also shown me the dorms, and where the container with all my stuff in it was waiting to be unpacked. OSIRIS had sent a collection team to my house to get my clothes and those things they or my parents thought I might need. I hadn't opened it yet and, given the way my mom and dad had insisted I wasn't staying, I suspected it would be missing a lot of things I might want.

When I got back to the dorm room I was going to be sharing with Jeda and two other boys, I found it empty. I'd never been so glad not to see anyone in my whole life. It meant I could skin out of my jeans, brush my teeth in the attached bathroom, crawl into bed, and pretend to sleep. It wasn't until I was finally drifting off for real several hours later that I realized I still didn't know where the AMO was.

Somehow, it no longer seemed to matter.

10

Out of This World

Combat with Dinnerware.

That's what finally got me out of my dorm room again, two days after my arrival at the AMO. I'd taken one day more than Mike had initially offered me, because I simply felt too angry to deal with it all. The school doctor said I could take an entire extra week if I needed it. But how do you skip a class entitled Combat with Dinnerware?

That was the name of one of the workshop classes in the Topics in Heroing sequence for incoming students—Fridays 10:00 a.m. for course weeks three through nine. Topics in Heroing didn't work like the classes I'd had at my regular school. Instead of the whole semester you might spend on something like American history, it was a blocked-out hour each day where different instructors came in and did a workshop on something Masks needed to know. Some of the classes were a one-time deal only, like Capes—Flashy but Fatal. Others might go for two or three sessions. Those mostly ran on Tuesdays and Thursdays.

The more intensive ones, like Combat with Dinnerware, ran weekly for a month or two, usually Monday/Wednesday/Friday. I'd already missed the first sessions of Bantering Basics and Costume Maintenance—the other two weeks-three-through-nine extended sessions, but I could catch up next week. Whenever I could manage to forget about that awful Captain Commanding video and my other problems, I found myself really looking forward to my time at the school.

I took advantage of the doctor's permission to skip my 9:00 a.m. math class, and there were no 8:00 a.m. classes. *How awesome was that?* Professor Matheny told me it was because OSIRIS research showed that making teen Masks get up too early degraded their performance on standardized tests and power control. The latter could lead to things like major fires or the destruction of expensive government equipment. So, it was official school policy to let sleeping teenagers lie.

When I finally crawled out of bed around nine thirty, I put on jeans and a dark green Captain Commanding tee—turned inside out, so you couldn't see the Captain's face and logo. It made me furious to have to wear his brand at all, but I didn't have much choice. Whoever packed for me hadn't included many unmarked shirts, and almost all of my tees featured the Captain one way or another.

Since I didn't want any connection to him after seeing that altered video feed, I had a major wardrobe problem. Eventually, I was going to have to figure out a better solution than wearing all my shirts inside out. But for today—given how awful I felt—I figured simply getting to classes would provide challenge enough.

As I pulled my socks on, I couldn't help notice the pile of bright yellow message slips on my desk. Each marked a call from my parents, calls I had simply refused to take. I still didn't want to talk to them. Not after the way the last time had gone, and especially not after seeing that video and knowing what they must believe about me now.

My cell phone was sitting there as well, turned off now that it was tuned to use the school's booster antenna. Which reminded me that I really ought to make an effort to find out where I was at some point, for my own curiosity if not for my parents. I glared at the yellow slips for several long beats, then quietly pushed them off the back of the desk. They fell into the dead space between it and the wall. I would call my parents later, after I'd settled in a bit.

When I got to class, I found that my plan to quietly slip into the back row of seats was a nonstarter. There were no seats. The room was set up like my grandmother's dance studio. There was a hardwood floor and mirrors on three walls. The fourth had big sliding doors—open now to reveal stacked gym mats. Jeda was working with two girls and my second roommate—a fifteen-year-old named Eric Anwyn—was pulling the mats out and setting them up.

There were a bunch of other kids, too, but Eric and Jeda were the only ones I knew by name. I backed into the corner and tried not to make eye contact while I waited. Even with my eyes down, I could see the class was made up of a wider-than-usual assortment of ages, everything from me and my roommates on up to a couple of girls who I would have guessed were close to twenty. Most of the other students were wearing costumes of one variety or another, which made me feel even *more* out of place. But about two minutes after I slipped in, Jeda came over to collect me.

"Hey, it's great to see you up and among the living. Come on, Mike had to run to the office for something. Let me introduce you to some of your fellow minions-in-training while we wait."

"I don't know," I began, but Jeda was already dragging me over to where he had left the two girls with Eric.

"Hey, Alissa, meet my new roommate, Evan." He pointed me at the taller of the pair, a pretty, muscular girl with deep black skin and short curly hair somewhere between an Afro and a crew cut. She was wearing a black-and-gold uniform in one of the combat-grade sports blends like Invulycra with Armex reinforcements. She looked to be a year or two older than the rest of us.

"Handle's Emberdown when I'm in uniform; I heat things up." She turned an exasperated eye on Jeda. "Speaking of handles, that's how you *should* have introduced me."

Jeda shrugged. "It's silly."

"It's protocol," she answered stubbornly.

"I haven't got a handle yet," I said, offering her my hand to take the heat off Jeda. "I . . . don't really know what all of my powers are. They're kind of erratic."

She smiled. "Don't worry about that. They mostly are when you're first getting started. I'm sure they'll settle in after a while."

Jeda turned to the second girl. She was skinnier than Alissa, and shorter. But that hardly registered. What really stood out was the eight-inch mohawk and all the piercings. She wore a studded leather jacket with the sleeves hiked up to expose intricate tattoos on her forearms—a wolf on the left, a dragon on the right. I wondered how she'd gotten her parents to agree to them.

Jeda nodded at her. "Mel, Evan. Evan, Mel. It's short for Melody."

"But don't ever call me that," she said, her voice surprisingly deep. "I freaking hate it. I'm not all that fond of Mel either." She glared at Jeda before turning a stern eye on me. "Handle's Night-Howl, 'cause I'm a werewolf. 'Howl's what I prefer. In class or in costume, folks mostly go by handles and I *always* do."

"Nice to meet you, 'Howl. Your tattoos are *awesome*."

For the first time she actually smiled, it made her look a lot younger—my age maybe—and a little less scary, but only a little. "You'll do."

"You know Blindmark already," Jeda indicated Eric, who had changed out of his regular jeans and tee in favor of a stylized martial arts outfit. "Now, who else . . ."

But as we were talking, another student had drifted over, cutting in now, "You're that kid who wrapped a piece of rebar around Spartanicus's head the other day, right?"

"Uh, yeah," I said over my shoulder.

Apparently, despite whatever was being said out in the normal world, here at the AMO the real story was getting around. That was a relief. Maybe my peers wouldn't think I was quite as much of a giant dork as the rest of the world did. With a smile, I turned to face the new . . . guy . . . girl . . . other? I wasn't sure how to place the person I was talking to. Their features were androgynous, as was their body shape under the loose fitting cargo pants and sweat shirt.

The effect was greatly enhanced by a slow but constant series of changes to skin color, hair length and curl, cheekbones, nose. Everything about them was continually shifting, so that what had been a slender boyish blonde when I first caught sight of them was already turning into a more feminine brunette with café-au-lait skin.

"Name's Blurshift," they said in a musical voice that walked the line between genders. "Shapechanger. No handle, no other name. All that stuff is bull."

"Blur has dibs on the fourth bunk in our room," said Eric, injecting himself into the conversation for the first time. "If they ever decide to be a boy, that is." His tone was more bemused than anything.

"Ours, too, if they go the other way," added NightHowl, and she actually laughed. "Blur's the perfect roommate. Never there to hog the closets."

"Love you, too," Alissa said, sarcastically.

'Howl rolled her eyes. "You know what I mean."

"So you're not . . ." I trailed off as I realized I was about to ask Blurshift something that could well come off as rude. "Uh, sorry. That was impolite. I'm not used to . . ."

"This?" Blur touched a finger to their chin and arched an eyebrow that shifted from brown to black. "No one is." Blur laughed. "Not at first anyway. Don't worry about it. 'Howl's right. You'll do."

Where the conversation would have gone next, I don't know, because Professor Matheny—Mike—arrived at that very moment and told us to line up on the mats.

He was wearing his old Minute Man uniform, instead of the jeans and button-down he usually sported. The outfit was a bit scuffed up here and there, and perhaps a touch tight across his middle, but otherwise he looked good. Every inch the classic Mask, from the tips of his red boots to the double *M*s of his crest—the first huge, the second tiny and connected to the first by cartoon lines that somehow conveyed shrinkage. The one difference from the old pictures I'd seen of him in his heroing days was that he'd doffed his cowl.

He was carrying a clear plastic bin filled with a weird assortment of junk. It held everything from scratched-up old silverware, to an ancient issue of *Mask Monthly*, and a couple of cans of sardines. He set the bucket down, flipped the lid off, reached in, and pulled out a tin fork.

"This," he said, "is a deadly weapon in the right hands. I know that sounds silly." A few of the students chuckled and Mike grinned as well. "But it's also true. Look, not everyone can punch through steel plate like Captain Commanding, or throw around plasma balls like Flareup. Heck, most of us don't even have the martial advantages of something like a Foxblaster."

His expression grew more serious. "Frankly, most of us are a lot less super than that . . . and when I say most of *us*, I also mean most of *you*. For whatever reason, much of the younger generation of Masks—that's you—are not nearly as tough as your predecessors were at a similar age. How many of you think you could take a hit from Spartanicus like Quick here did and not wind up in a wooden box?"

The whole room turned and looked at me while I tried to sink into the floor. "I didn't exactly bounce back from that gracefully," I mumbled when that didn't work.

Mike nodded, his expression still serious. "I'm glad you recognize that." He looked at the rest of the class. "After Spartanicus blasted him, Quick spent ten days in a cocoon in a coma. He barely made it."

"But he *did* make it," said Jeda. "Sounds like he's a plenty tough hombre to me."

"He got lucky, Speedslick," replied Mike. "Agent Brendan was the first OSIRIS operative on scene. I've read her report. This is what it had to say on the topic: 'Subject Evan Quick is in deep coma after his encounter with Spartanicus. His odds of survival are currently estimated at sixty-three percent. They are that high due entirely to having had his powers accidentally boosted by Mr. Implausible at the time of the blast. Odds of subject's survival without that boost estimated at point zero-zero-zero-two percent.'

"Pretty ugly, huh?" No one answered, and Mike continued, "But those are still better odds than mine in that same situation. I don't even have Quick's baseline healing factor. Neither do most of you. That doesn't mean the Hoods will take it easy on you. Being a Mask is a very dangerous business, one which is likely to get more than one of you killed."

Mike stopped talking to let his words sink in. The room got very quiet and I wasn't the only one looking at my feet.

"Good, that's the response I hoped I'd get. It means you're listening *and* thinking. Which brings us back to this." He brandished the fork. "I know it doesn't look like much, but there are a lot of things you can do with a fork in a fight." He shifted his grip so that he was holding the back end out like a knife. "It's not very sharp, but it's thin, and it's strong enough to punch in under someone's ribs and up into something vital, or into an eye."

He flipped it around again. "Or, if you're small, it's pretty much a trident." He shrank down—a bizarre thing to watch given that he was such a bear of a man to start with—and gripped the fork like a spear. He looked for all the world like a prop from the world's tiniest gladiator movie.

"A fork for a trident?" Blurshift said doubtfully. "You're a pretty awesome teacher, but that seems a little weak."

Mike laughed and grew back to regular size. "You're skeptical, and reasonably so. But, this fork saved my life once." He dropped the fork back into the bin and pulled out the old *Mask Monthly*, opening it to a page flagged with a sticky note. "Look."

The note marked a two-page article with the title "Minute Man Forks His Way Out of His Last Minutes." He shook his head. "I never could get through to *Mask Monthly* that it was *my-newt man* and not *mih-nut man*—drove me crazy."

Below the main headline was the opening, "Minute Man knocks the stuffing out of the Fluffinator. Armed only with a fork, the miniature Mask takes down killer teddy bear."

"I popped its stitches."

"I don't know," said Blindmark. "Good against a remote-control bear is one thing. Good against a living, thinking opponent . . ."

Mike shook his head and rolled up the magazine. Then, moving with a speed that surprised me, he jabbed it toward Blindmark's midriff, tagging him just hard enough so that he gave out a little *whuff* as the air left his lungs.

"Hey, no fair," he said. "I wasn't ready." Mike raised an eyebrow at that and Blindmark blushed. "Yeah, the Hoods aren't going to wait for me to go into a battle trance either. Point taken."

"Good." Mike set the magazine back in the bucket. "Look, I'm not saying that any of you is going to take on someone like Spartanicus or HeartBurn with a magazine and a fork. That's simply not going to happen, though I did once knock Mr. Implausible out with a small bucket of squid, three chopsticks, and a spoonful of malt powder. What I'm trying to do is get you all to think in terms of using every available tool to save your own lives."

He reached into the bucket and pulled out a plastic picnic knife. "Given any choice at all, this is not the weapon you want to bring to a gunfight. But if that fight comes to you when you're eating tuna salad in the park, you may not get the choice. You have to be ready to turn any old thing into the weapon that wins your battle. For the rest of the hour, I'm going to go through a whole list of daily items and demonstrate how to turn them to your advantage. Dental floss doubled up a few times makes a dandy garrote. Body spray quickly becomes a flamethrower. Jet cheese can destroy your enemy's traction.

"Here"—he pulled out a spoon—"let me give you a demonstration. Speedslick, hit that target-dummy button, would you?"

He pointed and Jeda blurred across the room. A half second later a door opened in the ceiling and a surprisingly lifelike mannequin descended. It was made of some soft material that looked much more like flesh than plastic.

"Start with grip. The best way to use a spoon as a weapon is to place the bowl of the spoon in your palm with the back side against your skin. That lets you brace the tip of the spoon against the heel of your hand. Now, the next bit will vary a bit depending on how your hand is shaped, but for most of you, you'll want to make a fist around the spoon with the handle sticking out between your middle two fingers like so."

He held up his fist with the handle sticking out like a long steel spike. "See how nasty that looks? And it's only a spoon. You're going to use it to punch through one of the soft spots on your target."

Mike suddenly lunged forward, throwing an underhanded punch that stabbed the end of the spoon into the dummy's belly right below the breastbone. There was a soft pop in the instant before the more meaty sound of Mike's fist hitting the mannequin's skin. As he pulled his hand back, a big drop of blue gel welled up from the hole where the spoon had gone in.

He touched it with his other hand. "This is probably the easiest target for a spoon. It's central, it's low, you can do a fair amount of damage if you angle the handle up toward the heart or into one of the lungs. That said, there are several more dangerous targets if the situation calls for."

Mike struck again, this time driving up under the mannequin's chin. "If your spoon is long enough, you can punch it up through the roof of the mouth and into your opponent's brain. That's generally fatal.

"If you don't want to kill someone, but you do need to put them in the hospital you can also go for the kidneys." He leapt forward, catching the dummy by the neck and spinning around it to plunge the handle of the spoon into its back below the ribs on the right side. "Or you can always go for an eye."

NightHowl grinned. "Gruesome!"

"It is," agreed Mike. "Flatware is great if you want to go for real injury. If you're looking to incapacitate, you want something in the plates or platters family. Or a vase is always good. Everyone will get a turn, but who wants to try the spoon first?" He held it up and Speedslick blurred his way to the front of the line.

As Speedslick went all sewing machine on the mannequin, Mike continued his lecture. "Starting next week, you'll be spending time in the school's battle simulation rooms, either with me for improvised weapons practice or with Professor Ivanova or one of our other teachers for your powers and martial arts drills. We'll set you up with various combat situations you're likely to encounter as a Mask and teach you how to fight your way out.

"In my class you will practice identifying everyday items that are potential weapons and using them against attack bots and your fellow students. As a mental exercise, tell me what you might do with this packet of dried sea monkeys . . ."

The rest of my day felt more like a typical school routine, with all the usual sorts of classes. Only three things really stood out as different from my old school. First, the colorful costumes and battle suits worn by many of the students. Second, the small but constant demonstrations of powers: like the geometry teacher, Professor Bankole, floating worksheets out to her students on a translucent blue platter that she projected from a gem embedded in her forehead. Or the pretty, older girl with skin the color of silver who blurred away down the hall when I made eye contact with her. Third, I got really, really tired of having to add "no handle" to every introduction.

"Man, I need a Mask name soon," I said after about the three dozenth time it happened. I turned to Jeda—*Speedslick*, I mentally corrected myself, also for the three dozenth time. We were walking down the hall after our last class of the day, history. "You want to help me come up with one?"

He frowned. "I'd love to, but it doesn't work that way."

"What do you mean?"

"Official handles are assigned by OSIRIS based on powers or affiliation."

I stopped dead. "Wait, we don't even get to choose our own secret identities? That blows!"

"You didn't really think someone like HeartBurn chose her own name, did you?" said Jeda. "Come on, *HeartBurn*?"

"But HeartBurn's a Hood. Why would she have an OSIRIS-given name?"

"Because she's an AMO grad like most of the younger Hoods," said 'Howl, walking up from behind us. "I think half of 'em go bad because they don't want to play second fiddle to some pathetic older Mask like Rockmeister or Farflung while they wait to get their Mask license."

"Mask license?" I said. "Like driver's license? You're kidding, right?"

'Howl rolled her eyes. "Wish I was, but it's the truth. First, you

108

have to get a sidekick's permit. Then, you do the whole minion thing until your Mask mentor says you're cool or you save the world or something fancy like that. Depending on when one of the official Masks takes you on, that can happen anytime between the end of freshman year and sometime after graduation. Then you still have to take writtens and practicals before they license you. It totally blows monkey chunks."

"How come I've never heard *any* of this?" I demanded. "I thought I was the ultimate Mask nerd."

"Nobody talks about this stuff to outsiders," said Speedslick. "Not if they want to stay on OSIRIS's good side. And *everyone* wants to stay on their good side, even most of the Hoods."

That brought me up short. "Really, why? I mean, I can see why the good guys don't want OSIRIS on their case. But what's up with the bad guys? Isn't taking people like Spartanicus down a big part of OSIRIS's job?"

'Howl and Speedslick looked at each other. Then, both looked around shiftily, like they were making sure no one was listening.

Finally, 'Howl, said, "Come on, let me show you something," and started walking.

"Where are we going?" I asked.

"You'll see," she growled.

Then she shut up and wouldn't say another word as she led us through a maze of doors and passages, several of which were marked with phrases like "authorized personnel only." Eventually, we came to the base of a narrow spiral ramp and started up.

After what must have been ten floors of steady climbing with no end in sight, I finally asked, "Where *are* we?"

She countered with a question, "You ever hear of the AMO before you got sent here?"

"No." I hadn't—or I'd have been begging my parents to send me here, powers or no.

"And you're a self-admitted Mask nerd. Seem a little strange to you?"

"When you put it that way, yeah."

"So, you want to know why *no one's* ever heard of the AMO?" she continued. "I mean, a whole freaking school full of baby metas just learning how to handle their powers. People like Emberdown, with her lasers and fire bursts. Or Sparkle. You know Sparkle?" She glanced at Speedslick.

"Dude's a living firework," he replied as we turned onto another flight—this one with a door at the top.

"'Zactly!" she said. "Now, how do you hide something like that from the world?"

"I don't know," I answered.

"Like this." She pushed open the door and gestured me through.

I froze with one foot on the threshold. Beyond, there were stars. Nothing but endless, impossibly bright stars. 'Howl gave me a gentle shove and I stumbled forward into a huge domed room something like a greenhouse. The door opened out of a small shed-like structure in the center of a slightly sunken well at the center of the dome. Above, the sky was blacker than I'd ever seen it.

"This is how you hide a school like the AMO from the world," said 'Howl. "By putting it on another one."

"Where . . ." I couldn't even finish the question as I stumbled forward up the low ramp that climbed out of the well. I was too awestruck.

Speedslick put his hands on my shoulders and very gently turned me around. That's when I sat down on the floor because my knees gave out. A huge arc of red-brown desert dominated the view on that side.

"Is that Mars?" I whispered.

'Howl nodded. "Welcome to the moon of Deimos."

11

Be Careful What You Wish For

"But the gravity feels normal and . . . ," I mumbled, barely coherent in the face of the sheer glory of the warrior planet hanging above us. "How is that even possible?"

"Don't ask me," said 'Howl.

"Some *very* super-Mask with gravity powers probably," answered Speedslick.

"But how did we *get* here?" I asked.

"Oh, right, you missed that step by arriving in a cocoon," said Speedslick. "There's a big steel tube thing at OSIRIS headquarters in Heropolis, looks like a giant cannon complete with shells as big as an elevator compartment. You step into one on Earth, there's a mondo-big noise and ten minutes of elevator music, and then you step out in the arrival well here on Deimos."

"OSIRIS built this place?" I still couldn't get my knees to let me stand back up. "On one of the moons of Mars?" I suppose that explained the weird lack of any smell to the place—constantly recycled air.

"Yep," said 'Howl. "As a freakin' *high school*. And they've kept it completely secret for twenty years or more. Now do you see why even most Hoods don't want to seriously piss off OSIRIS?"

I looked up at Mars and slowly nodded. "But I'm still confused about one thing. I thought OSIRIS was supposed to keep the Hoods under control."

"Officially, sure," said Speedslick.

"And unofficially?"

He did one of his high-speed shrugs. "That's a harder question. Sometimes, from the inside, it looks an awful lot like they *want* all those Hoods running around wild."

"Why would they want that?"

"Nobody knows," said 'Howl. "Nobody knows."

"But that's what you believe?"

She nodded.

What had I gotten myself into?

〰〰 〰〰

When I got back to my room after my Monday classes, I pulled my laptop out of its bag and climbed up onto my bunk. It took a little while to hook up to the wireless, and even longer to open my webmail account, but then what could you expect . . . Mars! Freaking Mars.

There were about fifty messages from my mom and dad, and a dozen or more from reporters, but not one from classmates back at my old school. Still invisible, I guess. I moused over the most recent e-mail from my mom four or five times without opening it, then shifted to a different window in my browser to noodle around on the Web. But that didn't last long.

Somehow, playing around on my favorite Mask news and gossip sites seemed silly when I was sitting on a bunk at the School for Sidekicks. How fresh could all their insider news really be when they didn't even know this place existed? Didn't even know how it all *really* worked, with stupid hero licenses and Mask internships, and, well, everything!

I went back to my mail. The heading on my mom's most recent message said, "Please." That's all, "Please."

I closed my eyes as I clicked on it, trying to imagine what I wanted it to say. But I didn't even know. Somewhere in the past couple of days I had lost touch with the part of me that wanted things. I guess that wasn't surprising considering that if you'd asked me two weeks ago what I wanted most in the world I would have said *this*. What I had right now.

I was living my dream. Powers, other Masks my own age to hang out with, saving the life of Captain Commanding. More than my dream really. Mars. I was going to school on one of the moons of Mars! *That* was beyond anything I had even imagined wanting, but I felt almost numb when I tried to think about it. There was too much at once.

But I knew that no matter how weird I felt right now about the break with my parents and well, everything, that I wouldn't give any of it up if you gave me the chance to make it never have been.

Stay.

I *had* to stay.

I opened my eyes and started reading my mom's e-mail with the subject line that simply said, "Please":

Evan,

I don't know if you've read my other messages or not, and it doesn't matter. My message is the same as it's been from the first moment, though I hope I can express it better now that I've had more time to think.

I love you. I'm frightened for you. I want you home.

When we talked last, you said that you were a Mask now, that nothing could change that, and that you had to find out what that meant. I didn't take that well. Neither did your father. I said some things I shouldn't have. You're not a freak. You're my son.

No matter what else is true about you, you're my son and I love you.

I'm not going to say that I'm all right with you becoming a Mask. I'm not. I never will be. It's simply too dangerous for me to accept. Yes, you're metahuman. There's no denying that. But that doesn't mean you have to put on a costume and battle evil. We can fight the Franklin Act, I'm sure we can. We just have to find a brave enough lawyer. You can still live a normal life . . . a safe life. No one even has to know you have powers. Not yet, maybe not ever.

You're too young to be making these kinds of

decisions. Come home to us. Put it aside for a few years, and then we can talk about it again.

I just want my boy back. Is that so terrible a thing that you won't even answer my e-mail?

Oh, please, come home, Evan. Please.

Mom

I closed my laptop and slid it under my pillow where I didn't have to look at it. Then I climbed down from my bunk and walked out into the hall. I didn't know where I was going, I only knew that I needed to move. Couldn't they see how important this was to me?

I must have walked for a couple of hours without paying attention to much of anything before I finally ended up standing and staring absently at what looked like a giant bank-vault door somewhere down in one of the deep basements. I had encountered several similar places in my wanderings without really paying much attention, but something about this one brought me back up to the surface for some reason. It felt vaguely familiar, if you can say that about your umpteenth blank vault door in a featureless fused-moon-rock hallway.

There was no handle for opening the vault, just a hand scanner and a microphone like the high-security setup Mike had used to open the door from Backflash's superweird lab space. It might even be the same door. I really hadn't been paying enough attention to my path to know where I was.

The AMO was really, really big. Huge even. I'd seen some of that when I arrived, but in the days since I started classes I'd barely left the areas around the dorms and main classrooms, except to go down to the battle simulators for practice or up to the sky dome to look at Mars. There was plenty of weird to see just doing that, but basically it was an area only about twice the size of my big urban junior high back home. This was the first time I'd wandered farther afield since bouncing back from my Captain Commanding letdown, and now I knew that there were miles of tunnels in the deeps as well as at least four more of the big sky domes.

I also suspected that gravity did some very strange things in the depths. I had never once felt pulled in any direction but down toward the floor, but I was pretty sure that at least two of the domes I'd been in had floors at pretty severe angles to each other—though you couldn't see one from another. For that matter, some of the deepest passages had floors that visibly curved downward in both directions.

"What the plan, *Quick*?" The question came in a female voice, silky and smooth, yet somehow a bit snippish at the same time.

"Huh?" I looked around to see who'd spoken. I was alone. "Is . . . is someone there?"

A patch of empty space about three feet in front of the vault door suddenly lit up with purple flashes like one of those plasma balls. A hundred little arcs of lightning connected it to a thick cable running along the wall, nearly blinding me with their brightness. A moment later it vanished, leaving behind a girl at least a year or two older than I was.

She was tall and slender with long black hair and metallic skin the color of freshly polished copper. Her eyes were a deep mossy green with huge pupils, and she wore a black-and-green uniform that mirrored her hair and eyes. She was simultaneously alien and beautiful, and I couldn't help but swallow.

Flailing around for some response, I stammered, "Do . . . do I know you?" Not that I had any doubts that I'd have remembered it if I'd met her earlier. I simply didn't know what else to say to the prettiest girl I'd ever seen.

Her only reply was a slight lift of her eyebrows and a tightening of her lips—somehow managing to convey with that subtle change of expression that I'd asked her the stupidest question in the history of stupid questions. I blushed all the way down to my toenails.

I looked away. "I guess not. I'm Evan Quick."

"I know." Nothing more, just a flat declaration that made me feel even stupider.

"Ah, you, that is . . . uhm . . ." I couldn't think of a graceful way to either exit the conversation or go any further, so I blurted, "Who are you?"

"You really don't know?" I shook my head. "They call me Burnish."

"Nice to meet you." I extended my hand, but she ignored it.

"What are you doing here, Quick?" She held up one hand to indicate the vault door. Lightning arced from it to the polished metal surface. Her skin shifted from copper to mirror-bright stainless steel—and I suddenly realized she might be the silver girl I'd seen earlier.

"I don't know," I said. "I was just walking. I don't even really know where here is."

"Why am I not surprised?" Her lips tightened again.

She took a long step toward me and, without thinking, I moved backward. She smiled a grim smile and I suddenly felt very alone and more than a little bit threatened.

"Have I done something to offend you?" I asked.

She nodded, but didn't say a word as her hands tightened into fists. I was bracing myself to get the stuffing beat out of me when the vault door made a harsh metallic clunk. Burnish reached out to touch the nearby conduit. Lightning arced at the contact and her skin shifted back to copper. For a moment, purple plasma danced its way down her arm to touch her neck and chest, but then she swore and pulled her hand away and it faded. Behind her the vault opened.

As it swung aside, a woman came forward to the threshold. I recognized her immediately, though I hadn't seen her since my first day at the AMO—Backflash. There was something about her that didn't invite forgetting. So, it *was* the same door.

"What are you children doing down here at the school-side door to my lab?" she asked, her tone vague and almost sweet.

"I'm kind of lost," I said. "I was walking and I forgot to keep track of where I was going."

Burnish didn't answer, and the woman didn't press, though I had no doubt she noticed. "What are your names?" she asked.

"I'm Evan Quick."

"Oh, right, the new one," said the woman, "from the museum. We met last week, didn't we? The cocoon boy. Case number FLR871. Healing powers as well as intermittent bursts of heightened strength and speed."

She smiled at me. "The latter are pretty much par for the metahuman course, and are present to some degree in most cases. But your healing factor is unusual both in type and apparent strength. I look forward to seeing what happens with it when you enter stage-two development. What about you?" She turned to Burnish as the vault door closed behind her.

"Comendelia Waters," she mumbled.

"Ah, yes, HNL932. I knew I recognized you—catalytic metal-empath. Very interesting power. Or powers really, since they change as you shift metals. Very strong too, and so different from your mother's . . . or your father's, for that matter." The woman nodded to herself. "And that explains the two of you wandering around together as well. I'd wondered, considering the clear difference in your ages and relative training. Obvious connection, really."

"What is?" I asked, deeply confused.

"You saving her father's life, of course. I'm sure she has very strong feelings about the boy who saved Captain Commanding." A look of concern passed across her face. "You do remember that you saved him, right? I saw from the initial report that you had suffered moderate brain damage from the blast, but its placement and the thoroughness of your regeneration suggested it wouldn't significantly affect memory. Was the estimate in error?"

"No, no, my memory is fine." *Brain damage?* "It's only . . ."

I glanced over at Burnish, whose lips had now tightened them-selves practically out of existence, and I trailed off. Somehow I didn't think that any strong feelings Captain Commanding's daughter had about me at the moment were good ones.

"Excellent," said the woman. "Excellent, it's always nice to verify metahuman theory with actual physical results where pos-sible. Speaking of which, I should probably get on to my next task."

She started to push past us, and I realized I was about to be left alone with Burnish. "Wait!" She paused and gave me an ex-pectant look. I stammered out the first thing that came to mind, "Stage-two development? What does that mean?"

"You don't know?" Then she shook her head. "No, of course you don't. No reason for it. Not this side of getting your Mask li-censes and full security clearances anyway." She paused thought-fully before finally nodding. "I think I'll wait to let you find that out for yourselves. If your powers fail and you flunk out before it happens they'll have to scrub all of your classified memories, and it's always better to minimize how much they have to wipe. Now, if you two will excuse me, I really do need to get to my next meet-ing. Good-bye."

She headed off up the hallway without another word. I con-sidered quietly following along behind Backflash, but somehow I didn't think Burnish would have any trouble catching me alone again if she really wanted to. So I might as well see it through now. Once Backflash had vanished around the curve of the hallway, I turned back to Burnish, but instead of getting ready to pound me, she was staring blankly off into space. Eventually, she seemed to come back to herself.

"Are you still here?" she asked, her voice cold and bitter.

"I didn't think there was much point in running." The words came from the same place deep down inside that I had spoken from with Spartanicus—some inner font of reckless bravery that I could only tap into at the worst possible moments. "If you really want a piece of me, you might as well try to take it."

She sighed. "Not right now I don't. But we're not done, you and me. Not after you inserted yourself into my family's story back at the museum."

Great.

She reached out to the conduit again. Lightning arced and plasma flowed. This time she didn't stop and, as the purple light engulfed her, she began to stretch and twist. A moment later, there came a faint *fwoomph* of inrushing air as she suddenly flowed into the conduit.

The only thing she left behind was a whisper: "Tell anyone my name is Comendelia, and you're dead, Quick. Dead."

When I got back to the dorm, Speedslick was bouncing around impatiently outside the door to our room. "Thereyouare!"

"Is something wrong?" I asked.

Jeda slowed himself down and spoke more carefully. "Nope, but Mike wants to see you in his office like twenty-minutes-ago." His words started to run together again. "I'll-go-tell-him-you're-onyourway."

Jeda blurred out of focus and rocketed away before I could even think to say anything. When he hit the end of the hall his powers hiccupped and he *really* hit the end of the hall, bouncing off the wall with a *thud* and a yelped "ow!" But he never slowed down.

When I got to the office, I found Mike waiting for me in the doorway—Jeda had come and gone already. "Come on in. I'm glad they found you in time."

"In time for what?" I followed him through the door.

"For this, for starters," he slid a shrink-wrapped bundle across the desk—black, faintly squishy, and about the size of a typical school backpack.

"What is it?" I poked the bundle.

"Your uniform. I'd meant to give it to you once you settled in a bit, but my timeline got advanced."

"My uniform?"

"Yes, the one the machine measured you for that morning at Camp Commanding. Back when you first got your powers."

"I—" I stopped dead—so that really *did* happen. "I'm confused. When I went back to the building to pick up my uniform a couple of days later the whole place had changed into a set of restrooms. What happened?"

Mike looked very uncomfortable. "Your marker wore off."

"Marker?"

"Yes."

"What kind of . . . wait." An interesting thought occurred to me. "The machine does a lot more than measure you for a Mask uniform, doesn't it? It's the Hero Bomb, in ray form. *That's* why I was able to lift those barbells! And why I got my powers that day!"

Mike nodded reluctantly. "Yes. I said marker, but what I was really talking about was the charge from the hero beam. If you'd gone back within forty-eight hours, the doors would have detected the charge and you would have gotten your uniform." He took a deep breath and looked straight into my eyes. "You can't tell *anyone* about the hero beam. It's classified information, OSIRIS level 1A, which will buy any person who's not supposed to know it a memory purge. I know you don't want to bring that down on someone's head."

I had another leap of understanding. "But I'm not supposed to know about it either, am I? Why not purge *my* memory? It's the same reason Agent Brendan reacted so harshly to Captain Commanding's suggestion. It's something to do with being a meta, with how we react to memory alteration, isn't it?"

He nodded reluctantly. "You're a very smart boy, Evan. Too smart for your own good, probably. The memory ray is closely related to the hero beam. Using it on a fully activated metahuman can have *very* unpredictable results—as unpredictable as the original Hero Bomb. Powers get changed, amped up, lost completely. You could die, or go mad, or even explode with tremendous force."

"Explode?" I whispered.

"So they tell me."

"That's . . . I don't know. Wow." Another question occurred to me then. "Why me? The hero beam, I mean. Why pick me?"

"Genetic predisposition. The hand scanner that sizes you for your class ring tests for a bunch of gene complexes to sort out likely candidates at the same time. If you're a good bet for genetic enhancement, you get the fancy ring and the hero beam. If not, you get a plastic decoder ring and a gift certificate for a free meal at one of the vendors." Mike's phone chimed and he grimaced. "But we're out of time for now. We can talk more about this later."

"You promise?"

"Yes, I promise. But right now, you need to run to the bathroom down the hall and put that uniform on."

"Why?"

"Because you're starting your internship today."

"I'm what?! Three days ago you said it was too early for me to even be thinking about finding a hero to intern with. What changed?"

"Someone asked for you."

"Captain Commanding?" It burst out of my mouth before I could stop it. Even now, knowing what he had done, I couldn't help myself. Somewhere deep down inside, he was still *my* hero.

"No." Mike's voice came out flat and uninflected.

"Then who?" I'd never met any other Masks, and I couldn't imagine that my powers, such as they were, would generate much demand for me.

"Foxman," Mike said quietly.

I felt like someone had kicked me in the chest. "You're kidding. He's a failure, and a drunk!"

"No, Evan, I'm not kidding, and he's sober now—going on six months—or we wouldn't even consider him as a mentor. Now, go get your uniform on."

"But he's a complete washout and he's *never* had a sidekick. This isn't fair!"

"We *really* don't have time for this, Evan," Mike's voice took on a note of exasperation. "He's already arrived on the station. He's going to be here any minute."

"What if I don't want to work with him. Can't I refuse?"

Mike frowned and rubbed his forehead. "I wanted to wait to tell you this, and I wish I could do it gently, but there is no more time. No. You can't refuse. Not if you ever want to get your Mask license. The day you were sent to the AMO, Captain Commanding put the word around that he would take it as a personal insult if anyone accepted you as a sidekick. He blacklisted you. No sidekicking means no hero license."

"But then, why is Foxman . . . I don't understand."

"Evan, come on, you've already proved you're smarter than this. Foxman hates Captain Commanding's guts. He's not alone in that. Lots of Masks hate Captain Commanding, but Foxman is pretty much the only one who hates him more than he fears him. If you really want to be a Mask—and we both know that you do—Foxman is your only door into the game, and it's open right now. You can go and put that uniform on, or you can give up the dream. Those are your only choices."

I went.

12

Foxman Jr.

I took one more quick look at myself in the bathroom mirror. My costume was so cool! All black; Invulycra with thick Armex reinforcement in the torso and cowl and various other vulnerable points. It made me look about three times as muscular as I really was and *super* tough. All it really needed was a logo and a cape, and I would be *made* of awesome. For the first time since I'd arrived at the school, I felt completely good about the whole Mask thing.

That lasted right up until I heard "I think we'll call him *Foxman Junior*" coming through the open door of Mike's office as I returned from changing.

"What!" I couldn't help myself. The word burst out of my mouth. "Seriously?" I stepped into the doorway. "Foxman *Junior*?"

Mike was sitting behind his desk wearing the expression I'd come to associate with dealing with an "outburst" from one of us students. Foxman stood across the desk from him wearing his full battle armor, complete with the long-eared helmet and fluffy-look tail, all in red and white. As I spoke, the nearer of Foxman's ears rotated toward me, making a faint metallic grinding noise as it moved. He turned to follow his ear a moment later, and suddenly I found myself face-to-face with the most infamous of Masks.

"Is this him?" The question came out gruff and hard, not at all in keeping with the ironic grin built into the helmet's long muzzle.

Behind Foxman, Mike frantically signaled me to pull off my half mask and cowl. "Evan, this is your new mentor, Randall Hammer, better known as Foxman." I reached up and hooked my fingers under the cheek piece of my mask, pulling it back as Mike continued, "Rand, meet Evan Quick."

There was a pause as Foxman reached over and pressed a series of almost invisible buttons on the back of his left gauntlet. With a sharp clunk, the fox mask began to yawn, exposing the face within. The long muzzle slowly opened wider and wider, making a faint whirring sound as it did so. The top half slid up and back between his long ears while the bottom lowered to touch his chest. Eventually, the man inside the helmet was fully visible.

Randall Hammer looked like he could have been an actor once upon a time, a leading-man type. But that was years ago. Now the short hair held as much gray as black. His dark skin had developed deep lines at the corners of his eyes and mouth and across his forehead. His goatee and mustache were marked heavily with gray, as was the thick stubble across his cheeks and on his neck. Dark brown eyes looked at me out of bloodshot and yellowing whites. His expression was grim and it deepened his wrinkles.

"You have a problem with 'Foxman Junior'?" he growled.

I shook my head and hoped my eyes weren't betraying what I was really thinking.

"The storied name of Foxman isn't good enough for you?" he demanded.

I took a deep breath while I tried to think of an answer that didn't start out with something like, "No, Washed-Up-Man Junior doesn't exactly sing." Finally I settled on, "It's not that. I just think a hero has to have his own identity if anyone is going to take him seriously, don't you . . . sir?"

He frowned. "I've never liked kids. Really, why does anyone have them? Is it a sense of inadequacy? The need to leave a legacy beyond their own deeds? Mortality issues?"

He shook his head. "Not important right now. What is important, is how to deal with one kid in particular—you. It's good you're willing to stand up for yourself. I like that. Only up to a point, of course, but we can go with it till you get there." His words came out manic and staccato like a machine gun firing or like someone who's had way too much coffee. "I still think Foxman Junior has a nice ring to it. But if you can come up with something better, we'll try that. Deal?" He stuck out his hand.

I crossed my arms. "No 'Junior.' No way. No how." If I was going to stand up for myself, I might as well go all the way.

He raised an eyebrow speculatively. "Foxboy?"

"Absolutely not."

"Kid Kitt?"

"You're joking, right?"

"Brainstorming. Flufftail?"

"Forget it."

Foxman snorted, and his eyes went distant. Finally, he half smiled. "How about Meerkat!"

Where on earth did that come from? It was a little better, maybe, but . . . "I don't know."

"Foxman and Meerkat," he said, spreading his hands like he was painting it on a marquee. "Yeah, it scans." He nodded sharply. "We'll go with that."

I opened my mouth to protest, but Mike caught my eye and made a throat-cutting motion.

"I guess we can try it," I said.

"It's settled." Rand extended his hand again.

This time I shook it. What choice did I have?

"Okay, next point," said Rand. "We need to get your costume sorted."

I pointed at my chest. "I thought this was pretty good."

"For the basics, maybe. But we need to fill in the colors, make you a logo, add some ears to the cowl, equipment belt, Meerkat blaster, maybe some exoskeletal power boosters—"

"I kind of like the black," I interjected. "It's mysterious."

"It's clichéd," he barked. "You look like something out of a low-budget comic book starring some Mask who got hit in the head by one too many bats. The flying kind, not the ones used by overamped steroidal baseball players."

He started walking around me in a slow circle, lightly tapping the Armex across my chest and shoulders as he went. "We want a costume that goes with the Meerkat name. It'll have to complement my own uniform, of course. Maybe dusty gold with some red-brown stripes on the shoulders and thighs, shading across the neck and up into the cowl, contrasting boots and gauntlets, logo front and back of the chest plate, maybe echoed on the backs of your hands . . . Yeah, that could work. Come on, off to the booth with you."

"Booth?" The way he said the word, it sounded more than a little alarming.

Rand ignored me, turning back to Mike. "Everything's still in the same place it was last time I came up?"

"More or less," replied Mike. "Backflash has modified the controls a bit, but that's to be expected."

Foxman's expression darkened. "Born to meddle, that one, or she will be anyway. Or should that be, would have been . . ."

Mike started a bit, then glared at Foxman. "Rand, she's the director of OSIRIS."

There was something going on there, but I had no idea what. And I wasn't going to find out now, because Foxman looked at me, then nodded sharply.

"Right, right. Not relevant at the moment, though I'll probably have to restore the controls at some point. But not now. There's too much else to do today." Foxman grabbed my shoulders and turned me toward the door—there was no resisting the servos of his powered suit. "Costume and colors first, then back to the Den so I can show you around and lay out your new duties.

"Can you make a decent martini—no, of course you can't. Stupid question. You're what, eleven? Can't talk to you about martinis for at least seven or eight years, not without getting all sorts of horrible questions from the press about corrupting minors. For that matter, I don't drink anymore. Not since March.

131

That's when I got out of rehab, and this time I seem to be sticking with it. Twenty-third time is the charm. Go me. You know, let's just pretend I never said the bit about martinis."

Before I had time to even think about what to say to any of that, Foxman had chivvied me out of Mike's office and classroom, down the hall, and through a side door that led into another hall. We soon arrived at a door marked COSTUME LAB. Ten seconds after that, a huge glass tube was descending from the ceiling to enclose me, clanking horribly the whole way down.

"Is this thing safe?" I asked.

"Of course it is," replied Foxman. "I built it myself. Well, safe enough, anyway. You'll be fine. I do excellent work." He paused and looked thoughtful. "Of course, who knows what Backflash has done to it since then. Still, not to worry, you've got that great healing thing going on if anything does go wrong."

Not reassuring. Not one tiny bit. As the tube slid noisily down past my head, I thought about making a break for it. But somehow I didn't think that would go over well with the machine's designer. If Mike was right, and this really was my only chance at ever getting my hero license, that could be a problem. So, instead of bolting like anyone sensible would have done, I clenched my teeth and waited for the thing to close me in. I couldn't suppress a twitch at the thumping *hiss* when the tube sealed itself to the base pad.

Foxman said something to me, then turned to the control pedestal. At least, I think he said something. No sound penetrated the tube despite his lips moving. He mimed putting my cowl back on. So I did that. I couldn't see what his hands were doing, but within seconds lines of color were coiling and twisting through the walls of the clear tube. They looked like bits of colored string floating in a fish tank. It was actually kind of soothing.

Right up until the point where several of the strings shot out of the walls and latched on to my uniform to the accompaniment of a hideous crackling and sucking noise. It was the sort of sound you would expect giant electric leeches to make, if such things existed. If I'd had anywhere at all to go at that moment I would have gone there double-time. I didn't. All I could do was hold still and try not to freak out while the strings slithered back and forth over the surface of my uniform, slurping and sparking all the while.

Eventually, it was over, and the tube clanked slowly upward. It hadn't gone two feet before I grabbed the bottom and limboed my way out of the thing. A metallic gauntlet landed on my shoulder then, and I practically jumped out of my skin. But Foxman's suit was enormously strong, and his grip remained tight as he turned me first this way and then that.

"Let me look at you. Yeah, I like it. I like it a lot. Form *and* function, kiddo. Who's still got the old magic touch?" Foxman tapped his chest. "This guy does. And don't you forget it."

"What are you talking about? Huh?" Between my panic about being in the booth and my overwhelming relief after getting out, I'd entirely forgotten the why of the thing.

He shook his head despairingly. "Your uniform, Evan, your uniform. Keep up, here." A brief pause, as he canted his head to one side. "You do remember that's what we came for, right? No short-term memory loss from the tube? Because that could be a thing if Backflash messed up. No? Good. So, your uniform. Well, it's downright dashing, if I do say so myself. And I do. Oh, I do. Thirsty work though. Hmm."

He reached for something on his chest, and for the first time I noticed that he'd added a bandolier to his armor—a thick metal belt that ran from shoulder to hip and held a dozen canisters about a half the size of a soda can. His thumb touched the end of the third one down. It flipped open, dropping a six-ounce shorty of MaskerAde into Foxman's gauntlet and opening it in the process. The canister closed automatically as he lifted the can to his mouth and downed the energy drink in one long draft.

Foxman sighed, crushed the can, and tossed it over his shoulder. "Better! Now, march."

He gave me a gentle shove toward a full-length mirror that hung from a nearby stainless steel rack. He followed me over and stood half behind me, striking a heroic pose with his fists on his hips and his head turned up and to one side to make his jaw look stronger. I managed not to roll my eyes, though I nearly sprained my face doing it.

"Soooo, what do you think?" he asked.

"Give me a moment to take it all in."

Foxman had colored the bulk of my costume a deep orange-gold. The gauntlets, the boots, and the back and top of my cowl were all a dusky red, as were the stripes he'd painted across the shoulders and down the outsides of the thighs. They complemented the shinier reds of his own armor rather than duplicating them. He'd given me a sort of second mask in a black domino painted in around the eyes of the gold half mask—mirroring the natural bandit style of my new namesake.

He'd also done a stylized meerkat-head logo on my chest—basically a gold triangle with ears and a mask—all edged in red to make it stand out from the fabric around it. The symbol echoed his own fox-head logo to a degree I didn't like, but it still looked pretty seriously awesome on my chest. Or, it would have, if it weren't a tiny bit off center and slightly tilted to the left. Given time, that was going to drive me completely crazy. There were matching triangles on the backs of my gauntlets, though with less detail and better placed. I glanced at Foxman in the mirror and saw his carefully constructed heroic expression slowly deepening into a frown.

"I like it," I said quickly, "it works."

Apparently I didn't say it with enough enthusiasm, because the frown turned into a full-fledged scowl. "Works? Works? Visigoth! It's fabulous. Come on." Foxman hit the button that closed his helmet, turned, and walked away without another word or so much as a glance over his shoulder.

I trailed along behind him. Because, again, what choice did I have? He led me quickly through a series of corridors and doors. Many of the latter were marked AUTHORIZED PERSONNEL ONLY, which I was beginning to think of as the AMO's unofficial motto, since nobody I'd met yet seemed to think of themselves as *unauthorized* personnel.

Eventually, we arrived at a pair of curved elevator-style doors in an otherwise unmarked moon-rock wall. Foxman pressed another of those tiny near-invisible buttons on his right gauntlet. This time, the armored plates that covered his palm and fingers slid back, exposing the skin underneath and a OSIRIS ring, worn bezel down.

He pressed that to the panel beside the doors, and the mechanical voice did the "authorizing" dance I'd already become accustomed to. Blah-blah-authorized. Blah-subject number-blah. Etc. A moment later the doors slid open, revealing another, inner set of doors, which opened as well. He stepped through, again, without looking at me, as ignoring Evan seemed to have become the order of the day.

Beyond was a small cylindrical room perhaps six feet in diameter that came to a point above—like the inside of a bullet. When Foxman reached the far wall he turned back around to face me, but his helmet hid his expression. I followed and took up a casual stance beside him as the inner doors closed, shutting us in. An instrumental version of "The Girl from Ipanema" started playing through a cheap set of speakers above the door.

I pretended to be totally cool with the situation while not knowing what the heck was supposed to happen next. Then, a sudden earth-shattering bang startled me half off my feet. It was followed by the sensation of sudden acceleration, like we were standing in the world's fastest elevator as it shot off toward the four-hundredth floor.

That feeling of acceleration continued for perhaps thirty seconds, before my stomach did an amazing flip-flop as the transport shell rotated end for end and the gravity dropped to something like one-tenth normal. That lasted for another ten minutes until the trip ended as suddenly and noisily as it had started. This time, the bang sound sort of played in reverse—not quite "gnab." But something quite like it. I found myself torn between wishing the shell had windows and being very glad that it didn't.

The doors slid open to reveal a curved steel wall ten feet in front of us. When I trailed Foxman out the door, I nearly fell as my foot just suddenly stopped when it touched the floor. Yes, I know your foot always stops when it hits the floor, but this was different. There was no sense of resistance, no squish, or bounce, or rebound. It was like I'd put my foot into a six-inch layer of invisible Jell-O that suddenly hardened up the instant my shoe's sole hit the dull black surface.

"What the—" I mumbled to myself.

"Inertial damping field," Foxman tossed over his shoulder. "Shoot a bullet into it, and it will simply stop without flattening or bouncing. Big machine under the floor—gargantuan, really. Takes enormous amounts of power, too—runs off a core tap."

I wanted to ask more questions, but he kept right on moving. As I hurried to catch up, a noise from behind made me look around. A huge clawlike arm had descended from above—the noise was the sound of the claw clamping on a groove a couple of feet below the top of the bulletlike transport shell.

As the arm lifted the transport, I noticed that we were standing in the bottom of a sort of round, upside-down pyramid, like a funnel. We were at the bottom. The arm placed the shell on the step above us, where it slid slowly away, possibly on a conveyer belt of some kind. But Rand powered onward and I didn't have time to watch where it went.

He led me through a series of halls and doors out into a deep sunken plaza with small palm trees scattered around the stepped edges. The whole area lay under a thick glass roof. About halfway around the plaza from us was a curved door like the one we'd entered the shell through on Deimos. Above it a huge polished steel pipe like some metal chimney climbed up through the glass roof and continued on for another hundred feet. It cast a long shadow under the setting sun.

"Where are we?" I asked as I caught up to Foxman.

"OSIRIS headquarters, central building, Heropolis." Foxman tossed the words over his shoulder and continued walking.

Earth! "Two weeks ago I thought I knew everything there was to know about Masks. Now . . . ," I said, talking more to myself than to Foxman. "Why haven't I seen pictures of this place before?"

I almost ran into Foxman as he stopped and turned to face me. "The roof is mirrored glass. It and the chimney are covered by a directional chameleon field that uses the reflective surfaces to paint a very different picture for outside observers. Brilliant little technical twist on more traditional camouflage, designed and built by Foxhammer Industries . . . back in the days when there was a Foxhammer Industries." He sighed and looked unspeakably sad and distant for a moment.

"What happened?" I asked.

"The CEO and chief shareholder got distracted by, uh, other interests. The stock started to lose value, and *bam*, the board of directors turned on him. Injunctions were filed. Lawsuits ate up more of the company's value. There was a hostile takeover bid— pennies on the dollar. The CEO had the choice of selling out or taking the company into bankruptcy and hoping to salvage something from the wreckage.

"He was still distracted by those other interests, so he made the expedient decision. The wise decision. The wrong decision.

The new owners sold most of the company for parts and changed the name of what was left. And, thus, a great personal fortune and corporate success story was flushed down the drain along with a lot of hopes and dreams."

I didn't know what to say to that and a long awkward silence descended. Foxman finally broke it with a shrug.

"But that was probably more than you wanted to know. Come on, the *Flying Fox* is parked upstairs."

The *Flying Fox*! That sent a little slither of cold spiraling down my spine. Even a hard-core Captain Commanding fan of the sort I'd been until very recently couldn't help but be thrilled at the thought of actually taking a trip in Foxman's personal jet. It had been plying the skies over Heropolis almost as long as there'd been a Heropolis.

He led me through a bunch more corridors and through at least a dozen doors, many of them marked with the near-ubiquitous OSIRIS-AUTHORIZED PERSONNEL ONLY. Eventually, we emerged from a building that looked like a squat ziggurat into an open campus surrounded by other buildings of equally odd shape and design. Those included the giant faux chimney of the Mars-cannon, several grain-silo-like towers, a gigantic geodesic dome, and a featureless black cube. The *Flying Fox* was parked jauntily in the middle of it all, blocking most of a main sidewalk.

As we approached the slender red wedge with its fox-head profile, the jaw suddenly opened, lowering itself to the ground and extending a short tonguelike ramp.

"You'll have to duck," Foxman led the way up the ramp, "it's very low and tight in here."

He wasn't kidding; I had to travel the last few feet into the tiny cockpit almost on hands and knees. Inside, there was a small T-shaped space that ran between two low-slung seats back to a narrow cargo area behind them. Foxman was already settling into the left-hand chair as I rose out of my crouch.

Foxman pointed. "Strap yourself in. Right side is primarily for passengers, but there are duplicate controls in case something happens to mine. They're locked, but don't touch them unless I tell you to. This baby's more than a little bit tricky to fly and you don't want to mess with anything."

His voice sounded different somehow when he talked about the plane, more assured and less cocky. It made me want to listen to him in a way I really hadn't until that moment.

"Yes, sir."

"Good lad."

I started fastening the multiple safety belts in place. "Why is it so tricky . . . if you don't mind my asking?"

"Design trade-offs." He tapped the armored glass in front of him. "From the outside, this reads as an eye. I wanted any Hoods who saw her to *know* Foxman had arrived. So I went for the fox-head look." While he talked, he calmly checked the gauges and flipped various switches. "Problem is, foxes don't generally fly. She's a bit more aerodynamic than your average brick, but only a bit. You'll notice she has no wings to speak of."

"I'd always wondered about how that worked."

"Partially it's a lifting-body shape, what we call a flying wing, but mostly she gets by on raw power. Anything can fly if you strap big enough jets to it, and that was my solution for the *Flying Fox*. It's how my suit flies, too."

That was something else I'd always wondered about. "Why even have a plane? Why not fly everywhere in the suit?"

"Power. Or, not enough of it. The supercapacitors that run the suit can only hold so much juice. Flying burns it like you wouldn't believe. The *Flying Fox* is big enough to have its own on-board reactor. Not only does it get me places without running my capacitors down, I can actually charge up on my way. Same with the Foxmobile. It's much more about having a portable power generation system than the ride."

At that point, Foxman finished with his preflight check. "One more thing and we can be on our way. Gotta blow in the tube." He opened up his helmet, then pulled a plastic tube out of a device mounted on his control panel. "Breathalyzer. OSIRIS made me install one in every one of my vehicles after the IDS Tower incident. They wanted to make sure I don't drive *impaired*.

"They even made me put one on the armor. But don't worry, I'm reformed now." He bent forward to blow into the end of the cylinder.

"It's a wasted effort on their part either way, really," he continued as a green light blinked on the breathalyzer. "If I wanted to get around it, designing a filter that pulled the alcohol out of my breath would take all of ten seconds, and fabricating it would hardly take longer than that." He tilted his head to the side. "I suppose I could build a blood cleanser into it at the same time, which would at least give me a bit of a challenge."

He shrugged. "Sorry, problem-solving. Can't help myself, even when it's all moot because I'm not drinking anymore. Well, nothing alcoholic anyway." He thumbed the bandolier on his chest and took a long sip of the energy drink he pulled out. "I can't really help it—the problem-solving, that is. It's who I am. Foxman has to tech, just like Spartanicus has to villain, and Captain Commanding has to ego." As he said that last part, he stabbed a button on the console in front of him.

Sudden acceleration pressed me down into my seat and the plane leapt into the air. Despite the enormous kick of the jets, the cockpit remained almost eerily silent. Foxman leaned back in his seat, put one foot up on the edge of the dash, and took another drink just as the plane banked sharply to the right, barely missing a tower on the edge of the OSIRIS campus.

"Shouldn't you have your hands on the wheel?" I yelped.

"Don't worry so much, kid." He patted the control panel, then tucked his free hand behind his head. "This thing is a VTOL jet—that's vertical takeoff and landing—and it's got no wings. The whole thing runs on computer controllers. Barring some sort of computer malfunction, she drives herself. Which is for the best. There's not a human alive and very few metas who could pilot her any other way. I simply tell her where to go and she takes care of the rest. Like so: Take us home to the Den, baby, and keep a low profile!"

The jet, which had been steadily climbing up to that point, leapt forward and down, hugging the treetops as it headed for wherever we were going. Watching the controls in front of me operate themselves wasn't at all reassuring.

"What happens if something goes wrong with the computer?" I asked.

Foxman shrugged. "We pile into the ground at eight hundred miles an hour. But don't worry, you won't even have time to panic."

"Oh. Well, that's fine then." If Foxman recognized the sarcasm in my voice, he showed no sign of it.

13

The Den

The *Flying Fox* suddenly dropped like a rock, plunging straight toward the Mississippi. I screamed. Foxman laughed. The plane pulled up a few yards short of impact and the jets splashed muddy brown water across the cockpit windows. We skimmed along within a few feet of the surface of the river for a half mile or so, then pivoted sharply to the left, rocketing through a gap in the trees on the nearer bank.

Our speed dropped to practically nothing. The sun had finished setting while we were in the air, but the windows had changed color at that point and I could still see perfectly. The trees in the little wood stood mostly on hummocks of higher ground amid a scattering of shallow pools and stands of swamp grasses. We traveled another hundred feet or so under the cover of the trees before coming to a halt above a particularly large pool. The jets cut out and we dropped into water that quickly flowed up and over the sides of the plane, covering the cockpit windows.

As we hit bottom, mud swirled up around us, blacking out all view of the world above. I glanced over at Foxman, who didn't seem alarmed in the least, and tried to copy his relaxed attitude.

"What happens now?" I asked.

"That," he replied, as a pair of sharp metallic clunks sounded from somewhere below us.

The plane began to move again. This time, with something towing it. After about a minute, the mud cleared away. Bright white beams stabbed out from lights on the front of the *Flying Fox*. They illuminated a long, water-filled tunnel cut through gray-green stone. A set of steel rails ran along the bottom of the tunnel, accommodating whatever was transporting the plane. After a while, we slid up out of the water, passing from limestone walls to sandstone soon after.

"Where are we?" I'd seen depictions of the Den before, of course—in comics and on shows about the early Masks—but none of them had been specific about the location of Foxman's lair.

"Under Summit Hill in what used to be St. Paul. I lived in a mansion on the bluff once upon a time in a different life. There are still elevators leading up from the Den to the house, but I don't use them anymore. As much as the new owners might appreciate a visit from the fabulous Foxman, I'd rather skip the whole scene."

A huge set of steel doors loomed ahead, sliding neatly open as we reached them. They closed behind us as the *Flying Fox* slid to a stop in its hangar.

"Red leather walls?" I whispered, more than half speechless.

"Pretty amazing, isn't it?" Foxman grinned over at me as the ramp lowered between us.

"Yeah, that'd be one word for it." It was the gaudiest thing I'd ever seen.

"You don't like it?" He actually sounded hurt, and I shook my head quickly—after all, he *was* going to be *my* hero from here on out.

"No, nothing like that, I'm just . . . stunned."

Foxman pivoted out of his seat and slid down the ramp. "If you think this is something, wait till you see the rest of the place!"

There was a leather-covered bar beside the exit of the hangar and Foxman stopped to pull yet another can of MaskerAde out from a mini-fridge before opening the door and gesturing me forward. I stepped through into—I don't know—Xanadu?

My painter grandmother used to recite this poem to me every night at bedtime when I stayed with them:

> *In Xanadu did Kubla Khan*
> *A stately pleasure-dome decree:*
> *Where Alph, the sacred river, ran*
> *Through caverns measureless to man*
> *Down to a sunless sea . . .*

It went through my head again now as I surveyed the main chamber—at least I hoped it was the main chamber—of Foxman's Den. The cavern was huge and domed, easily big enough to hold my parents' entire house and yard. A gigantic central pillar rose up to the ceiling with supports radiating out and up from a point about two-thirds of the way up the pillar. It looked a bit like the spokes of an umbrella blown inside out. Only, in this case, all the spokes and the central shaft had been sheathed in panels of some richly grained wood stained a deep red-brown.

More wooden paneling covered the bottom ten feet of the encircling wall. Above that, and rising all the way to the center of the dome, was hundreds of square feet of deep blue leather with what looked like gem stones sparkling here and there in the patterns of the constellations. The floor was an incredibly intricate parquet-quilt-work incorporating thousands of little hardwood fox-head logos.

There was an enormous fountain in one section. The water came in through the open mouth of a six-foot-tall bronze fox head on the wall. It cascaded down from there through a series of levels to a large koi pond, exiting eventually as a small stream that flowed out through a low arch. An entire pack of bronze fox sculptures fished and splashed in the fountain and along the edges of the pond.

A bar and kitchen with thick granite counter tops centered another area, while an open living-room-like space big enough to seat thirty on its blue leather couches took up a third. An area covering one-quarter of the circle was given over to a combination crime lab, machine shop, and manufactory. The floor in this last area—demarcated by a boundary of darker wood in the parquet—looked unnaturally shiny.

The whole place seemed inhumanly clean, actually—given the scale. Or, perhaps, free of filth and dirt might be a more accurate description than clean. There was clutter covering every flat surface that wasn't the floor. Even there, drifts of papers and small herds of bric-a-brac consisting mostly of endless cans of

MaskerAde, dog-eared books, or open magazines clustered themselves around much of the more comfortable-looking seating.

It was quite the strangest mess I'd ever seen. Not a spot of dirt or dust or a single filthy plate or empty glass anywhere, but endless piles of clutter. Fascinated, I crossed to the nearest heap of books and lifted off the top couple volumes. The ones underneath were as free of dust as those on top.

"I don't get it," I said, barely even realizing I was speaking while I dug deeper and deeper into the pile.

"Don't get what?" Foxman sounded looser and more relaxed than he had at any time that afternoon.

"How your mess can be so clean?" I dropped the books back into a rough pile.

He finished off his third can of MaskerAde in a bit over an hour—which would have had me buzzing around like a hummingbird—and smiled a rather smug sort of smile. "Wait for it."

"Wait for what . . ." I trailed off as a faint mechanical whirring drew my attention toward the fountain.

One of the bronze foxes had left its place at the pond. It trotted toward me now, its metal tongue a-lolling and its tail a-wagging. It went to the pile I had disarranged and reared back on its hind legs. The toes on its front paws extended into fingers and the pad formed a thumb. It very carefully resorted the pile into the exact configuration it had held before I messed with things. As it picked up each item it lifted them to its nose, where, with a vacuum cleaner noise, it sucked off any hint of dust before replacing it. When it was done, the fox returned to the edge of the pond and froze.

"The master computer laser maps the room once every fifteen minutes or so," said Foxman. "If it finds anything out of place, one of the Foxbots restores it to its rightful order. Once a day, the entire pack goes through and dusts and vacuums the whole place. They also deal with any dirty dishes or other unsanitary messes."

"And the piles of books and notes and things?"

"That's my filing system. The computer knows I don't like to have my creative tools disarranged—it's like moving bits of my brain around—*very* disruptive to my thinking. So, it leaves my diagrams and references and other stuff exactly as I placed them. When you moved that stack, you triggered the motion sensors. There's been the occasional avalanche over the years, and it knows that I would prefer that it restored everything to exactly the way *I* left it."

"That's amazing!" It really was. Despite the clutter and general air of decayed glory that hung about the Den, I was impressed.

Foxman smiled. "Come on, I bet you could use a sandwich or something. Even if I hadn't taken you away from the AMO at dinnertime, I know I never got enough to eat when I was your age." He canted his head to one side. "Hmm, nutritional deficiencies as a contributing factor to my later problems with alcohol and emotional issues? Nooo, my baseline nutritional needs were more than adequately taken care of. Ridiculous hypothesis. Still, what about microdeficiencies? Flag for later research?"

I was about to tell him I didn't need anything when my

stomach made a sad little whining noise, triggered apparently by the mention of food. "All right, thanks."

"There's no need to thank me. Feeding you is part of my job if you're going to be my sidekick—and I think you are, since that's the best way to stick it to Captain Commanding." As we crossed into the kitchen, Foxman snapped his fingers three times quickly. "Before I forget again, Denmother, this is my new intern, Evan Quick, code name, Meerkat. He has level-three clearance as of this moment. Make him feel at home."

"Yes, sir." The voice was clean and clear and mechanical, utterly devoid of any human intonation. "How may we accommodate you, Master Quick?"

I didn't know what to tell it. "Dinner?"

"Cold or hot?"

"Hot? What can you make?"

"American, Chinese, Indian, Italian, and Thai provide the bulk of the food that Foxman normally eats, but I can offer other options based on my most common ingredients. I can also send out for further ingredients if needed, but that will increase production times to levels beyond the optimal parameters established by my programming."

"Pizza?"

"Excellent choice and one of my specialties. Size and ingredients? Style? Spicy, standard, or white?"

"I dunno, twelve-inch pepperoni and mushroom? Spicy, Chicago style? Can you do that?"

"Of course."

Robotic arms extended themselves from the central counter,

pulling ingredients out of the huge stainless steel fridge, and utensils and dishes from various cabinets. They began assembling a pizza for me. I was entranced, and would happily have sat there to watch the whole thing if Foxman hadn't tapped me on the shoulder.

"Come on, this'll take a while. Let me show you the rest of the place."

As he led me through the manufactory, I noticed a quilt wrapped around a breadbox-size object on one of the consoles. Curious, I moved closer. Faint voices seemed to be coming from within.

"What's that?" I pointed at the quilt.

Foxman looked down at his feet as a blush spread across his cheeks. "Nothing much, Foxsnooper. It's a multiband communications monitor, descrambler, and code breaker. I could do better now." He didn't say anything more, but he didn't move on either, just kept looking at his feet.

"Why the blanket?"

"I got tired of listening to it, but couldn't quite bring myself to shut it off either." He sighed and picked a half-full can of MaskerAde off a nearby workbench, idly rolling it between his hands. "Oh, go ahead and take the stupid quilt off already. We both know you're going to do it as soon as I turn my back if I don't let you do it now. We might as well get it over with."

I lifted the blanket, exposing a streamlined black-and-red box fronted with a screen and a fold-down keyboard. The faint voice I'd heard earlier came through clearly now, an OSIRIS agent— identified by a crawl at the top of the screen—detailing the escape of some Hood called the Fromagier. It didn't sound all that interesting, so I tuned it out as I sat down and looked over the equipment.

A double row of function keys across the top of the keyboard were labeled things like "Local police band" and "OSIRIS scrambled" and "Scan for keywords." The last of those was currently lit up. So was another, marked "Signal anomalies." The screen displayed an overhead map-view of Heropolis sprinkled with hundreds of colored dots spanning the entire rainbow. A large X on the map in the Summit Hill area clearly showed our own location.

As I watched, a bright red dot appeared on the screen perhaps eight blocks from our current location and began blinking. When it did so, the voice coming out of the monitor switched from the OSIRIS report to the smooth mechanical tones of Foxman's Denmother.

"Point seven-two-two second alarm system carrier interrupt at grid point three-three-one-seven —Spinnaker residence. News article cross-reference indicates J. P. Spinnaker and family are vacationing on the family yacht in Dubai. Interrupt time is consistent with a computerized alarm bypass device manufactured by Dactolory Systems Inc. Odds of break-in in progress seventy-eight percent."

Foxman took a sip of his drink, then made a face. "Flat, ugh."

"Aren't you going to do something about that?" I pointed at the scanner.

He shrugged. "I'm sure the local police can handle one little break-in."

The computer spoke again. "Highly unlikely, sir. Police band

152

monitoring shows no calls relating to Spinnaker house. Cross-checking to the private security firm in charge of monitoring the alarm system likewise shows no activity."

Despite the inherently emotionless nature of Denmother's tone, I thought I detected a hint of reproach there.

"We've got to do something!" I jumped out of my chair, looking around for options.

"Really?" asked Foxman, his expression doubtful and sad. "Really?"

I couldn't believe how outraged I felt at his indifference. "We're Masks. We fight crime. It's what we do. Come on!"

He sighed and tossed back the rest of his MaskerAde. "All right, if you insist." He jerked a thumb over his shoulder. "Foxmobile's through the far door—we'll need it if we're going to get there in time."

The leather walls in the garage were pool-table green and studded with heavy brass nail ends. The car was exactly as it always appeared in the vids and comics, a low-slung bright red wedge that shared the fox-head styling of all Foxman's gear. As I admired the car, Foxman pushed a button on his wrist, opening the gull wing doors. He climbed in on the right side. It wasn't until I got in on the left and discovered myself behind the steering wheel that I realized he'd chosen the passenger seat.

As the doors hissed closed I turned to Foxman. "What's going on? I can't drive."

He shrugged. "I'm a has-been, and you're the one who wants to fight crime. In my book that means you're driving. Well, unless you'd rather turn around and go back to your pizza?"

"I'm thirteen! I don't even have a learner's permit!"

"It's really not all that hard, or shouldn't be for a hotshot young Mask fresh from the AMO. Gas pedal's on the right, brake's on the left. Steering wheel's in the middle. If you've ever played Mask Racers on your game console, you know the rest. But, it's up to you." He gestured at a box on the dashboard, his expression mocking. "Blow in the tube and go stop a crime, or turn around and let Denmother get your dinner."

"I do have a couple hundred hours in Mask Racers," I ventured.

He reached over and hit a small black button beside the steering wheel. The big leather-covered garage door started to crank itself upward. "Then it's like you've already driven the Foxmobile dozens of times, isn't it? Are you going to take us out, or what?"

It was the "or what?" that got me. It had such a sneer in it that I couldn't turn away, even if my heart was beating a million beats a second and I wanted to roll down the window so I could barf. So, I didn't tell him that I'd only ever played the Foxmobile in the races that required it for unlocks, or that I drove the Commanding Car the rest of the time. I didn't mention how terrified I was. I just blew into the tube and hit the gas when the engine started. The seat kicked me in the backside, and padded steel restraints dropped down in place of seat belts as we shot forward along another tunnel. The stone walls blurred around us.

"How fast are we going?" I squeaked.

"Speedo's on the lower left." Foxman sounded bored.

"One hundred and thirty!?"

154

"Might want to tap the brakes before we hit the street. But only a tap, mind, or we'll spin into the wall."

There was a horrible grinding screech, and we slowed remarkably as I stomped on the brake, fishtailed into the wall and then slid fifty feet diagonally, dragging the corners of the car along the walls all the way. The speedometer was reading thirty-five when we finally straightened out a moment before I noticed the brick wall at the end of the tunnel a few yards ahead—

Brick wall at the end of the tunnel!!!

I screamed and stomped the brake again. We slid into the wall anyway . . . and right on through without any sense of impact, or raining bricks, or anything. A split second of darkness and then we were skidding out into the end of a small tree-lined cul-de-sac with a concrete retaining wall suddenly visible in the rearview camera. What. The . . . ?

"Holographic projection," said Foxman. "With a real concrete-surfaced steel plate underneath, but that opens automatically whenever the Foxmobile is close enough. Oh, and don't worry about the scrapes in the armor and paint," he added sarcastically. "It's only a few thousand dollars worth of damage and I can always fix it up tomorrow. Also, you might want to actually start moving, if you're planning to *catch* the bad guys. Gas is on the right. Don't push it so hard this time, unless you *want* to engage the rocket assist again."

I didn't run into anything else and I did eventually get us to the blinking marker on the on-board map system, but that's about all the good I have to say about the next few minutes. As we rolled into the long driveway of the Spinnaker mansion, I glanced over at Foxman, who hadn't made eye contact since I bounced off the wall. After the way he'd mocked me up to this point I didn't want to talk to him again, but I'd never done anything like this before. Not for real anyway.

"What now?" I finally asked.

"Push the blue button on the left side of the console," he said in the same bored tone he'd used earlier.

I looked around and found the button, a palely glowing circle labeled FOXDAR. When I hit it, the central display screen blinked several times, then shifted to a sort of ghostly schematic view of the house ahead of us. Two transparent figures—outlined in red— were busily pulling stuff out of what looked like it might be a safe and stacking it on the floor . . . maybe. The view was hazy and small.

Foxman took a sip from his umpteenth MaskerAde, then leaned forward and tapped a virtual button on the right side of my screen. A menu opened over the picture. MAP PROBABLE ESCAPE ROUTE was the top line, and he selected it before the others had a chance to register. A green path marked itself out inside the building and 85% PROBABILITY flashed across the screen. It started at the burglars and ended at a window on the ground floor.

"Select the exit window in the diagram," said Foxman, settling back into his seat.

I touched a finger to the screen and was answered with "glass removed."

"Drive us around back."

So I did that, parking us a few yards from the window with the cutaway pane. Then, under Foxman's direction, I pushed the button marked FOXAMELEON MODE and we settled in to wait. We weren't there long before a couple of black nylon duffels came sailing out to land on the ground. A moment after that, the first of the two burglars followed, a slightly tubby white man in his fifties. I reached for my door handle.

"No!" Foxman spoke quietly but sharply. "Don't be a fool. Wait till the second one comes out. Then push the big red shiny button."

I was about to ask what big red shiny button, when I saw that the middle third of the screen had become a glittering red circle with the legend APPREHEND FELON? in black across the center. As the second burglar—pretty much a skinnier, seedier version of the first—came out the window, I hit the button.

Something low and in front of me clunked. Twin streams of scarlet foam shot from somewhere near the headlights, hitting both men and covering them in sparkling goo from about mid chest down. Before either of them could do much more than yell startled obscenities, the foam expanded like a marshmallow in a microwave. In less than two seconds flat both men were encased from the shoulders down in rigid bricks of glittering foam. More foam stuck the bags in place.

I reached for my door handle again.

"No, stay in the car."

"Why?" I was confused. "Do I need to hit another button?"

"Nope, but you do need to drive us back to the Den now."

"What about the burglars?"

"What about them? Denmother will phone in an anonymous tip as soon as we're clear. After that, the police will collect them. We're done. We might even make it back before your pizza goes cold."

"But—but—don't we have to *talk* to the police or the press or anything?"

He tilted his head to one side and raised a very skeptical eyebrow. "You're a smart kid, but a little too earnest yet, so I'm going to walk you through this once. But only once, so pay attention. I am—not to put too fine a point on it—a has-been whose Mask license is, well, not quite suspended, but not exactly in good standing either."

He pointed at me. "You are a wet-behind-the-ears newbie, with no driver's license, no Mask license, and as yet unprocessed internship papers. You are also illegally and very badly operating a car that both the Defense Department and OSIRIS classify as a military assault vehicle. Add in the fact that as your mentor I had to sign about four hundred pages of consent forms swearing to god and the AMO that I wouldn't allow you within a thousand meters of a crime scene before your fifteenth birthday, and what exactly do you think the police are going to do when they find us here with those guys?" He pointed at the criminals.

I swallowed hard. "Arrest us?"

"Bingo." Foxman touched the tip of his nose, and it was only then that I realized he'd never even bothered to close his mask. "Now, take us home."

14

Don't Tell Anyone Official

I didn't say another word, just blew into the tube, started the car, and, with much screeching and jerking, got us turned around and headed out. As we pulled into the cul-de-sac that led back to the Den, I heard police sirens start wailing in the distance. I'd intended to pull over and have a chat with my new "mentor" then and there, but decided to wait until we got off the street. Ten feet past the entrance to the tunnel, I stepped on the brake and brought us to a slow stop—I was already getting better at this.

"What's wrong?" asked Foxman.

"You said your Mask license wasn't *quite* suspended. What did you mean by that?"

"I thought it was pretty obvious, kid." He pointed at the breathalyzer on the dashboard. "I'm a formerly drunken wreck and not fit to hero in public yet. If you don't believe me, ask Captain-freaking-Commanding."

It was my turn to raise an eyebrow. "And?"

He sighed. "And OSIRIS would prefer not to have to publicly

bust my chops. When I had my little chat with Special Agent Brendan a few years back, she let me know that if I kept my head down, *and* I didn't get caught doing anything OSIRIS would have to take official notice of, *and* I agreed to the breathalyzers for all of my 'mobile crime-fighting platforms,' then OSIRIS wouldn't pull my license."

"But aren't you sober now?" I asked.

"Well, my rehabilitation does seem to finally be sticking this time around, thanks to my discovery of the unholy elixir of concentrated caffeine and ridiculous amounts of sugar that comes in a MaskerAde can. But I am still not in good aroma with the powers that be, and I would really prefer not to have Captain Commanding come around to give me another of his lovely lectures on how a True Mask Behaves."

I could see that, especially now that I knew how Captain Commanding behaved when the cameras weren't running. "But won't the police know who foamed those bad guys?"

Foxman shrugged. "There are a half dozen of us who use something like that goop. As long as I don't give them any reason to actually run lab tests on the stuff, they can officially "assume" that it was Foamaster or the Foaminator, or some other Mask with foam prominently mentioned in their handle. Besides, it's only one incident. Probably, no one will notice."

"But I want to fight crime!" I said, a little startled by my own anger. "That's the whole *point* of being a Mask. If I'm going to be your sidekick, I am *not* going to sit in the Den and eat pizza and play nice. We are going to get out and do things!"

Foxman looked startled, then bitter. He sneered, "Really? What makes you so sure of that?"

I had a sudden insight. "Because you want this as much as I do."

He blinked. "How do you figure that?"

"If you didn't, you could have stopped me at any time. You're twice my size and about a hundred times as strong. You didn't have to let me get into the car. And, once we were in the car, you didn't have to let it move. Tell me you couldn't have stopped me at any time."

Foxman shrugged and looked away. "Believe whatever you want."

"Then, I *believe* that we're going to fight crime together because that's what Masks and sidekicks do, even washed-up has-been Masks and underage sidekicks with wimpy powers."

"All right, kid, if that's the way you want it. We'll try it, though I think you're going to be doing most of the driving." He snorted. "Literally and figuratively."

"That's fine by me."

His answering smile was more than a little sad. "You've got a lot of fire in your soul. That's good, but, well, never mind. I'll just say that you remind me of the me I wish I'd been at your age, and leave it at that for the moment. Now, do you want to go eat your pizza? We can work out what it is you're going to actually do around here after that."

"All right."

I couldn't believe I'd won the battle that easily. Then I looked at the bitter, poisoned expression on Foxman's face and decided maybe the battle I needed to fight wasn't exactly the battle I'd thought it was.

As soon as we got out of the car, Foxman grabbed another can of MaskerAde. He finished that one as Denmother served up my pizza on the breakfast bar, then started another.

"Why aren't you vibrating your way right though that stool?" I asked around a mouthful of excellent pizza. "Whenever I drink that stuff I get all shaky and then crash like a container of eggs dropped out a second-story window."

"I was pretty shaky for a while about thirty-five hours ago, but now I'm barely able to keep my eyes open."

"Wait, how long have you been awake? And how much of that have you had?"

"Maybe two gallons. Denmother, how long have I been awake?"

"Fifty-seven hours, forty-eight minutes, and seventeen seconds, judging by the change in your breathing as you were first waking up, sir." Again that neutral voice sounded somehow disapproving.

Foxman turned to me. "Fifty-seven hours, forty-eight minutes, and twenty-three seconds as of right now. Which might explain why I feel like I'm about to melt." He snorted and quirked up the corner of mouth. "Well, that and the fact that these energy drinks have some rather idiosyncratic effects on the metahuman metabolism."

"Idiosyncratic?"

"Weird, bizarre, erratic, varying wildly from meta to meta, freakish—" He tilted suddenly on his chair and started to snore.

Before he could fall off, one of Denmother's food prep arms shot out and caught him by the shoulder.

"Is he going to be all right?" I asked.

"Eventually," replied Denmother, and I thought I detected a note of long suffering there.

I finished my pizza to the accompaniment of Foxman's snoring. It was the first chance I'd had to think since I ran into Burnish and Backflash in the tunnels of the AMO. And I had a *lot* to think about: There was the fact that the Captain had a daughter who apparently hated me almost as much as her dad did. The mess with my parents, and what they must believe about me after seeing the video that Captain Commanding faked. The weird way Foxman talked about Backflash. The revelation that the uniform-measuring machine at Camp Commanding was really a new version of the Hero Bomb.

It was all way too much to make sense of, and I found the various ideas spinning around in my head and banging together aimlessly like ice swirled in a glass. It made me dizzy.

When I finished my pizza, I turned to my new mentor. *Now what?* I had no idea what my duties were supposed to be or anything. "What *am* I going to do around here?"

Foxman suddenly jerked upright, blinked several times, and started talking in mid-sentence like he'd never fallen asleep, "See also: strange. Some metas even find MaskerAde to be calming. Wait, what was the question?"

"I asked you what I'm going to do around here? Officially, I mean. What are my duties?"

"I really don't know what you're going to do. If I were Captain Commanding, I could always have you polish my ego in between telling me how awesome I was, but well—bastard—him, not you."

His eyelids sagged and he tilted again, but didn't actually start snoring this time.

With an obvious effort, he lifted his chin and forced his eyes to stay open. "Actually, you know what, kid? I think I'm going to send you home now, and we can talk about it later. I really didn't think this through beyond how much it was going to piss off our beloved Captain, and I'm clearly in no state to figure it out now. Why don't we talk about it tomorrow, or Wednesday, or whenever I'm supposed to have you next?"

"But it's not even seven," I said. "What do I do until then?"

"I'll send you back to the school. I promised I'd do that every night anyway. Well, weeknights, the ones you're with me. That's how it normally works, or so I'm told. You take classes during the day, then come out here and practice your heroing with me several evenings a week and on most weekends. Come on." He stood up and started walking toward the hangar.

"I didn't expect it to be like this," I said, more to myself than anything.

But Foxman turned back toward me, and the look on his face was the same unspeakably sad expression he'd worn when talking about his lost company earlier. "No one does, kid. No one does."

I had already half strapped myself into the passenger seat of the *Flying Fox*, by the time I noticed Foxman wasn't actually settling into the pilot's position. Instead, he'd flipped out a console and started typing something into it while he sat on one armrest.

"What are you doing?"

"Lean forward and look into the screen in front of you," Fox-man said through an enormous yawn.

Something about our most recent exchange had drained me of any will to argue, so I did as I was told. A bright light mounted above the screen flashed on and an electronic voice said, "Commencing facial and retinal scanning, please don't move." I froze, and a few seconds later the light blinked out. "Biometric data stored under code name 'Meerkat,' level-three vehicle access granted."

"There we go. The *Flying Fox* will now take you from the Den to OSIRIS and back anytime you ask her, as well as to other destinations as I designate them. You're good to go." He closed his eyes for a long moment, and I thought he'd gone to sleep again, but then he blinked and started slowly down the accessway.

"Wait," I said. "Is there anything I need to do to fly it? And when do I come back? And—"

"Don't worry, kid, she flies herself. But I thought I told you that already. Maybe I didn't? No, I'm sure I did. Either way, now you know. As for the rest, I'll set up a schedule with Minute Man for the days you're here and he'll take care of things on that end."

He slid a couple more feet down the ramp, then stopped and looked back. "Oh, and remember not to tell *anyone*, official or otherwise, about catching those burglars. Seriously. You're not supposed to have any contact with Hoods or other criminals until you get your provisional Mask license or sidekick's permit, or whatever they call it now. And you're not even eligible before you turn fifteen."

Then he was gone, and the ramp was closing. Two hours later, I was back on Deimos. Time from the Den to OSIRIS: less than ten minutes, counting the tunnel. Time from OSIRIS entrance to the teleport cannon: one-hour forty five, counting the hour and forty minutes I spent detained by the guards and going through all the processing that Foxman was supposed to have taken care of on our way *to* the Den. In the course of which, I got an in-depth tour of the detention facilities at OSIRIS headquarters, and the spaces between there and the Mars cannon. Whee.

"How'd it go, how'd-it-go, how'ditgo!?" Jeda speedslicked around me about a dozen times as I came in the door of our dorm, quite literally bouncing off the walls as he did so, since the room wasn't all that big.

"Whoa, dude, chill." I waved my arms in a stopping motion. "What are you talking about?"

He stopped running in circles, but continued to bounce back and forth heel-toe-heel-toe. "Your-first-outing-with-Foxman! Duh. What was it like? He used to be such a heavy hitter, and that's cool even if he's past it now. Is he as much of a wreck as they say he is? Come on, spill. Mostly us sidekicks get stuck with second stringers, like Emberdown getting paired up with Watchdude. Or Blindmark and total newb KataKitty—she can't be two years out of her own internship. Talk! Did you catch some bad guys?"

"Give the guy a chance to take his suit off, Jeda." NightHowl was sitting cross-legged on the upper bunk that was reserved for Blurshift in male mode. "We've waited five hours, we can wait another fifteen minutes."

Blindmark was lying on the bunk beneath her, reading a book

in Braille on his minitab and apparently ignoring the rest of us, though that part could have been entirely pretense and there'd be no way to tell. While Eric couldn't see anything through his own eyes, his powers allowed him to use those that belonged to others whenever he chose.

"But I wanna know what happened now!" Jeda's voice came out just short of a wail. Then he shrugged with that incredibly quick up-down motion of his. "All right, fine, fine, you-can-change. But hurry up about it, all-right."

I laughed. "All right, I'll hurry."

I liked Jeda, but patience was not his strong suit, or maybe it was. Maybe he was incredibly patient, but ran through it as quickly as he did everything else. Given the speed he mostly lived at, waiting fifteen minutes might feel like waiting fifteen hours did for the rest of us. It was a weird thing to realize, and it really did make me move faster, scooping up a tee and some sweat pants, before I ducked into our little bathroom to change.

When I came out, NightHowl had been joined on the upper bunk by Emberdown. The older girl frowned. "Why do you always wear your shirts inside out, Evan?"

Jeda spun around so fast that he did three full revolutions before coming to a stop facing Alyssa. "His first day with a real Mask and the thing you want to know is why he's a fashion casualty? Where's your sense of mystery, girl?"

"If his first day with Foxman was anything like mine with Watchdude, there's not much to tell. You fill out a bunch of forms and you get seven different versions of the responsible-use-of-powers lecture. Where's the mystery in that? Right, Eric?"

Blindmark didn't open his eyes or even shift position, but he did say, "Truth, sister."

"Is that what *you* did?" Jeda asked me. "Because that'd be totally boring, and one thing I can't imagine Foxman being is boring. Guy's supposed to be a train wreck!"

"Well, I did fill out a lot of forms." I could see Jeda start to deflate, and NightHowl's expression closed up, so I hurried on. "But that wasn't until after I left the Den."

"You got to go to the Den?" asked NightHowl. "That's pretty cool. Place looks awesome in all the cartoons. Are those anything like the real deal?"

"Kinda, yeah. It's got all the lab stuff and garages and hangars and boat docks they show, but it looks way less high-tech, more like something out of a big Bollywood flick—all bright colors and fancy-schmancy architecture. Place has leather walls and parquet floors. Oh, and robots. Bronze foxes that double as statues in the koi pond."

"There's a koi pond?" said Emberdown. "Seriously? Man, that makes the little fish tank in Watchdude's Guard Shack sound even lamer than usual. What else?"

So I gave them a quick description of the Den, and Denmother, the *Flying Fox*, and the Foxmobile, and even my pizza, because Jeda wanted to hear about the robo-kitchen. Blindmark kept right on being too cool for the rest of us— reading, or at least pretending to—I didn't know enough about Braille to tell. And somehow in there I found myself talking about the Foxsnooper and the burglars and Foxman telling me that if we were going to do anything about them, I was going to have to drive.

"Wait," said Jeda, "*you* got to drive the Foxmobile? The real honest-to-god Foxmobile? That is so awesome!"

That's when Blindmark finally bothered to say something again. "Give it a rest, Jeda. There's no way even a maniac like Foxman is going to let some thirteen-year-old kid drive his car."

I was about to say something like "that shows what you know," when I remembered Foxman reminding me not to let *anyone* know about our adventures. So, I snapped my mouth shut instead.

Blindmark set aside his minitab then and sat up, turning to face me without opening his eyes. "Or did he?"

I just shrugged, knowing that Blindmark would be looking at me through at least one of the others. "I'm not saying anything about that."

"He did, didn't he?" said Blindmark.

I looked at the floor.

Blindmark shook his head. "I'm not sure who's stupider here, Foxman or you . . . *Meerkat*."

The way he said my handle made me want to change my name, or maybe punch him in the nose. "You going to snitch on me?" I asked.

I could see Blindmark roll his eyes through closed lids. "No. I might think your Mask is an idiot for risking his license that way, and that you're even more of an idiot for doing something that might keep you from ever getting one, but I'm no rat. OSIRIS knows way too much about what we do without me helping them out. Honestly, I don't think there's a kid in this school who would snitch on anyone for anything where it comes to OSIRIS."

Emberdown nodded. "Amen to that."

There was something about the way Blindmark said "OSIRIS" that made me blurt out, "You don't much like the way they run things, do you, Eric?"

"OSIRIS?" Blindmark finally opened his eyes, and though I knew he couldn't see, I felt like he was looking straight into my soul. "No, I don't. You shouldn't either, little Meerkat. The Franklin Act gives them way too much power over people like us, and I don't think they're very responsible in the way they use it. Did you know that Spartanicus has already escaped?"

I blinked. "What? No way! When?"

"This afternoon, while you were out catching petty burglars with Foxman."

"Meta*max* prison, my aunt Fanny," said Emberdown. "Those places are more like short-term hotels for Hoods. Nobody ever stays locked up."

"No one competent, anyway," said NightHowl. "It's like OSIRIS *wants* them to escape." I was reminded of what she'd said about Hoods the day she and Speedslick took me up to the surface and showed me Mars. "I think there's something rotten at the core of OSIRIS."

A thought occurred to me. "Any of you ever go to Camp Commanding?"

"Sure, lots of times," said Speedslick. "Why do you ask?"

"I'll get there. Anyone else?" Everyone but Blindmark nodded. "Any of you 'win' a uniform?"

"I did," said NightHowl. "The measuring booth creeped me out something fierce."

"Me too," said Speedslick.

"Not me," said Emberdown.

"Not there," said Blindmark. "Tell me about this measuring booth."

So I did, including the itching sensation.

"Sounds kind of like this truck at the mall in Chicago," said Blindmark. "My mom got a free invite to have the whole family laser-fitted for clothes. No more guessing what size everyone was, just step into the booth and you can order anything you want to wear online after that. A whole bunch of e-tailers had signed on to the new system. It's the itching that reminds me of it, because my parents said they didn't get the itchies. But I sure as heck did."

"They had one of those trucks come to my school in DC," said Emberdown. "Itchies and everything. Now you've really got me curious, Evan. Where are you going with this?"

"That booth is the new version of the Hero Bomb," I said. "It's a ray now, and OSIRIS is using it to *make* metas."

"That's a mighty big jump you just made there," said Blindmark. "But it makes sense. You got any proof?"

"Mike pretty much admitted it when I asked him. He said he'd tell me more about it later if I insisted, but I don't think I want to remind him that I know about it if I don't have to. He said it was classified OSIRIS A1 and he seemed very worried about talking about it."

"I wonder what else they're hiding," said NightHowl.

"I don't know," I replied, "but I think we need to find out."

15

School Daze

School . . . The AMO was the most amazing place I'd ever been in my life. Bits of it blurred by like something out of *Scenes from a Week of Classes at the School for Sidekicks*:

Putting on a cape is like sticking a "kick me" sign on your back.

Bullet holes in Armex are remarkably easy to patch. You simply . . .

A well-timed quip can save your life.

A domino mask is pretty much the same as no mask—you might as well pretend that glasses and a different hair style will protect your secret identity.

No one knows for sure why most Mask-built technology can't be mass-produced, though one popular theory holds that gadget-driven Masks are really using technokinetic powers that manifest themselves as shiny hardware.

High-end superspeed without some sort of concomitant friction reduction—usually of the general slipstream or vacuukinesis types—is a fast track to sudden human combustion.

The spork is the most underutilized flatware item when it comes to combat.

And some of it dragged—my math classes, for example.

But what I liked the most was learning to do things that no other school would have taught us. Things like the care and feeding of uniforms.

Professor White held up a small power buffer. "I know Metamorphosis Day is still a couple of months away, but there will be a major memorial held here on Deimos as always. You'll want to look your best with most of the major Masks a-visiting, and Invulycra and Armex take a lot of work to clean and buff properly."

I know, I know, cleaning technology doesn't sound like the most exciting thing since ever, but when he said that a bell went off in my head. I realized I now had the answer to the M-Day Mystery. When meta activity went dark for a day, *this* was where they all went! And this year, I would be among them. How amazing was that?

~~ ~~

There we were, walking down the street, me, Speedslick, Emberdown, NightHowl, Blurshift, and Blindmark. Heropolis, downtown east, near the capital. Not that far from the museum, actually.

We thought we were ready for anything, but we didn't even see it coming, not even Blindmark with his fancy optical telepathy. Just *bzzt* and a huge green flash that put Emberdown out of it before things really even started.

Speedslick reacted first—go figure—blurring away ahead of us. Briefly. Whether Spartanicus had anticipated him or it was plain dumb luck didn't really matter. The results were what counted, and Speedslick versus the banana peel and its buddy, the concrete wall, was a short and ugly fight.

I dived behind a parked car as the second blast came in. It wasn't elegant, and NightHowl landed on top of me when she had the same idea, but the beam that KO'd Blindmark missed us both. I'm not sure what happened to Blurshift at that point. I lost sight of them, and, *poof*, gone.

"What was that?!" NightHowl demanded angrily from her place in the middle of my back.

"Spartanicus," I said over my shoulder.

"Are you sure?" Her voice slipped an octave higher. "That can't be right!"

"If there's one thing I'm *sure* of about this Mask business, it's what it's like to have Spartanicus taking pot shots at you."

A heavy *thump* sounded from somewhere on the other side of the car.

She scooted off me, staying low and angling forward to the next car in the row. "We're not ready for this!"

Before I could answer, a deep gravelly bass spoke, "No, children, you aren't. You never will be."

The car I was hiding behind rose up on one end as Spartanicus lifted it aside. But I was already moving. With NightHowl going forward, I scrambled back, ducking around behind the tailgate of an old station wagon. I don't think the scarred Hood saw me.

"Hide-and-seek won't save you for long," Spartanicus said, hurling the first car aside. "Why don't you come out and get this over with? I promise none of you will be seriously injured."

"What about Emberdown?" NightHowl yelled from somewhere on the far side of our attacker—brave but stupid.

"The girl is merely unconscious," said Spartanicus, followed by something else I missed as I scrambled under the delivery truck behind the station wagon.

When I peeked my head out past one of the wheels, I saw Spartanicus heading to the center of the street, his head turning this way and that as he looked for NightHowl. Now would have been a great time for an energy beam or sonic blast or, well, anything really. Unfortunately, my powers didn't include anything by way of a ranged attack. If I was going to do something that Spartanicus would even notice, I had to get in close. Just like last time.

As I looked around for a route that might let me do that and arrive in one relatively leak-free piece, I spotted Emberdown. She didn't look unconscious. She looked dead, with blood leaking from her nose, and an obvious dent in her forehead. Blindmark lay nearby, likewise limp and bloodied.

I went from frightened to furious in about four-fifths of a

second. The six of us against Spartanicus was so ridiculous there wasn't even a word to describe how unfair it was. Like a bunch of Chihuahuas taking on a grizzly. We couldn't possibly win, but I was too angry to give up. When I felt my meager powers welling up in response to that fury, I charged. I knew it was insane when I did it, but I couldn't help myself.

Pivoting on the heel of one hand, I launched myself out from under the truck and onto my feet. I had enough presence of mind to try to run quietly, but that was all the caution I could manage. I didn't even have a weapon. If I'd been more than about twenty feet away, or Spartanicus had been more on his guard, I'd never have made it. But, I don't think he really saw any of us as a threat.

When I was five feet behind him, I leapt into the air and made my best attempt at one of the flying side kicks that Professor Ivanova had been drilling us on. For once, I got the move about right. The heel of my right foot connected with the back of Spartanicus's head with a really satisfying crack. Unfortunately, it was the sound of my foot breaking.

Spartanicus barely moved. No, cancel that. My kick barely moved him—half an inch, no more. Yet, somehow, he managed to spin and catch me by the calf of my kicking leg before I could drop back to the ground. I ended up hanging head down by one leg.

"Still more brass than brains," he said almost gently. "That's going to cost you badly some day."

"Not today?" I asked, somehow managing to keep the shake out of my voice—maybe because the pain in my foot was distracting me.

"No."

Spartanicus froze then and another voice spoke from his lips, "That can't be right." It was Backflash—I recognized her accent. "Why didn't he kill the boy?"

The sky above me suddenly pixilated and vanished, leaving behind a high-domed ceiling of fused moon rock. The cars went next, exposing NightHowl as she crept toward Spartanicus's back. Then the buildings, leaving only the street and the people in it. For one brief instant, the bottom five feet of the street-light right behind Spartanicus remained, then it slowly shifted from steel gray to the urban camouflage pattern of Blurshift's uniform.

Blurshift was holding a heavy tire iron. "Really, you're going to freeze the simulation now? Two more seconds of slow shifting and I'd have had my shot. I was practically on top of him!"

The street vanished at that point and Emberdown, Blindmark, and Speedslick—all unharmed—got up from the KO positions they'd assumed when the sim declared them casualties. Spartanicus remained—though a much more plastic-looking version, as the holographic overlay faded out, taking much of his apparent animation with it.

The main door slowly opened then, and Professor Ivanova stormed into the huge room and stopped in the middle, looking up. "Backflash! You are interfering with my training regime again." The tiny Russian combat instructor's hair was on fire. Literally. A long burning mane of yellow flame roared and snapped behind her like a banner in the wind. "Why is it this time?"

The Spartanicus dummy spoke again. "There's something wrong with the programming. Give me a moment."

Ivanova said something very fast and very angry in Russian, but then crossed her arms and assumed a patient waiting posture. I felt a lot less patient myself, but then I was hanging upside down from the fist of a large robot.

"What's going on?" NightHowl asked me very quietly as the others came to stand around the deactivated combat bot.

"I don't know," I replied equally quietly. "But is there any chance you guys could get me down?"

Blindmark shook his head and tapped the robot on the biceps. "This is a Mark IX attack drone, designed to spar with heavyweights like Captain Commanding or Burnish. Short of disassembly, none of us is going to get it to let go of anything it doesn't want to."

"I don't understand," Backflash said as she walked in through the same door that Ivanova had used. "It shouldn't have reacted like that at all."

Ivanova's hair flared wildly, but she took a deep breath and spoke calmly. "Again, I ask: Why is it that you are interfering in my carefully calibrated training schedule? None of these children should even be in the same room with a Mark IX, much less one programmed to simulate the powers and temperament of Spartanicus. They are still untrained—fragile. They could have been hurt or even killed."

Backflash ignored Ivanova in favor of the combat drone. "Chest port open," she ordered, and the whole front of its torso swung to one side. "Skull port as well." The face flipped up and out of the way, exposing a sensor array. "Oh, and drop the boy."

It did, and I landed hard on my shoulders before flopping onto my back. I ought to have seen it coming and rolled out of the fall, but I'd been so busy twisting around to look into the thing's chest cavity that I simply didn't have time to react. Before I could even try to get up, Ivanova was there, kneeling beside me.

She put one hand firmly on my chest. "Your foot, I heard the break on my monitor. How is it?"

I wiggled my toes, and found that the pain had faded, though my boot felt a bit tight. Quite possibly that had to do with the increasingly familiar sensation of scabweb wrapping my injuries. "My healing mojo kicked in, I'll be fine."

"That is good." She caught my hand and pulled me to my feet as she returned to her own. "We will discuss your actions in the session tomorrow." She swung a hand around to take the others in. "All of your actions. Given the circumstances and the surprise, you did . . . not badly. But that is for later. For now, you are free to use the rest of the hour however you might like. I need to have words with Madame Backflash."

The director of OSIRIS was neck deep in the chest of the Mark IX, and had been mumbling to herself the whole time. Things like, "Shouldn't have reacted like that. Not in the programming. Why not simulated lethal force? Some sort of feedback loop with the preserved imprint from Bittersharp? Self-connect to the newsweb? It makes no sense."

Professor Ivanova broke in then, tapping her on the shoulder. "What makes no sense, Madame Director, is your interfering in a training sequence without at least warning me."

Backflash pulled her head out of the bot's chest. "Don't be silly, Irina. It makes perfect sense. If you'd known about it, your

179

reactions might have given something away to the trainees, and I wanted total surprise. I've been working on the Spartanicus emulator on and off for years, and it's a rare opportunity for me to spring it unanticipated on someone who's actually faced off with him and lived. I couldn't pass it up. The risk of permanent injury or fatalities was acceptably low given the potential rewards."

Ivanova took a deep breath like a woman about to start shouting, then paused and looked over at us. "Did I not tell you all that you were free?"

I nodded and saw several of the others doing the same. "You did."

"So, be free. Fly away. Shoo. Do whatever you want as long as it is not here." She pointed firmly at the exit and this time waited to see us start moving before she returned part of her attention to Backflash.

I wanted to drag my feet and listen in some more, but it was quite clear that we'd be in trouble if we hung around even one minute longer.

"What was that about?" NightHowl asked as we went through the door.

I shrugged. "Beyond what we overheard? Who knows."

We turned left, still in a loose group, passing down another of the moon base's endless corridors. This one had heavy blast doors spaced out along both sides, each leading into another of the school's battle simulators. Several of them were designed to provide unusual environments, including the tank, which allowed for various combinations of underwater and boat fights.

"We've only got about twenty minutes of free time," said

Emberdown. "That's barely enough time for a real vid. So, what do we do with ourselves?"

I'd been idly watching the occupancy lights on the sim rooms as we passed them. Red for in use, dangerous, do not enter. Yellow for occupied, limited entry. Green for available. Now I had an awesome idea.

"What about that?" I pointed at a particularly large door ahead on the right, its green light shining away. It was the low-grav simulator, which was one of the only places where the tiny moon's gravity acted the way it ought to. "Speedslick could run and grab us a volleyball or something."

I'd barely finished speaking when Jeda blurred away down the corridor, the greens and golds of his costume flickering now and then as his powers hiccupped and he briefly slowed.

"I don't know," said Emberdown. "We're not really supposed to use the sims without permission."

NightHowl rolled her eyes. "Did Professor Ivanova tell us we could do whatever we want, or did she not?"

"That's good enough for me," said Blurshift, unlocking the vault-style door latch. "I'm in."

Emberdown looked at Blindmark, but the other older student shrugged. "Why not? We do sort of have permission. I think that's enough to keep us out of real trouble as long as nobody gets hurt."

"All right." Emberdown sighed. "But let's try to be careful, okay?"

"Of course," replied NightHowl. "I'm the soul of caution. Now, how do you get the holo-projectors to cycle random environments?"

Thirty seconds later we were playing a sort of mishmash of dodgeball, tag, and kill the quarterback in very low gravity on what looked like the surface of Earth's moon. Two minutes after that, the environment shifted to something that could have come straight out of the Colliding Galaxies vid franchise complete with starfighter flybys. And, two minutes after *that*, we were duking it out in what could best be described as a miniature Tokyo scaled as though we were all two hundred feet tall.

Totally awesome!

The next afternoon, when we arrived for Professor Ivanova's class, I asked her, "What happened yesterday with the Spartanicus simulation?"

Her hair flared for a moment and she said something in gutter Russian under her breath, then she shrugged. "According to our director, I am not needing to know. So, we will talk about what you did right and what you did wrong, and then we will not talk about it anymore to spare my blood pressure. Start with your approach. Emberdown, you begin. How could you have done better yesterday?"

"Not dying without so much as laying eyeballs on my killer?" she said glumly.

Ivanova frowned. "Well, yes, this is truth. But it is not all the truth. You died in part because you were not paying proper attention. None of you were; I will show you." She waved her hand and a miniature version of the scene from yesterday sprang up in holographic projection.

"Here is the cityscape. As you are walking along the street, do you see where Spartanicus entered?"

"No," said Emberdown. "I *still* don't see . . . wait. On top of that skyway! No wonder I missed him."

Professor Ivanova nodded. "Now you see why I always, always tell you to keep an eye on the sky. You cannot trust that Hoods will approach you on your level. Not even the ones who don't fly. Blindmark, what should you and Emberdown have done differently yesterday?"

"Besides keeping an eye out upward? To start with, I should have kept shifting my focus. It's fatiguing to keep jumping eyeballs, but it gives me a much better chance of spotting someone coming in. I know it wouldn't have worked on the Mark IX since it doesn't actually have eyes, but in a real-world situation, I might even hop into an enemy's point of view by chance, and that'd come in very handy."

"Good, what else? You and Emberdown made one critical mistake none of the others did."

"Don't freeze," he said harshly. "I should have grabbed a piece of cover like NightHowl and Meerkat or faded instead of simply standing there like an idiot."

"Excellent." She turned to Emberdown. "Why did you two freeze where the others did not?"

Emberdown raked her fingers nervously across the top of her short afro. "Honestly?"

Ivanova quirked an eyebrow. "Of course."

"Too much time in the sims, I think. The young 'uns are only just getting their first experience in the battle simulations. They don't know what should and shouldn't be there. That green flash freaked me out. It's Spartanicus's signature attack, and I knew that you wouldn't throw the heaviest of heavyweight Hoods at a team with four first years in it. So I didn't know what was going on, and instead of reacting to an attack, I stood there like an idiot trying to figure out what was up with the sim."

Ivanova turned her gaze on Blindmark.

"That's me, too, though with less thinking and more panicking," he said, his voice small. "Honestly, it's embarrassing to get shown up by a bunch of rookies like that."

"Any conclusions?" she asked, widening the question to include all of us.

I raised my hand cautiously.

"Meerkat?"

"Sims ought to have a wider range of scenarios? You know, to throw in more unexpected stuff." It sounded kind of feeble when I said it out loud.

"Yes, they ought, though that's not what I was thinking. Anyone else?"

Blurshift spoke up. "More real-world training? Get out of the sims and into the field."

"Very good," said Ivanova. "Also, you did the best of any of the group yesterday. Your shifting powers are not strong enough for full-on transformation into other shapes, but you made excellent use of what you had, first blending into the crowd and then working your way closer to Spartanicus under cover of camouflage. Much smarter than what Meerkat pulled."

She turned a very hard look on me. "What you did was brave,

but stupid. Very, very stupid. You could have died yesterday, and not merely in simulation. A Mark IX is too dangerous to be loosed on any of you. Though you had no way of knowing that was what you faced, you all made a huge mistake yesterday and I will be marking most of you D-minus for Unscheduled Extra-Credit Sim Spartanicus-Alpha. All except for Meerkat, who gets an F."

"What!" I couldn't help myself. "Why?"

Ivanova's face went as grim as I had ever seen it. "Because yesterday, in simulation, you committed suicide. D-minus for the group, for not doing what you should have done the second you saw Spartanicus—run away! F for the foolishness of attacking him without the slightest hint of a plan. I will *not* see my students throw their lives away."

"But—" I began, but Ivanova's hair flared and she made a sharp chopping motion that made me bite off my argument.

"No buts. Yesterday you did something stupid by needlessly charging someone who could kill you as easily as slapping a mosquito. You chose to pursue conflict in a no-win situation. Do not repeat your mistake by arguing with your teacher. Unless perhaps you would like to add detention to your F? Understood?"

I nodded. I didn't like it, but I did it.

16

The Foxman Theme

Then, it was Friday morning, and I hadn't heard another thing from Foxman, or from Mike *about* Foxman. I was beginning to think I'd been dumped as a sidekick. But, as Combat with Dinnerware finished up, Mike waved at me to stay after.

"I had a little chat with Rand this morning," said Mike. "He says he'll have the *Flying Fox* waiting to pick you up at OSIRIS headquarters at four thirty." Mike frowned. "I might have yelled a bit, and I don't think he much approved, since he sounded like five miles of bad road."

His frown deepened. "I know that he's reformed himself, but I'm still not entirely comfortable about handing you over for an entire weekend. On the other hand, I don't know what else to do if we're going to salvage your chances at becoming a Mask." Mike sighed. "He did seem on top of things the day he asked for you to come intern with him, but I just don't know."

"I'll be all right," I promised.

Honestly, Foxman wasn't nearly as hard to deal with as

figuring out what do about my parents. I still didn't know what to say in my e-mail to them, and with each passing day it got harder. Now I had to figure out how to explain why it had taken me so long to get back to them in addition to what to say to Mom's e-mails to me. Things had gotten so bad on that front that even opening my e-mail program made me want to barf. It was much easier to simply pretend everything was fine at home and not deal with it, except when I remembered. And then it wasn't.

"Evan, are you all right?" Mike asked, leaning forward.

"Yeah, I'm fine. Shouldn't have eaten so much for breakfast is all. It'll get better in a bit."

"Ah, I see." His eyes met mine. I could tell he didn't believe me, but he didn't push it. "Make sure you remember to bring your uniform along when you head for OSIRIS. Oh, and your laptop and a couple changes of clothing, since you'll be staying through Sunday evening. Rand and I put together a schedule and duties list for your internship when we had our little chat. I'll write it up and get it e-mailed to you when I'm done with classes this afternoon."

I flinched when he said the word *e-mail* but I don't think he noticed. "Thanks, Mike, I really appreciate it. Is there anything else you need to talk to me about?"

He frowned and pursed his lips, but he finally shook his head and I ducked out the door. I was going to be late for my next class—one of my civilian-side courses—American Government, with an emphasis on its impacts on metahuman issues. We were going over the Franklin Act this week, and the way Professor Vang explained it, the law sounded even worse for minor Masks than I'd gathered from my own reading.

Vang gave me a hard look when I came in, but didn't actually scold me, as she was busy drawing a diagram showing governmental authority over various metahuman issues. I tried to pay attention, but found I couldn't focus at all. Talking with Mike had really pulled my worries about my parents up from the depths where I'd been hiding them from myself, and now I couldn't think of anything else. I *had* to write that e-mail, but I just couldn't.

The whole rest of the school day went like that, with my classes blurring past and the sick feeling in my stomach getting worse and worse. By the time the bells rang at the end of the day, I was about ready to barf in my book bag. That's probably why I didn't see Burnish until I ran right into her in a mostly empty hall on the way back to my dorm room.

No, that's not quite true. I didn't see Burnish until I was flying backward down that hall with a huge numb spot in the center of my chest where she'd hit me with some sort of electrical blast. Even then, I only had a blurred impression of tangled black hair whirling around an angry expression on a face the color of polished copper.

I went from sick at heart to completely enraged in three-tenths of a second as all my frustrations with everything suddenly found a target. As I did so, I felt the world sort of slow down around me. I had time to look down and see that a big chunk of my shirt had burned away. The skin underneath was cracked and blistered, but there was no blood. Instead, a gooey gray ooze came from my pores. I had time to turn in the air, twisting as Professor Ivanova had shown us, so that a wild tumble turned into a triple cartwheel that ended with me on my feet facing back the way I'd just come.

I started back toward Burnish and, if I wasn't quite as quick as Speedslick, or even me that day at the museum, I was still moving faster than a speeding bicycle. I didn't have a plan or anything—I was too angry for thinking—but I knew I didn't want to let Burnish get away with what felt like a sneak attack.

As I got within striking distance, Burnish reached over and touched the front of the nearest locker. Instantly, her skin shifted from shimmering copper to the dull color of oiled steel. With her other hand she casually caught me by the throat and lifted me off the ground, holding me out at arm's length in front of her. That's when I learned the difference between my more-powerful-than-a-really-butch-lawn-tractor muscles and real Mask-grade superstrength.

I was strong then, stronger than any normal human by a factor of two or three at least, but Burnish in her steel shape was strong enough to pick up a bus and throw it. She didn't squeeze—or she could have killed me, easy—but she didn't let go either. And I could no more pry her fingers loose of my throat than a beaver could have chewed through a steel bar. It really drove home the lesson of Ivanova's F.

"Nice try," she sneered, "but nothing like good enough to get you into the big leagues. Maybe if you keep sucking up to Fox-loser, he'll build you a suit that lets you pretend you have real powers. In the meantime, watch where you're going, and stay out of my way."

That made me even madder, but try as I might, I couldn't do anything to pull loose of Burnish's vastly stronger grip. Given the length of her arms I couldn't even reach her with my fists, and pounding on her forearm only bruised my hands.

"Burnish, put Evan down." Mike's voice—flat, quiet, gentle even, but with real iron underneath. "Now."

"Don't you mean Meerkat?" She spoke with a bitter, dismissive snap, but she did put me down.

"Does that look like a uniform he's wearing?" Mike asked.

Burnish shook her head. "No."

"And class is over for the day. Speaking of which, the rest of you need to find something else to do. Now."

I hadn't noticed until then, but maybe a half-dozen students had gathered around us in a semi-circle. At Mike's words they scattered. Mike didn't speak again until there were only the three of us left.

"So," he continued. "No class, no costume, no outside assignments. No handle. Which means that right now Evan is officially a civilian, *and* that you were using powers on a civilian."

"He doesn't look like much of a civilian to me." She tapped the center of my chest where a thick gray web completely covered my injury.

"Using powers on a civilian?" I asked.

Mike sighed. "You never did read the AMO handbook I gave you, did you, Evan?"

"I'm working on it," I mumbled, though I'd pretty much forgotten about it entirely till that very moment.

"Well, you clearly haven't worked your way as far as chapter two," he said in a tone that made me blush. Then he turned his eyes back on Burnish. "As for you: passive powers invoked defensively don't count, and you know it, Burnish. Unlike Evan here, *you* grew up knowing it. Don't play at ignorance."

Burnish took a deep breath and nodded. "I'm sorry, Mike."

He raised an eyebrow, and she sighed. Then she turned to me, and with a look that told me she'd rather eat dog droppings, she added, "I'm sorry, Evan. I shouldn't have used powers on you like that."

"That's a good start," said Mike. "You and I are still going to have a very long talk in my office, but for my part I think we can skip reporting it officially for now."

"Thank you, Mike." This time Burnish's voice was sincere. "That's really kind of you."

Mike's frown lightened, but didn't go away. "I know you're in a tough place here at the school given who your parents are, Burnish, and why you never, ever wear civvies. I don't want to make your life any harder than it already is. But going after Evan like that is completely unacceptable behavior, and it would be even if he *was* in costume. He's a brand-new student with sidekick-level powers, and you're a third-year Maskweight. What were you thinking?"

Burnish looked at me and then at her feet, and she didn't look up again or say another word. Mike's expression went thoughtful as he glanced back and forth between the two of us.

"How does your chest feel, Evan?" he asked.

I tapped the center of the scabweb where my healing power had coated my skin. It didn't hurt, and I could already see the edges starting to peel up. "I'm fine."

I wasn't really. Not inside, where Mike's gentle dismissal of my "sidekick-level powers" had stung my pride even more deeply than my inability to do anything against Burnish. But I couldn't tell *him* that, or let Burnish see that those words had hurt me more than her lightning.

"Then you need to get changed and head for the Den ASAP. But I'll want to talk with you about this when you get back Sunday evening. I'm not going to escalate things on my own, but you have to decide how you feel about what happened with Burnish and whether you want to take it further. Using powers on a civilian is a serious offense, even if you're only a civilian by school courtesy in this case."

Burnish actually flinched and her lips tightened, but she still didn't look up or speak. I wasn't entirely sure what the whole "civilian" thing was all about, but I suspected that if I pushed it I could get Burnish in a world of hurt. That was *very* tempting, and I made a mental note to pack the handbook with my other stuff for the weekend so I could find out more.

But then I thought about who Burnish's dad was, and how big of a jerk he was, and about how bad I felt about the mess I was in with *my* parents. I paused then, as I realized that some of her problem with me might be tangled up with how she felt about her dad. Maybe when he blacklisted me, that made her feel like he'd be proud of her if she beat me up? I didn't know who her mother was, but I got the feeling that was even more of a sore spot than

Captain Commanding. As much as I wanted to lash out at her, I found that I couldn't do it.

"As far as I'm concerned, this is over," I said. "She didn't really hurt me, just made me mad and ruined a Captain Commanding shirt I didn't like all that much anyway. Whatever you want to do about it is fine with me."

Though Burnish didn't otherwise move, her eyes flicked from looking at her feet to looking at mine and I could see the tension go out of her back and shoulders. Mike nodded for me to go then, so I went.

This time, knowing what to expect, I had a lot more fun riding in the *Flying Fox*. I even put my hands on the controls and pretended I was flying it, though I made darned sure I didn't actually put any pressure on anything. For a few brief minutes I even forgot about the mess with my parents.

What peace it brought me started to fade soon after I hauled my stuff out of the plane. To start with, Foxman wasn't there to greet me. Instead, Denmother had one of the little bronze Foxbots waiting to lead me to my rooms—a huge suite behind a hidden door in the library area of the main dome.

It *was* pretty cool to see a set of bookshelves slide silently aside to let me pass into the modestly sized parlor that centered my five-room suite. I also had a large bedroom with a huge canopy bed in the center, a bathroom with a soaking tub big enough for a small swim meet, a walk-in closet with three more versions of the Meerkat costume neatly arrayed on their own racks, and an office/workroom that was larger than any two of the other rooms combined. I suppose the big-time secret hideout was one upside to being relegated to sidekick status.

Once I'd gone through the whole suite, I tossed my backpack on the bed and went back out into the parlor. On my side, the door was hidden by a broad fireplace with a very convincing holographic fire burning in the hearth. As I approached it, the fires parted like a curtain and the back wall slid aside to let me out into the main dome.

When I asked Denmother where to find Foxman, she directed me to the trophy room and another concealed door—this one hiding beneath a marble coffee table—that slid aside to expose a set of stairs. The steps spiraled down into a large and dimly lit round room. Various pedestals and glass cases filled with random bric-a-brac stood scattered around the space.

Foxman, or—considering his lack of costume—Rand, sat with his back to the stairs in a big overstuffed chair that had obviously been dragged down from the living room above. He was wearing some sort of fancy patterned silk jacket. He didn't look up when I came down the stairs, though the light streaming in from the trapdoor must have alerted him to my presence.

As I got closer, I could see that he was just sitting and staring meditatively at the wall in front of him. A MaskerAde stood on the arm of his chair and a half-dozen crushed cans lay on the floor around his feet. Closer still and I saw that the wall itself was covered with tiny letters carved into the stone—names. I paused beside his chair, trying to figure out what he was doing.

Without looking up, he said, "Hello, Evan."

"Hello . . . Mr. Hammer."

"Rand. You're my sidekick now, and we're going to be fighting crime together. I think it would be better to skip the formality. Especially given your lack of a sidekick's permit and how very many laws we're going to be violating in the process. Don't you?" He sounded resigned and a little angry—not at all his usual manic.

"I guess so."

"You do still want to fight crime, I assume?" He stood abruptly then and I got a better look at his clothes, a thigh-length jacket belted with a silk sash, black silk pajamas, and worn leather slippers. "Well, other than the violations of the Franklin Act that we are going to commit while doing it. Fighting that particular bit of crime would be self-defeating. Quite literally."

I nodded. I'd been badly stung when Burnish mocked my comparative lack of powers, and even more so when Mike casually dismissed them as well. I wanted to—I don't know—redeem myself, maybe? I'm not sure what I wanted exactly, but I suddenly knew that I needed to make being a Mask *matter*. If I couldn't do that, then all my dreams, and the rift with my parents, and . . . well, everything, was all meaningless. And I absolutely couldn't bear the thought of that.

"It's the only thing that makes any sense to me right now," I said after a moment.

"Hold on to that!" Rand's voice was fierce in a way I hadn't heard before. "Hold on to that and never let it go." But he didn't move, and I could see his eyes drift back to the wall. "I did and, hmm, never mind." He still didn't move.

"Are you all right?" I finally asked.

"Yeah." He nodded. "As much as I ever am, anyway. Come on, I'll suit up and then I guess we can go right some wrongs, however minor."

I wanted to ask about the names on the wall, but Rand's attitude and the expression on his face when he looked at them convinced me now wasn't the time. A few minutes later, I stood in the manufactory watching as a dozen robotic arms deftly assembled the Foxman armor around Rand, who had put an Invulycra jumpsuit on as a base layer. The whole operation took less time than it took us to walk up the stairs from the trophy room.

The Foxmobile had been fully repaired since my last visit, and it didn't show so much as a single scrape. Foxman blew into the tube himself this time. But he still made me drive because "You're the one who wants this. I gave up years ago, and I'm not buying back into the whole thing now."

For the next three hours, we quietly patrolled the streets. As soon as I started the car, Foxman had pulled up a menu labeled "Foxouflage" and selected "Bread truck." We didn't actually encounter any crime, but then it wasn't yet dark. Just before the sun went down, we headed back to the Den for dinner. I would have preferred to keep going, but Foxman insisted that proper meals were part of the deal he cut with Mike.

"Low blood sugar is bad for crime-fighting," he said. "It'll make you stupid and shaky. Speaking of which . . ." He pulled a MaskerAde from his bandolier and drained it in one go.

"Are you sure that stuff is good for you?" I asked.

"I'm *very* sure it's not," he said, making a face.

"Then why don't you drink something else?"

"Why don't you shut up and drive the freaking car!" he snapped, turning away from me and staring out the window.

The rest of the trip back to the Den passed in a long and uncomfortable silence. Great, now I'd screwed things up with my parents *and* my mentor. By the time Denmother had served us each a plate of Vietnamese chicken lo mein, my stomach felt so horrible I couldn't even *imagine* eating it.

After a few minutes Denmother asked, "Is there something wrong with the meal, Master Quick?"

"No. It's fine."

"But you're not eating. If you don't like lo mein, I can make you something else."

"No, I like it fine. I'm just not hungry."

Foxman had gotten yet another energy drink to go with his dinner, focusing on it with an intensity I'd hoped would keep him from noticing me picking at my food. Now he set it aside and gave me a speculative look.

"Look, I'm sorry I yelled at you, but . . ." He sighed. "Let's just say that was a really stupid question to ask a drunk, especially a dry drunk, and leave it at that. Okay?"

I nodded, and Foxman went back to eating his food while I went back to pushing mine around the plate and wishing I knew how to handle my parents. After a few minutes he looked up again.

"What's chewing on you, kid? I'm thinking it's more than getting yelled at by one old has-been."

I looked down at my plate because the edges of my eyes had suddenly started burning. I wanted to talk to someone about my parents, needed to, really. But at the same time I didn't want to let anyone into a pain that felt so personal and private.

"Kid, I didn't agree to take you on to be your friend. I did it solely to piss off Captain Commanding. I don't even like kids," he growled. "But, I *am* your designated Mask mentor, and the last thing in the world that I need to do is add another failure to what is an already epic list of guilts." Foxman sighed. "There isn't anyone in the world less qualified to offer good advice to an up-and-coming hero than I am. But there's also no one in the world who has less of a right to judge somebody else's failings either. So, cough it up. It can't possibly be as bad as all the stuff I've screwed up over the years."

I laughed, and it eased the burn in my eyes and the ache in my throat. I looked up at Foxman. "That's the least inspiring thing anyone's ever said to me."

He grinned. "Hey, I am the undisputed world champion of uninspiring. Not only am I an alcoholic, and a has-been, I'm also a raving egomaniac with delusions of grandeur. Or, I was at one time, anyway. I might be a recovering egomaniac right now—it's hard to say."

"You don't seem that self-absorbed to me," I said.

"Maybe not right at the moment, but how many people do you know who spent five hundred grand having the then-number-one-selling heavy metal band, Iron Ratt Riot, write them their very own theme music?"

"You have Iron Ratt Riot theme music? Why have I never heard of this marvel before?"

"Because Iron Ratt Riot sent it to me the same day I almost

knocked the IDS Tower off its foundations. It was another two weeks before I was sober enough to notice I'd gotten the file, and at that point the only thing Heropolis wanted from me was that I dig a hole and bury myself in it. I never actually got to use the theme, which is a shame, because A) it rocks, and B) the upgraded speakers in my suit were a total waste of time and money."

"Suit speakers?"

He nodded and touched a button on his wrist. Plates slid aside on his shoulders, exposing a thin metal mesh. "Right there. Flat panel sound broadcast technology better than anything you've ever heard before."

"Play your theme song for me. I'd like to hear it." That would have been true even if I wasn't looking for anything to distract myself from my own worries.

He raised an eyebrow. "How about this: I'll play the Foxman theme for you, if you tell me what's got you feeling so messed up you can't eat Denmother's excellent cooking." He extended his hand. "Deal?"

I shook it. "Deal." But where to start . . . I chewed on my lip for a little while, then decided I had to cowboy up and simply start talking. "It's my parents . . . they don't really want me to be a Mask."

I waited to see if Foxman would say anything, but he only nodded for me to continue. So I did. Slowly and with a lot of long silences between the bits, I gave him the whole story. My dreams, my hopes, my relationship with my parents before and after the hero beam. Everything. I even showed him all the e-mails.

Finally, when I was done, I looked at him and said, "Well, what do you think?"

"I said right up front that I don't have any right to judge anyone, and I won't. That's a lot of pain you've got there, kid, with no easy way out. I've only got two things to offer on the subject that have any chance of being useful. First one's a piece of my past."

Then he went silent for so long that I finally said, "Which is . . ."

"That wall downstairs, the one I was staring at when you showed up. It's carved with the name of every person that died in the original Hero Bomb blast, and every person that's died because of metahuman activities since. You probably couldn't see it, but some of the names are in italics. Those are the ones I personally failed in some way. There's only one italic name on the M-Day part of the wall."

Again he went quiet for a long while. This time I kept my mouth shout.

"The name is Archibald Hammer, and he was my dad. We had a big falling-out when I was a bit older than you are. I'd just turned sixteen and he bought me a fancy car as a birthday present. After he left my mother, he spent a lot of money on me trying to—I don't know—buy off his guilt maybe. He was a very rich man. Anyway, I was mad because he kept giving me presents instead of his time, and I threw the keys down at his feet and walked away.

"That was in October of '88. For the next month and a half I flat refused to take his calls or talk to him. Then, on the Ides of December, someone put a bomb under the I-94 bridge. Afterward, I was a billionaire Mask and he was dead. I never got the chance to straighten things out with him. I don't know if I would have, or if we could ever have fixed all the stuff that lay between us, but I would have liked the chance to find out."

"I'll answer the e-mail tonight."

"Good kid."

"What was the second thing you wanted to tell me?" I asked.

"That there's nothing in the whole world for easing some of the sting of hard times with family like taking down a bad guy." He smiled grimly and finished his drink. "I guarantee that it'll be easier to write that e-mail after you've punched your first real Hood in the nose, and I know just the guy. Now, come on. The Foxmobile awaits."

As he got up, the speakers on his suit started blaring a heavy metal anthem.

17

Heroing Without a License

"Sweet barking cheese, Foxman!" Put that one down on the big list of things I never thought I'd find myself saying.

But then, I never expected to find myself battling vicious guard Gouda in the hideout of the Fromagier either. Sure, I knew that he existed in a vague sort of way, but until you've nearly been KO'd by a giant wheel of Wensleydale, it's hard to take someone seriously when their power is listed as "fromaginesis."

I threw myself to the ground as the Fromagier hurled a handful of Cheddar stars my way. Three of them clipped me anyway. Fortunately, the Armex reinforcements in my uniform blocked two. The remaining star grazed the lighter Invulycra over my left bicep, leaving a long shallow cut that bled wildly. It was nothing my healing powers couldn't handle, and the red vanished beneath a web of gray goo within a matter of seconds, but I played dead until he turned his focus back to Foxman.

Then I started creeping toward the side wall and the stairs that led to a catwalk overhead. The Fromagier was really out of my league, but I figured if I could drop stuff on him from above I might have some chance of taking him out. I'd just gotten to the first landing when the Gouda came at me. Three wheels of the stuff, all studded with spikes and raring to run me down. I had to throw myself over the railing to avoid their charge. I fell nearly fifteen feet, landing in a Dumpster full of discarded cheese seconds. Worst smell of my life, but it got me clear of the Gouda. It also took me off everybody's radar for a little while.

As I was climbing out, I picked up a long, slender brick of combat-grade Swiss. It looked like the unholy offspring of a hockey stick and a cheese press. Coming out of the back of that Dumpster did an even better job of moving me out from under the Fromagier's eye than the catwalk would have.

He was hunkered down behind a thick wall of case-hardened Parmesan that allowed him to lob Limburger grenades at Foxman without putting himself directly in the line of the Foxblaster. I waited till he was in the midst of throwing a particularly thick and aromatic barrage. Then I slid forward through the shattered remains of a double dozen Gouda wheels. I got pretty close, then had to duck under the workbench where the foul Fromagier crafted his cheese of mass destruction when a lull gave him time to look around.

I think the Fromagier might have spotted me, if Foxman hadn't picked that exact second to toss a smoke bomb into the Parmesan bunker and start firing the Foxblaster wildly. As the Fromagier staggered back from the wall of choking smoke, I leapt forward and smashed my Swiss brick against the back of his skull with all my might.

Both the Swiss and the Fromagier's thick Colby shock helmet cracked under the impact, and he went down in a boneless heap.

Foxman was absolutely right! It did make me feel better. Maybe our lack of the proper licenses meant we could never take any credit for bringing the rogue cheese fancier to justice, but I knew that I'd helped bring his reign of terror to an end, and that was enough. For the first time, the idea of being a sidekick seemed like something I might actually want to do.

But when we pulled back into the tunnel that led to the Den, and I remembered I had a much more personal challenge to face in trying to figure out what to say to my parents, my mood crashed and burned. Somehow I didn't think *Hi, Mom, I defeated an evil cheese-monger today, what did you do?* would make for a good opening paragraph.

"What am I going to tell my mom?" I said as I parked the car.

Foxman shrugged. "If I knew how to bridge that kind of gap I might have sorted things out with my dad while I still had time." He looked down into his lap. "Wish I could do more. Sorry."

"It's all right, you've already helped a lot. Thanks."

I headed for my room and my laptop. As I passed the communications monitor, I paused to listen to a report about Spartanicus breaking HeartBurn and Bagger out of the metamax women's facility in southern Heropolis an hour or so earlier. Currently, OSIRIS had no idea of their whereabouts. But I had a job to do, so I moved on.

～～～ ～～～

I had to suppress my desire to fling my laptop into the fireplace as I deleted my fortieth or so attempt at an opening paragraph. Writing a reply to my mom's e-mail just wasn't working!

I pressed my fingertips into my cheekbones and stared at the "Please" she'd put in the subject line of all her most recent e-mails. I didn't know how to answer that.

Maybe that was the problem. Maybe I needed to write my own message and not just respond to my parents. Maybe I needed to take control of my life and grow up a little. I could do that, couldn't I? Look at how well I'd managed against the Fromagier. I began to type.

Mom, Dad,

I love you. Don't ever doubt that.

But this isn't about you. It's about me. Whether you like it or not, I have the trigger genes for metahuman powers and they've been activated. No matter what else happens with the rest of my life, that's going to be true.

You've read the Franklin Act. You have to know what that means in terms of my legal status both here and in the wider world. Heck, you've been on the wrong side of it when they dragged you away from work. I am a "potential weapon of mass destruction," and subject to the internationally recognized authority of OSIRIS.

But ignore that for a moment. I know you'd defy the whole world to protect and take care of me. I have never

205

been in any doubt of that, or of your love. That's not what this is about either.

It's about growing up. No matter how much you love me and want to take care of me, someday I have to grow up. Everyone does. Maybe thirteen is earlier than any of us would have liked for me to take such a long step on that road. But this isn't about what we'd like either.

This is about what is. And thirteen is when my world changed forever, when I changed forever. I don't know if I'm ready for this, but it happened, and I have to make the best of it. I have to make the best of me.

Maybe I didn't really understand what being a Mask really meant before, maybe I don't even understand it now, but it's what I always wanted. You raised me to believe I could be anything I wanted to be. Now you have to let me try.

I love you both,
Evan

I didn't hit send right away, but not because I was scared anymore. I waited because I wanted to make sure it was really what I needed to say. That was something my mom had taught me—never send your reply to an upsetting e-mail without giving yourself time to cool down and read it again. If I was going to deal with my parents, I might as well try to live up to them, too.

Setting my laptop aside, I asked Denmother where Foxman was. I wanted to thank him for taking me out to deal with a real bad guy—it was exactly what I'd needed to put some spine into me.

Denmother told me Rand had crashed hard and she'd had the Foxbots put him to bed, so I headed to the trophy room instead. Directly in front of Rand's chair and about halfway up the granite wall was the name *Archibald Hammer*. It was easy to find. Despite obvious efforts on the part of the cleaning bots to keep everything looking uniform, the stone there was a little more worn than the names around it, like someone had traced it over with fingertips a hundred thousand times.

Between fighting with the Fromagier and writing the note to my parents I felt way too amped to sleep. I headed for the kitchen to make myself a sandwich. Well, technically, to have Denmother make me one, but the result was the same. My first taste of real crime fighting had left me with an itch to get out there again.

So I took my sandwich and a glass of milk and carried them over to the Foxsnooper and started playing with the settings. After listening in on the local police chatter, and switching from there to FBI official dispatches, I was scanning some eyes-only CIA reports on the screen when a red flag popped up in the corner of the touch screen.

I tapped it and it opened out to show "OSIRIS priority alpha scrambled traffic, decrypt?"

I tapped yes, and a moment later, the audio portion of the monitor's traffic switched over to a woman's voice saying, "Repeat, this is Special Agent Brendan and I have eyes on subject

Spartanicus." That made me lean in toward the speaker. "Target is having a glass of wine on the patio at Merik's. I have two snipers in position and I can either take him out or take him down. Requesting firing authorization."

"Agent Brendan, this is Hood Command. Stand down the lethal option. That's an imminent-danger-only request, and you know it. As for nonlethal takedown, I refer you to standing order 1-A re: Alpha- and Bravo-level Hood targets. In accordance with 1-A, I am forwarding your request directly to Director Backflash. I wouldn't get my hopes up if I were you."

Wait, what now? None of that made any sense, not unless Night-Howl's darkest suspicions about OSIRIS deliberately letting Hoods roam loose were true.

"Roger that, HC." Agent Brendan's voice sounded more than a little resigned. "Standing down sniper team Omega. Will await further orders on team Delta."

The monitor went silent for perhaps ten heartbeats while I tried to make sense of what I was hearing. Then it spat out a sharp burst of static before switching back to voice. I recognized Backflash's accent instantly.

"Agent Brendan, this is Backflash. Stand down Delta team as well, and close up the operation. Spartanicus is currently status free-range." Her voice came out crisp and hard with none of the distracted vagueness of our last two encounters.

Free-range? Did that mean what I thought it did? *Could it?*

"Ma'am, two guards were killed when he escaped—OSIRIS personnel," said Brendan.

"I'm aware of that, Agent Brendan, and I deeply regret their loss. I personally made the calls to their families, as I always have, and it never gets any easier. But I am also aware of the bigger picture. Given the ultimate goals of OSIRIS and our mandate, sacrifices are inevitable. You knew that when you accepted the promotion to special agent."

What ultimate goals? What mandate? It didn't sound like she was talking about any of the things I thought I knew about OSIRIS, not if letting Hoods run around loose was part of that.

While I was pondering, Brendan sighed audibly. "I understand that, Director, it's just . . . hard sometimes."

"If the job were easy we wouldn't need people of your caliber to do it. And if it were any less important we wouldn't be forced to do it at all."

"Yes, ma'am. Standing down team Delta now. Returning subject Spartanicus to free-range status. Brendan out."

The monitor went quiet and the red flag that had opened into a dialogue box closed and vanished. But I kept right on staring at the screen until I heard a throat being cleared behind me. I turned around to find Foxman leaning on the edge of a lab table. He looked old and haggard and his eyes were threaded with blood. His silk pajamas and the jacket thing that went with them were badly rumpled.

"It's one in the morning," he grumbled. "Shouldn't you be asleep? That is traditionally what one does at this time of night. Especially when one is a thirteen-year-old. I'm pretty sure that I remember that from being one of you, back . . . a really, really long time ago. I'm certain that I got more than one lecture on the subject from my mom. Not that I listened, or expect you to. But the social compact and my job as your mentor compels me to point it out. Heck, it might even be in that giant lump of paperwork Minute Man made me sign before handing you over. It being bed-time, a time for sleeping, and all that."

"Too wired and worried and, now, confused, to sleep," I said. "Did you hear all of that?"

"No, only the last few sentences. Maybe five, maybe six. Hard to say, grammar was never my best subject." He met my eyes as he spoke, but something about the way he said it made me think he wasn't telling the whole truth. "Besides, I am in the middle of the sugar crash to end all sugar crashes, and my brain's gone kind of fuzzy."

"So, what are you doing out of bed?" I asked.

"The bladder waits for no one . . . I got up to pee, and while I was in the bathroom Denmother let me know you were still out here. She felt that you ought to be in bed and that it was my job to see that you went there. I don't much agree, but then she piped in the audio from the Foxsnooper and I thought maybe I *should* come out and yell at you to go to bed." He yawned enormously, growled, "Go to bed," and turned back toward his own rooms.

"Do you know what they were talking about with that stuff about OSIRIS's goals and mandate?"

"No. Absolutely not. Even if I did, I'm pretty sure it's classi-fied. Which, by the way, is the case for *all* OSIRIS priority alpha scrambled traffic. You can get into a lot of trouble for breaking their encryption." He squeezed his face between his hands and frowned. "Oh, and I'm *very* sure that Minute Man's paperwork included me not giving out classified information to an unlicensed sidekick. You know, in case you were wondering."

I gave him a skeptical look. "So, that's a yes, then."

Rand held out his left hand and quickly counted the fingers before raising an eyebrow at me. "No, actually, I'm very sure that was a no. It even included reasons."

"Reasons for not telling me things, you mean. Not reasons for why you didn't know what they were talking about."

"Those aren't the same thing? No, I suppose they aren't. But the results are the same, more or less. I can't tell you anything because I don't know it, or I can't tell you anything because OSIRIS will roast me over a low fire if I do. There's no real difference from where I'm sitting. Well, except the bit where I get roasted . . . soooo, cancel that. See, I'm exhausted, I would never have made that kind of mistake under normal circumstances. What I meant is that there's no real difference from where *you're* sitting. No answers either way."

"Do you seriously expect me to believe that you care enough about OSIRIS regulations and enforcement to not tell me something because that would violate them?"

"No?" He sighed and his face went deadly serious. "How about believing I won't tell you something because you're thirteen, and I'm not willing to be the one to ruin your childhood. Will you believe that? Because you're thirteen, and I think you're a good kid—well, as good as it's possible to be for anyone in the category of 'kid' anyway—and I'm *not* willing to be the one who ruins your childhood. That's OSIRIS's job, I won't have any part of it, and I *really* need to go back to bed now." He scratched his ribs and turned toward his rooms.

"I need to know, Rand. I may only be thirteen, but I can handle this. I *have* to handle it."

He started to shuffle away.

"Please."

He paused and his shoulders slumped but he still didn't turn around. "I *can't* tell you. I . . . don't have it in me. Denmother, increase Evan's clearance to level two."

Denmother responded, "Noted."

"Will *she* tell me what I need to know?" I asked.

"No," said Foxman. "But if you dig through the level-two files, and you're as smart and mature as you think you are, you might be able to find out where to look for the real answers." He spoke bitterly then—almost angrily, "But don't blame me when you end up in the gutter drinking mouthwash out of brown bag before your fourteenth birthday. I won't be held responsible for you screwing up your own life." He started walking again.

"Thank you," I said.

But he didn't answer, just shook his head and kept going.

When he was gone, I looked up and said, "Denmother, I'm going to need access to all level-two material."

"There's a computer hookup in your rooms, Master Quick, built into the desk. You may view such material on the screen there or on your television."

"I guess I'd better get to it then. Thanks."

"You are welcome, Master Quick."

I woke up after noon with my head pillowed on the wireless keyboard that linked to the big television screen, which was now covered top to bottom in an endless repetition of the letter *k*. My head felt stuffed full of mostly useless information, and I didn't know a lot more about OSIRIS's "mandate" than I had the night before. But I did know where to look, and that was on Deimos. There was a lot more up there than just the school. Denmother wouldn't tell me what outright, but the hints I kept finding told me I had to dig deeper.

I didn't see Foxman again until almost five when he crawled out of bed to grab some breakfast. "Good morning," I said as he slumped at the breakfast bar.

"Go away, kid. I'm not really here. I'm really in bed. This is merely an interlude where I force some protein down my throat so that I feel less like a pile of goo when I get up tomorrow, okay? No one is home, so make like an amphibian and frog off." He made hopping away gestures with one hand.

"I'll go in a minute. But first I wanted to thank you for what you said and did for me yesterday . . . and, last night."

He turned a bloodshot glare on me. "What part of 'frog off' do you not understand, kid? You are my revenge on Captain Commanding, not my BFF, *capisce*?"

"All right." So, today was apparently a bad day.

I left him there and didn't see him again until Sunday morning when he acted as though he had no memory of any of our conversations this side of the fight with the Fromagier. Since I wasn't sure whether he was faking or not, I really didn't want to push things. What if he decided he'd gone too far by giving me level-two access to his files?

We went out on patrol, but it was a quiet morning in Heropolis, and we didn't actually do a whole lot of fighting evil. Before I knew it, it was afternoon and Foxman was escorting me to the *Flying Fox*.

"Did you send that e-mail to your parents?" he asked as the ramp came down.

I froze, because I hadn't. I'd actually managed to forget all about it in my obsession with the level-two materials, which maybe was a good sign. "No."

"Why not?"

"I . . . I don't know. I forgot. But maybe that's because I feel like it's missing something. I need to do *this*." I spread my hands to take in the *Flying Fox* and the Den and, well, everything. "But that's a hard message to leave them with. I . . ."

"You want to give them a peace offering," he said.

That felt right. "Yeah, I think that's it."

"Offer to fly them back here for dinner. That'll give you the home-ground advantage, and Denmother can cook up something special. We can send the *Flying Fox*. You won't even have to ride along."

"Thanks, that seems right somehow."

So, a few moments later, as the jet started rolling along its rails, I pulled out my laptop, added a P.S. to my e-mail, and sent it via the onboard wireless:

P.S. I know this wasn't what you wanted for me, but I'm interning with a big-name Mask now. He said that I should invite you to dinner at his secret headquarters if you're interested.

I'd finally managed to push that send button, and what I felt was mostly relief.

Considering Foxman's reputation, I wasn't at all sure how my parents would take the invite in the P.S. if they knew where they were going to dinner. Which was why I didn't mention him by name. At the same time, I did need to talk to my mom and dad face-to-face, and the Den seemed like a much better place to do it than OSIRIS headquarters in Heropolis, or worse, trying to get permission for them to visit me on Deimos.

All I had to do was imagine my mom punching some OSIRIS agent in the nose to see the sort of disaster a visit like that might turn into. Having them in the Den dealing with Foxman might be a disaster of a whole different kind, but there was much less chance of my parents getting tossed into jail for assaulting government officials that way.

Now that I'd committed to dealing with my parents, I just wanted to get it over with. As soon as I got back to my dorm room at the AMO, I opened up my laptop to see if my parents had answered my e-mail. This was all there was:

Dear Evan,

Your mother is too upset to respond right now, and I can't say that I blame her, though I do appreciate what you're trying to say with this note. We want to see you as soon as possible. When can we arrange this dinner?

Love,
Dad

I typed my answer immediately.

I'll check in with my mentor and get back to you ASAP.

Love,
Evan.

Then I sent a quick note to Foxman asking when would be good. So, there we were. Things were in motion and I would finally get this situation resolved with my parents. I ought to have felt great. Instead, I closed the laptop and started gently banging my head on my desk. Not entirely sure why it seemed like a good idea just then, but, hey, the banging seemed to help.

"You okay, Evan?" As usual, Jeda started speaking before I had the chance to register that he'd arrived, superspeed being what it is—even erratic not-so-superspeed.

"My parents want to have dinner with me and Foxman at the Den."

"The parents who completely lost it over you becoming a Mask?" asked Jeda. "That's going to end well."

"Thanks for your support. I really appreciate it."

He grinned. "Hey, man, I'm happy to be there for you. Do you think we'll be able to see the fireworks from here on Deimos?"

"Probably."

Someone knocked on our door.

"Come on in," said Jeda.

It was NightHowl. "Heard you were back, Evan. You got a minute?"

"Sure, why not." It wasn't like pounding my head on the desk was going to put off the impending disaster of my parents meeting Foxman.

She closed the door behind her. "Blindmark and Emberdown and I have been asking around real quiet like about those laser fitting-rooms and the booth at Camp Commanding. About half the kids here didn't go through either one."

She held up a hand to stop me before I could say anything, and continued. "But most of those who didn't reported similar itchy feelings after going through one of those fancy new airport scanners or an oversize 'metal detector' at school. We only found five students who didn't have an experience like that between the ages of thirteen and fifteen, or at least didn't remember one. Two of *those* didn't get their powers until seventeen. I think you're right about the hero beam and about needing to learn more. But where do we start?"

I thought about what I'd learned in Foxman's files. "I have some ideas."

18

Lasagna at Ten Paces

"Boom, baby. Boom!" NightHowl sounded more than a little maniacal as she pointed a finger at the big steel vault door in the depths of the AMO—the one that led to Backflash's lab and . . . Well, not knowing what all it led to was *why* we wanted to get the door open. "That's the way to open it up. Boooooom!"

Emberdown shook her head at her roommate. "Even if any of us had that kind of power, it'd be foolish to use it that way. We need to do this quietly."

"She's right," agreed Blurshift. "We have to be subtle if we don't want to end up as premature entries on all those Hood wanted lists."

"I know." NightHowl sighed. "But a girl can dream, can't she?"

I couldn't really blame her. The vault door was going to be a big problem, but it was one we had to solve if we wanted to get anywhere. The OSIRIS facility on Deimos was huge, and the School for Sidekicks only made up a tiny portion of the whole if our calculations were right. Even when you counted in all the battle-simulation rooms and power-testing studios, there was an awful lot of the volume in the eight-mile sphere that was simply inaccessible to students.

How much of that lay inside the core vault where Backflash worked and how much lay beyond it in the main OSIRIS labs was anybody's guess. We'd never even have figured out how much was on *our* side without the inertial mapping device I borrowed from the electronics lab in the Den and Speedslick's footwork.

That level-two clearance Foxman had given me was coming in very handy. I wouldn't have known inertial navigation from black magic without Denmother's advice on how to map out the school. It also meant that I'd been allowed to bring a bunch of toys home from the Den after my most recent visit, including a remote link to the monitoring system and another to Denmother herself.

Now we had a rough map of the AMO portion of Deimos. It showed that all the wandering I'd done the day I found out what a giant turd Captain Commanding was had taken me through less than ten percent of the small moon. How much of the rest was hollowed out was an open question, but one we couldn't answer without finding some way around the vault door that led to the core and Backflash's lab.

"Blindmark?" I asked.

He shook his head. "Nothing. I can't sense a single set of eyes beyond the door. Of course, that's not a huge surprise. There's something about the walls here on Deimos that blocks my powers where normal stone doesn't. Could be that door is more than plain old steel, or there might just be a sharp bend in the passage on the other side, or maybe no one's in range."

"The door is definitely more than plain old steel," a sardonic voice said from above.

It was followed by a flash of purple plasma flowing out of the conduit to form itself into a copper-skinned heap of trouble.

"Burnish." Emberdown nodded at the other girl warily, while I slid behind Blindmark, hoping the Captain's daughter wouldn't notice me.

"Emberdown." Burnish inclined her head. "NightHowl. Blindmark. Blurshift. Weasel-bo—no, sorry, *Meerkat*. I keep getting that one mixed up."

So much for *that* hope. I stepped into the open again.

She continued. "And Speedslick's down around the corner, almost like he's playing lookout. Quite a party you've got going on." Her voice sounded casual, almost sweet, but her expression was the same angry, thin-lipped glare she always turned my way. "I'm half offended I didn't get an invite."

"What do you want?" I asked.

"I'm tempted to pretend I don't know what you're on about, Quick. But that would prolong the amount of time I have to spend talking to you, and it's just not worth it. What I want to know is what you've been doing down here this week. First Speedslick started bouncing around the tunnels like a Ping-Pong ball fired out of the Foxblaster. Then you all start skulking around the vault door here every other hour. Makes me wonder what you're up to. Especially after those oh-so-subtle questions you were all asking last week about my daddy's *lovely* amusement park and its uniform machine."

NightHowl snarled and leaned toward the older girl, but

Burnish just laughed. "Oh please. You couldn't take me on your best day, 'Howl. Not even if your little werewolf fantasies were true. The lot of you are a bunch of never-gonna-happens and why-bothers, just like ninety percent of the rest of the losers at this school. I could tear all of you in half without breaking a sweat."

I stepped between NightHowl and Burnish. "If we're all such losers, why are you here?"

"Because you know something, Quick. About all this." She threw a gesture that took in the whole facility. "I don't know what it is, but I want to, because the whole system is made of garbage, and I need to know why."

"Then why don't you ask your daddy?" NightHowl's voice dripped with poison as she slipped past me. "Oh, right, because he doesn't even acknowledge your existence."

Burnish didn't say a word, just reached over and touched the vault door, shifting from copper to bright steel and balling her fists.

NightHowl spat on the floor in front of Burnish's feet. "Truth hurts, doesn't it?"

"'Howl," I said quietly, putting a hand on her shoulder. "Stop. She'll beat you to a pulp." I turned to Burnish. "Then they'll throw *you* in metamax, and everyone loses."

Burnish took a deep breath but opened her fists. "Don't. Talk. About. My. Family."

NightHowl's lip twisted into a snarl but she kept her mouth shut and grudgingly backed up. I tried not to melt from relief because we still had a ways to go to keep this from blowing up.

"You want to know what's going on?" I asked. "All right. I'll

221

tell you, but not here. Someplace a bit more private would be much better."

And that's how I ended up alone with the scariest and prettiest girl I'd ever met, sitting on my bed in the dorm while I showed her what we'd found out so far. When I was finished, she nodded.

"There's a lot there to digest, Quick. Don't do anything stupid for the next couple of days while I think about this, OK? I might have a way to get that door open short of blowing a giant hole in it, *and* I might be willing to give you a hand there. But don't think this makes us friends, even for a second. I'm still going to twist you into a pretzel when I get the chance."

Then, without another word, she hopped down, crossed to the door and left.

Denmother's voice spoke into the silence Burnish left behind her: "Message from Foxman, Master Quick." A page of text appeared in the air in front of me, projected by the Foxmail unit on my desk.

Meerkat,

Have blocked out this weekend for dinner with your parents. Make the arrangements and give Denmother a menu.

Foxman out.

The angry centipedes fought another battle in my stomach as I typed a quick message to my parents.

Mom, Dad,

Dinner Saturday. Will send a plane to pick you up at six—
don't ask. I can't even begin to explain in e-mail.

Love,
Evan

My mom's response a few minutes later was equally terse.

Evan,

We'll be waiting. This better be *some* explanation.

Love you too,
Mom

I spent the next hour trying to imagine ways to get out of the whole dinner thing, but all the convincing ideas involved me ending up dead or in the hospital. I wasn't *quite* that desperate yet. *Give it a couple days*, said a voice deep down in the back of my head.

～ ～

"Are you ready for this?" Rand slammed back a can of MaskerAde as we watched the empty *Flying Fox* rolling away down the rails that led from its hangar.

"Not even a little bit."

"Neither am I. You know, it's not too late to grab the Foxmobile and sneak out the back." He half turned toward the door, then stopped and turned back. "Or, would that be completely irresponsible?" I didn't answer, but he nodded and said, "You're right. You're right. That'd be completely irresponsible, and I'm only semi-irresponsible these days, so no can do."

I looked at him. "Semi-irresponsible?"

He nodded. "Absolutely. It's part of the deal I agreed to when I talked Minute Man into helping me piss off Captain Commanding by taking you on as my teen sidekick. He tried to sell me on fully-responsible, but I explained that was a non-starter, and countered with almost-entirely-lacking-in-responsibility. We haggled it out from there."

"That's reassuring."

"Well, *I* certainly thought so, but I'm not sure Minute Man agrees. You're *sure* we can't just run for it? Of course you are. They're your parents, after all. If they were *my* parents, I'd run for it. Well, if they were my parents, anyone would run for it. My parents are dead, after all, and zombie parents coming after you is all kinds of bad news."

"I . . . what?" Trying to follow Foxman was making my head spin.

"Keep up here. Zombie parents equal bad news. Eat your brains and then yell at you for not cleaning your room. Nobody wants to deal with that."

That's when it hit me. "You're as nervous about this as I am, aren't you?"

"Me? No. Well, yes, actually, I am. Maybe more. I haven't met anyone's parents in ages. Not since I was dating, and that was always a disaster. The meeting-the-parents thing, I mean. The actual dates were fine . . . usually. Not sure if disaster thing was about me or about the parents of the sort of woman I was dating. I'd like to think it was them, but I was never very good with my parents either. So, that's a tough sell. What do you think?"

"I think this is going to be a disaster."

"Good, then we're on the same page." He popped another MaskerAde out of his bandolier. "If we're not going to make a break for it now, we should probably have an escape plan. It works with Hoods, it should work with parents, right? So, when things go completely off the rails, you say, 'Mars, really? I didn't know they had blizzards this time of year.' Then, I'll signal Denmother to fake a priority Omega alarm—the planet itself is at risk—and we bolt for the Foxmobile. What do you think?"

I thought it was crazy. *Tempting* but crazy. "Uhmm."

"You're right. The code phrase is way too long and hard to remember. I should have thought of that, myself. Good catch. Let's go with 'No, no, everything is going great, Mom.'"

I found myself nodding. "That certainly has the benefit of being something I don't expect to say for real."

"Okay, we'll stick with it."

"How long do you think it will take for the plane to get back?"

"Hard to say. Half an hour. Maybe more. Depends on how long it takes your parents to get in. I find that's the big factor with the *Flying Fox* and remote pickups. A lot of people don't want to get into a plane with no pilot."

"I can't imagine why."

"Was that sarcasm? Because it sounded like sarcasm to me."

"It was sarcasm."

"Good, I'd hate to think my filters were that far off." He knocked back the rest of his MaskerAde. "You're a very sarcastic kid. Did you know that? Probably good in a sidekick, well, unless you wanted to go for the boyish enthusiasm thing. But that'd probably be bad for a man with my ego, so better to go with sarcastic. Feature, not a bug. I like that."

"So, this is . . . nice." My dad looked like he'd swallowed a half a lemon as he touched the red leather wall of the hangar. "Very retro–lounge lizard . . ."

"Thanks." Foxman adjusted the domino mask he'd slipped on while we were waiting—after noting that it was hard to eat dinner through a full-face helmet. It made a strange contrast with his armor. "That's not really the effect I was going for, but I appreciate your take on the style, Mr. Quick."

"Call me Martin, Mr. . . ." My dad trailed off rather hopelessly.

Rand pursed his lips. "Probably best to stick with Foxman. If I told you my real name I'd have to kill you, and that would make dinner a little awkward." He grinned at his own joke. Neither of my parents joined him, and I saw a little bead of sweat appear at his left temple and roll down past his ear.

As he opened the door to the main dome I heard him mutter,

"Oh good, flashbacks to *my* parents. They never thought I was funny either." Aloud, he said, "Come on, let's go through to the dining room. We wouldn't want to keep Denmother waiting."

"Denmother?" my mom asked as she stepped through into the huge domed room beyond.

"My AI. The robot who runs the place, Mrs. Quick." Not to mention the robot who'd done stellar work at clearing all the half-empty energy drinks and other wreckage away before my parents got there.

"That's *Doctor* Quick," my mother growled. Then she paused and took a deep breath. "Sorry, academic reflex. Why don't you call me Madeline."

"Thank you, Madeline. I don't think Meerkat told me his mother was a professor. What's your doctorate in?"

"Meerkat?" The growl was back in her voice. "Is that what this ridiculous outfit is about, Evan?" She poked me in the Armex-covered ribs, but I barely felt it—score one for the Armex.

"It's my code name, Mom, my handle. All Masks have them." Then I turned to Foxman. "She's a mathematician. Actually, so is Dad."

"But I didn't get the Ph.D.," he replied. "Bailed out after my masters to become an actuary."

"What's your education, Mr. Foxman?" my mother asked.

"Well, if you want to get technical about it, that'd be Doctor Foxman as well. Double Ph.D. in mechanical and electrical engineering after a triple B.S."

"Triple B.S. sounds about right," said my mother.

"Mom!"

"Evan, I am not going to pretend that I'm happy about you becoming a Mask."

"Dear . . . ," my dad mumbled.

"Don't you dare *dear* me right now, Martin." She turned a hard look on Foxman. "And you! What madness possessed you to think it would be a good idea to get a thirteen-year-old involved in crime fighting? Were you drunk?"

Foxman held up an armored finger. "Actually, that wasn't me. That was OSIRIS. I merely agreed to take Evan on as my intern after he'd already enrolled in sidekick school. Oh, and, rather surprisingly, no."

"No what?" My mother demanded.

"No, I wasn't drunk. I'm sober now. Six months and change. I don't think that even OSIRIS would turn a thirteen-year-old over to an active drunk with an energy cannon and a combat jet. Not that I'd bet money on that."

My mother gave him her best over-the-glasses death stare. "If that's your sense of humor, I don't find it very engaging . . . Dr. Foxman."

"I wasn't trying to—I mean—I—serious there—" Foxman ground to a halt. "Hang on a second. I think I'm doing this wrong. I'm treating you like parents, and I'm terrible with parents."

"We *are* parents," my mother said frostily.

"Well, yes," he agreed, "but not mine. And I've been dealing with you like you were. Which is, maybe, where I went wrong with *them*, too. Have to think about that. Later, when you're not here. Right now, I'm going to try something new and treat you like people. I do all right with people. So, first"—he peeled off his domino and extended a hand—"Hi, I'm Rand."

My mother looked nonplussed, but my dad stepped into the breach. "Hello, Rand, I'm Martin. I take it from what you were saying about OSIRIS a moment ago that you don't think they have the best judgment about how to handle kids like Evan?"

"I don't think they have the best judgment about anything."

"Then why work with them?" asked my mother.

"I don't."

"And yet, here you are with my son as your intern straight from OSIRIS."

"Oh, mentoring Evan has nothing to do with dealing with OSIRIS. That's eighty-three percent about pissing off Captain Commanding."

"What are you babbling about?" My mother's voice was rising into the danger zone, and I noticed my dad very quietly sliding out of the blast area. "Why on earth would Captain Commanding care that Evan's interning with you?"

I decided it would be an excellent time to join my dad. Maybe I could show him the garage.

Foxman frowned. "Didn't Evan tell you about Captain Commanding blacklisting him after the Captain faked that video at the museum?"

"Evan James Quick, you stop trying to sneak away this instant! You, too, Martin." My mother turned a very stern look on me. "What's he talking about?"

I looked at my feet. "The video from the museum isn't exactly what happened. At least, not the bit where Captain Commanding crashed through and saved the day. It was more . . . complex than that."

Foxman raised his hand. "Can I cut in here for a second? Because I grabbed the original security-camera footage from the museum before it was erased. If you'd like to see the whole thing as it really happened, I can do that." Foxman looked at me and shrugged. "Well, *I* didn't do it myself, but Denmother is programmed to automatically capture anything that has to do with Captain Commanding. Mostly, I delete it right away, but anything potentially embarrassing gets archived for future use."

"Why would the real footage be embarrassing for the Captain?" asked my dad.

"Because your son saved the lives of everyone in that museum, including a certain masked red-white-and-blue jerk." He looked at me out of the corner of his eye. "To tell you the truth, that's the other seventeen percent of why I agreed to take you on." He smiled wryly at my mom. "I have to admit that it was mostly to piss off Captain Commanding, but the part where your son has the makings of a real hero? That didn't hurt."

"Show me this video." There was a cold anger in my mother's voice—the kind she normally reserved for deans and other academic administrators. "Now."

Foxman nodded. "If you insist. Denmother."

When it was over, my mom, who had been pacing back and forth through the whole thing while making the occasional worried noise, stopped abruptly. "Roast that man." Then she fixed her eyes on me. "I am not at all happy with the way your life is going right now, and I will *never* condone this Mask business, but that was terribly brave of you, Evan. Not very bright perhaps—goading a man like Spartanicus—but you acted in a way that makes me almost as proud of you as it makes me frightened for you."

"You did well, son," my dad added.

My mother rounded on Rand, "And you . . ." Then she sighed. "I came here planning on ripping you up one side and down the other. Now I have to thank you for trying to do right by my son, even if it is for the wrong reasons." She rubbed her temples. "I could really use a drink."

"Alas, I can't help you there," said Foxman. "There's not a drop in the whole place. I don't suppose you drink MaskerAde?"

"To calm down?" She looked incredulous.

"Good point. How about a glass of sparkling juice?"

"I guess that will have to do."

If you'd told me the evening would end with my mother giving Foxman a hug and my dad shaking his hand before they headed back to the hangar I'd have called you a liar. But maybe that's because I underestimate the value of being reasonable.

When we got to the hangar door, Foxman made a transparent excuse and left me with my parents.

My mother gave me a hug, then stepped back, but kept her hands on my shoulders as she looked me squarely in the eyes. "Evan . . ." She shook her head. "I was about to say that you were my little boy, but that's harder to do now that I have to look up a bit to meet your eyes. It's harder still to admit you might be growing up as well as getting taller, but this last month hasn't left me much choice—"

She stopped speaking and my dad stepped up behind my mother and quietly put his arms around her waist. "Given *us* much choice," she corrected herself. "We weren't ready for this, for you to develop powers, and, well, all of it. I don't think any parent would be ready for one of their children to have to take on so much risk or responsibility at such a young age."

I broke in. "Mom, it's not *that* much risk, and there's almost no responsibility. They won't even give me a real sidekick's permit for another two years. It's not like I'm supposed to be out fighting crime." Sure, I *was*, but it definitely wasn't like I was *supposed* to be. And I certainly wasn't going to tell *them* that. Not yet anyway. "I'm just going to a different kind of school, sort of like a gifted and talented program. I mean, it's on Mars and all, but—" My dad lifted an eyebrow at me, and the absurdity of what I'd said brought me to a sliding halt mid-sentence.

"On Mars?" My dad's voice was incredulous.

"Well, Deimos, really. Didn't I mention that bit?"

"No." He looked cautiously down at my mother—who had gone completely silent—like a man who realizes he's holding on to a ticking time bomb, and he sighed. "No, you didn't."

"Mars," she whispered. Then she took a deep breath and gave me her best dubious-mom-face. "We'll have to discuss that, and this whole sidekick's permit thing as well, but later. I was talking about risk and about responsibility and I want to finish that thought first, because it's got nothing to do with where you go to school, or what the government licenses you to do."

"It doesn't?" I was confused. "What *did* you mean then?"

"Power. You may be taller than I am now, but you're still

thirteen, and that's so very young to have the kind of power that you do now. That day at the museum you hit another human being in the head with a piece of rebar. You hit him hard enough to bend steel, Evan. You also knocked that horrible woman down by throwing a hundred-pound chunk of concrete at her. Think about that. If you did either of those things to a normal person, they'd be dead right now."

"I, uh, I hadn't thought about it that way." It was a very sobering realization.

"I wish that you didn't have to, but that doesn't change things. You now possess the ability to effortlessly kill another human being. It's like holding a gun or getting behind the wheel of a car. Except your abilities are inherent. You can't ever put them aside or step out of the driver's seat. That sort of strength comes with enormous responsibility to use it well and wisely every second of every day."

I swallowed and looked at both my parents. "I'll try, I promise."

My dad spoke then, "We know you will, son. We both love you, and we believe in you, even if we did say some things we shouldn't have when this first came out. Honestly, I think that's some of why we were both so upset. We've watched you grow up, seen how you play, and what matters to you. All those Masks Versus Hoods video games—you were never ever willing to play a villain. It's always been clear that you have a strong sense of justice and duty, and that you wanted to be a Mask to protect others."

"But why would that make you upset?" I asked, more confused than ever.

"Because we know that it means that having powers will lead you to put yourself at risk," said my mother. "And not just physically. If you have powers and you use them, you're going to end up in situations where you will have to hurt other people, possibly very badly. That's going to leave scars in here." She put her hand on my chest. "Scars that no amount of regeneration can ever heal. Neither of us wants that for you, Evan."

"I can see that." I nodded because much of what had happened between us suddenly made sense to me in a way that it hadn't before. "But it's what *I* want for me. I always have. I have the chance now to help people in ways I never could have before, and even if you're right and I don't, or can't, completely understand what I'm taking on yet, I believe it will be worth the cost."

"I hope you're right, son, I really do." My dad frowned a very worried frown.

"Either way," my mother added, "we'll try to support you as best we can. Because, no matter what, you're our son, and we love you."

19

In Deep Water

"Say something funny, Quick!" Professor Roadhouse, who had been walking back and forth at the front of the classroom, suddenly spun on his heel and pointed a finger at me.

I felt sweat break out on my forehead as I desperately tried to come up with something better than, "I—uh—what?"

Before I could get there, Roadhouse shook his head. "Not *Quick* enough, eh, Evan?"

The rest of the class laughed as I blushed deeply. "I guess I wasn't ready." Combat Quipping was my second-least-favorite class after math. My name had made me more the butt of jokes than a deliverer of them.

"Do you think that the Hoods are going to give you time to get ready, Quick?"

I shook my head. "No, sir—"

"Of course they aren't. The whole point of Quipping for Combat is rapid response and preemption. A well-timed joke can put an enemy off-balance for that critical moment that saves your life or even wins you the fight. Tell me, Quick, do you know what the most critical element of comedy is?"

"I . . . that is, no, sir."

"Then, since I am your teacher, and you're supposed to be learning here, why don't you ask me?"

"Now, sir?"

"No, yesterday, Quick. Of course, now!"

"What's the most important element of—"

"Timing!" he said sharply, cutting me off. Again, the rest of the class laughed. "Not *Quick* enough, again, young man. You'll have to do better than that if you ever face a real enemy."

"I did well enough against Spartanicus!" I blurted out, too angry to think it through.

Roadhouse snorted. "Of course you did, and there's all that video to prove it, too."

"That's . . . I . . . uh . . ."

A sudden squeeze on my shoulder made me glance to my left. Speedslick sat on that side of me, and now he shook his head very slightly. He was right, and though I hadn't seen him move, I was sure he'd been the one to squeeze my shoulder. With an effort that was going to cost me a good bit of teeth-grinding later, I shut my mouth.

Roadhouse raised his eyebrows, "What's that, Quick? I thought you had something to add to the discussion."

I shook my head and looked down at my desk. After a moment, Roadhouse found a new target. Jeda had been right, trying to verbally fence with a professional wit was a losing battle. Even if I had done fairly well matching wits with Spartanicus, the spark

I'd had then didn't seem to come with me to Roadhouse's class. Maybe I needed to be in real danger for it to kick in. Roadhouse wasn't actually a threat to anything but my ego.

～～～

"No, Roadhouse is a jerk," NightHowl said as we made our way up the ramp toward the nearest of the domes on Deimos's surface. "I hate that class. All he does is make fun of us and pretend that's going to save our lives some day."

"It might," I said, though I wished I didn't have to admit it.

"What do you mean?" Speedslick looked over his shoulder as he pushed open the door to the sky dome.

"I think the main reason Spartanicus didn't kill me that day at the museum is that he found me amusing."

"Are you actually defending Roadhouse?" demanded NightHowl.

"No." I threw myself down on the rough industrial carpeting and looked up at Mars overhead. "Not really. He's funny, but he's a terrible teacher, and I don't think he's doing anything to make any of us better banterers. But I do think it's true that saying the right thing at the right time might save your life."

NightHowl flopped down a few yards away. "Maybe, but if Roadhouse can't actually teach funny, how does his class help us against the Hoods?"

"I don't think it does," I replied.

She growled low in her throat. "But you just said you thought that—oh, never mind. I see where you are going with this, and I think you're kind of full of it."

Speedslick laughed as he sat down. "Now, there's something I can agree with."

"What, is it International-Pick-on-Evan Day or something?" I tried to kick Jeda, but he simply blurred out of reach before I connected.

"Nah," said NightHowl. "You're just such an easy target, it's hard not to pick on you sometimes."

"Ah, gee, thanks. And I didn't get you anything." She didn't answer that, and neither did Speedslick. We all just settled back to look at Mars and the stars, a pastime that never got old.

I had half drifted off to sleep when a familiar accented voice spoke sharply into my ear, "Subject FLR871, Evan Quick, please report to my office at once."

"Office, what!" I jackknifed into a sitting position and looked around. No one else was in the dome with us. "Did you hear that?"

"Hear what?" asked Speedslick.

NightHowl appeared to have drifted off and didn't respond. I was trying to think of something to say that didn't sound like, "Is the voice in my head bothering you?" when it came again.

"I'm on your suit com," Backflash said into my ear. "I overrode Foxman's security, and I'm waiting for you. I'm a busy woman, I don't have much in the way of free time, and I want you in my office. Ideally, five minutes ago. It's right under my lab. I know you know where that is, so come on down. You are in deep trouble already. Don't compound it by being late."

The voice cut off and I bounced to my feet as my stomach told me that someone had decided to breed giant centipedes in there.

"What's up?" NightHowl asked blearily.

"Backflash wants to see me in her office." I swallowed. "Now."

"Oh." Her face visibly paled. "Is this about—"

I made a desperate cutting motion. "I have no idea what it's about, just that I'm in trouble, and I need to get going." I figured Backflash must be on to our plans to break into her lab, but I didn't *know* that, and I sure didn't want to give it away if she wasn't.

"Now," said the voice in my ear.

It was a long way from the dome down to the vault door, and I had plenty of time for the centipede colony in my stomach to form up into teams and engage in epic battle. Somehow I managed not to barf, but I really wanted to. How had she caught us?

The box beside the vault door flashed at me as I approached, so I put my palm on the reader and said my name into the microphone.

After a brief pause, it responded: "Handprint verified. Voice verified. Retina scan initiated. Updating user profile. Retina scan verified. Subject FLR871 verified. Bittersharp special exception status verified. One-time one-way authorization for central core verified." The door swung open. "Reminder FLR871: passthrough closes special exception."

From there, it was a short march down the hall to the big globular room where Backflash did most of her work. The Mark IX Spartanicus unit was waiting for me at the end, which somehow made everything that extra bit worse.

"Come with me," it said in the Hood's gravelly voice.

It immediately turned and plunged into the maze of alien shapes and colors that made up Backflash's experimental setup. I didn't have time to really look at anything, but I did trigger the Foxcamera on my utility belt to take pictures as we went. *We needed info, and besides, how much more trouble could I get into?*

The Mark IX led me down a spiraling ramp on the far side of the globe, taking me through the thick transparent floor and down to a fantastically out-of-place office cubicle setup in the middle of the lower chamber. Backflash, who was working on something at a nearby lab bench, glanced up as I arrived.

"Sit." She pointed at an office chair facing the desk in the cubicle. "Wait. I'll be there in a moment."

The Mark IX pulled the chair back for me. Then, it settled into an arms-crossed/waiting pose directly behind the chair. Having that creepy mechanical Spartanicus hovering over me gave the whole thing a bizarrely nightmarish tinge. I could actually feel my knees shaking by the time Backflash finished what she was doing and came to sit down at her desk.

She steepled her hands in front of her chin and gave me a hard look. "*You* are a problem."

I swallowed, but didn't know what to say to that, so I kept my lips zipped and tried to hold eye contact.

"You see," she finally continued after about a thousand years of sweaty silence, "I had a long chat with the Fromagier this morning."

"You what?" I exclaimed, startled into speaking—that wasn't what I'd expected at all. "I—uh—yeah, that."

"Ah, good, you aren't going to try to lie to me about your

activities. That will make this less tedious. Our charming cheese-monger had a lot to say about Foxman and his young sidekick, and how unexpected your arrival at his lair was. I found it to be a very interesting conversation considering that your provisional internship papers are in this folder here." She set a file on the desk and flipped it open.

"Yes. This does seem to be them. I note that there's no formal approval date here, and that, as yet, they lack an authorization from the chancellor of the AMO." She turned the papers over, exposing the back of the folder. "I also note that the place where the school's copy of your sidekick's permit would go is empty. Perhaps that's because you are two years away from being old enough to file for one? What do you think?"

"That could be it, yes." To my horror the words came out light and almost playful, not in the respectful way I'd intended. "Might also be because I haven't applied for one yet. I don't suppose there's some way for fifteen-year-old me to do that and then send it back through time to now? Because that'd save a lot of trouble." *Great, I really* can only do banter when I'm in danger. Worse yet, I *can't not. I am sooo dead right now.*

Backflash closed the file sharply. "Do I take it that you think you're funny?"

Somehow, I managed to clamp down on the impulse to say, "If the jokes don't work, I could always juggle." I wanted to believe that was because I recognized verbal suicide when I saw it, but I was pretty sure it was simply because I didn't know how to juggle.

Backflash paused as though she were waiting to see how I responded.

Shut up, Evan, shut up! Shut up, shut up, shut up! Miraculously, I managed to follow my own orders . . . this time.

When I didn't say anything, she nodded. "Better. If my life were simple, you would be on your way to a juvenile metamax facility right now. Unfortunately for me, my life is never simple. You are a problem, but one with no easy solution."

"I don't understand," I said, because I didn't. Not even a little bit.

"Foxman is valuable to me. Or, rather, Rand is. When he is on form, there is no better engineer in the world. I *need* him to be on form. Sadly, the last few years have not seen him at his best. Even his recent sobriety has not returned to me Rand the builder, and I had begun to believe that I would never see him again. But then you came along, and suddenly Foxman takes down the Fromagier. Foxman, who has not captured a major Hood in over five years."

"So, I must ask myself, is it the protégé who has given him the kick in the rear that he needs to start climbing out of the pit? If it is, then I should not be too quick to throw you away. Understand, that by yourself and with almost any other Mask mentor, you would be in juvenile detention now. For Rand's sake I will suspend your sentence for the moment, but know that it is only suspended and that I *will* enact it if you give me reason."

"I . . . what are you going to do with me now?"

"I'm not sure. You have potential, and I would like to believe that you will grow into a model Mask. I would like to, but I'm not at all sure that I do. I also do not think that you will learn what is needed merely from a lecture, so I am trying to decide how best to make the lesson stick."

Backflash shook her head. "Really, Spartanicus, you should know by now that you can't defeat me so easily. Can't we talk, as we once did? You were a good man, and could be again. You know why I do what I do. Let go of your hatred and guilt and help me as you did then."

Spartanicus glared at her, but didn't immediately attack again. "I'm done with the 'lesser' evil, Backflash. I will do what has to be done my way, and without you or your Fascist boy scout, Captain Commanding, or I will die. Those are my only options."

"They aren't, you know. Not unless you choose it. Don't make me kill you."

"You already destroyed me once, and I came back. Don't bet that I won't do it again."

"That was a unique circumstance, Spartanicus. If I have to kill you again, it will be the last time. But I don't want to do that. I don't want to see a single drop of metahuman blood spilled unnecessarily. Not yours, not the boy's here, not even our resident psychopaths' like Cannibal Carnie. Work with me. Show me what you've done with the Mark IX—it might save us when the time comes."

"I don't think so," said Spartanicus. "The route I took to get here is highly improbable."

"Ah." She nodded. "You've used Mr. Implausible again . . . and the Fluffinator, I would guess. In which case, you're right, not broadly applicable. So, what now?"

"Now you die!"

Green beams flashed out from Spartanicus's palms. The one that punched through my heart came as a complete surprise—he'd moved his hands so slowly I hadn't even seen it coming. Backflash seemed to have been caught off guard, too, because she slumped forward as the green spear half severed her neck. I felt searing pain as—

I was fine. Spartanicus's beam passed through the space I'd just occupied when Backflash yanked my chair out from under me. As I landed on the floor, she turned back to face Spartanicus, her expression grim and wild.

"I believe that we are done here," she said.

The Mark IX lay on the floor, its face and chest panels open, its electronic innards lying scattered beneath it. Backflash stood above me, her hand clasping mine, though I had no memory of taking it. She pulled me to my feet effortlessly, and I could tell that she was much stronger than I was at my best, though I doubted she was in the same category as Captain Commanding or even Burnish.

As she set me on my feet, she touched the fingers of her other hand to my temple and said, "Remember."

I felt cold lightning jump from her fingertips deep into my brain, freezing something that had already begun to slip away. "What did you do to me?" I whispered.

"I wanted you to remember what you have seen here today," said Backflash. "I believe it will provide you with the lesson I mentioned earlier. Without my intervention, Spartanicus would have slain you, twice over. Not for anything you have done or are, but simply for what you would have seen had he succeeded."

"I still don't understand," I said.

"I am a timeshifter," said Backflash. "I can step backward through the doors of eternity and change the past. When I do that, the only ones who can remember the future that now will never be are those I wish to bring with me. Today, that's you, because I want you to keep doing whatever you're doing with Rand, and I need you to understand that I should not be crossed."

"How far back can you go?"

She gave me an enigmatic look. "What I tell you now, I tell you to set the lesson. Don't make me regret that. Usually, I only move a few seconds, but I have not yet found my limits. I come from a distant future now dead. What I do here, I do because I have seen what will happen if I don't, and it is too horrible to imagine."

20

Fire, Aim, Ready

Dying twice left me completely and utterly flipped out, and I didn't want to be anywhere near where it happened. I went straight from the lab to the gravitic cannon by the shortest possible route—do not pass Go, do not collect your gear, just skedaddle. It didn't even occur to me that I'd skipped out on the rest of my Friday classes until I was halfway to Earth.

When I arrived at the Den, I pelted into the main dome and yelled, "Rand! Rand, where are you? I need to talk!"

There was no answer.

"Denmother, where's Rand?"

"He's not here," said the mechanical voice.

"Well, where is he? I need him."

"I'm afraid that I don't know, Master Quick."

"What, why not?" Denmother *always* knew where her maker was, and I really wanted to talk to him.

"It's the weekend of his birthday," replied Denmother.

"I think I missed a step there."

"I'm sorry, I don't understand what you're asking, Master Quick."

"I asked why you didn't know where he was, and you told me it was his birthday. How are those things connected?"

"Rand told you about what happened with his father and the car." It wasn't a question. "Each year on his birthday, Rand puts on his armor, takes a car of the exact make and model his father gave him that day and he drives away from the Den. When he comes back—sometimes days later—he does so without the car, a red '88 Corvette."

"What happens to it?" I asked, genuinely curious and somewhat surprised that I could think about anything but my own recent deaths. *Own. Recent. Deaths. How does that phrase even happen?*

"I don't know for certain, but if one were to do a news search for that model car on the dates of his drive, there is an excellent chance that one would find a news item about such a car being totaled in a horrendous accident that never involves other cars or a driver's body being found."

I looked at the central pillar where Denmother's primary processing units were housed. "And has *one* done such a search for this year?"

"One has not yet. Rand only left a few hours ago, and the accidents rarely happen within a thousand miles of Heropolis."

"What sorts of accidents?" I asked.

"All sorts, Master Quick. Running into bridge abutments, going off cliffs, driving onto the firing range of an army base in the middle of mortar practice. The list is long and varied."

"And he's not going to be back today?" I tried to push aside the feeling of my own death with very limited success. I was going to need a big distraction.

"Nor likely tomorrow either, Master Quick. I'm sorry. I have a lunch prepared for you now if you'd like. I made one of your favorites while we were talking."

I was about to say no when I realized I was starving. Apparently dying made you hungry—and that thought was so ridiculous that some of my flip-out vaporized in the face of its absurdity. After all, no matter what had happened on Deimos, I was fine now. Without another word, I headed for the kitchen, where I found a gyro and fries waiting.

Once I'd eaten, I felt much more human, and my family tendency toward reasonable started to reassert itself. I mean, does it really count as dying if it happened during a time that never actually existed? Or would that be: wouldn't have existed? Or . . . My head was spinning. How do you even talk about bits of futures-past of the sort I'd just experienced?

A thought occurred to me. "If Rand hates the car so much, why not simply blow it up?"

"I really don't know what his thinking is, Master Quick, but I do know he doesn't like to talk about it. The one time I suggested that setting the car up for target practice in the weapons range would be a simpler mode of destruction, he shut my speakers down for a whole week."

"Wait, we have a weapons range?!"

"Yes, Master Quick, it's about thirty meters below the trophy room, and walled with Indestructabilium. The armory is also housed there."

That sounded amazing. "Can I see it?" Maybe I could try out the Foxblaster or something. Blowing stuff up seemed like a great way to get my brain to focus on something other than having died.

"Accessing the facility requires either level-one access or an override code," replied Denmother.

There went that idea. "I guess there's absolutely no way I'll get down there then."

"Not at all, Master Quick. As a level-two-access designee, you can request an override code under any number of circumstances, from emergency invasion of the Den through incapacity on the part of Mr. Hammer."

"I didn't know that. Would any of those options be available to me at the moment?"

"Allow me to check, Master Quick." There was a brief pause. "Yes, there are several that might be appropriate to the current situation, starting with communications-blackout case three. I have attempted to contact Mr. Hammer multiple times since you arrived, but all of his com equipment appears to have been shut down or sabotaged. As his designated sidekick, you may request temporary level-one access to the Den's physical plant and most of the equipment under the circumstances."

"Most?"

"Yes. Case three assumes short-term communications failure on Mr. Hammer's part only, and no life-threatening emergencies.

For full access to all Den facilities and capabilities you would need to assert case one, which can only be validated if Mr. Hammer is missing in action and presumed incapacitated or dead, or if you can demonstrate an imminent threat to Mr. Hammer's life, which could only be addressed by granting you full access."

I decided not to ask about case two. "What do I need to do to get case three validated?"

"I have already determined that Mr. Hammer is currently out of contact. At this point all you need to do is ask."

"I'm asking." I mentally crossed my fingers.

"Processing . . . case-three access granted. What are your orders, Master Quick?"

"Show me the armory."

Ten minutes later I was standing in the armory and looking down the sights of a device that Denmother had called the Foxfire. "How does it work?"

"Attach the tanks. Point the barrel at the target. Pull the trigger. High-pressure flames shoot out the end."

"Sounds easy enough. May I try it?" I figured I knew the answer—no one is going to hand a thirteen-year-old a flamethrower to play with. But I had to ask.

"I don't understand the question. You already have case-three access."

I managed to suppress a whoop of triumph. "I'll take that as a yes. Let's test this puppy out!"

"What sort of targets would you like, Master Quick?"

"What are my options?"

"For the Foxfire, Mr. Hammer is quite fond of using fiberglass Captain Commanding units."

"Like the ones at Camp Commanding?" I asked.

"Precisely, sir."

"Hooah! Set 'em up."

A few moments later I was standing at the firing line and sighting in on the nearest target. I pressed the trigger and *FWOOOOM!*

Turns out that a high-pressure, weaponized, fire-delivery system is not quite the same thing as the sort of flamethrower seen in games and vids. It's much more like a rocket . . .

"Are you all right, Master Quick?" The voice sounded tinny and far away, and it took a good three or four beats before I really registered it.

"Yeah . . . I mean, I'm fine. I think." I sat up and did a quick check to make sure all my limbs were still intact. "Yep, I'm good." I leaned down and rubbed at the soot covering my boots. "It's a good thing Armex is fireproof.

"And blast resistant," I said a few seconds later. I could feel a big patch of scabweb slowly hardening on the back of my head where I'd smashed into the back wall of the weapons range, and I was pretty sure I'd find more elsewhere.

"Yes, Master Quick." Denmother actually sounded slightly chastened. "I failed to take into account your youth and lack of education. I should have warned you about Newton's third law of motion."

"Say what, now?"

" 'For every action there is always an equal and opposite reaction: or, the forces of two bodies on each other are always equal and are directed in opposite directions.' "

"Which means?"

"That, in the absence of stabilizers of the sort built into Mr. Hammer's armor, or powers of strength, density, flight, or traction in the appropriate degree, the Foxfire will act much like a personalized rocket pack. One that lacks any sort of computer guidance controls or steering mechanism."

"It *was* a heck of a ride," I said, then laughed. Now that I was sure it wasn't going to kill me, the whole thing seemed a lot more awesome than it had while I was flying backward on a giant column of flame. "Not your fault, Denmother."

"Not entirely, perhaps, but I should not have *assumed* that you had taken into account all appropriate factors before pulling the trigger."

I wondered about Denmother's emphasis. "I didn't know computers could assume."

"It's not precisely the same thing as a human would mean when using that word, but it's the closest analogue I could find. The subroutine responsible for the failure has been excised and a new one substituted. It will not happen again."

"What else can I try out?" Might as well get the most out of a weekend at the Den without adult supervision. Besides, there were plenty more Captain Commanding figures to blow up.

Later, I sat in my rooms with a repeater for the Foxsnooper and listened in on the OSIRIS secure lines. After my experience in Backflash's lab, I was hoping to hear more about what

Spartanicus was up to. While I didn't get any direct reports on his whereabouts, there was a good deal of chatter about the gang he'd used at the museum.

Things like HeartBurn and the Fluffinator breaking into the Colonel Cuddlebear warehouse—without running afoul of the Colonel this time. They'd made off with a mobile plushie manufacturing unit—one of those semis you see at county fairs where people can order up a custom Cuddlebear Mask plushie. Or, Mr. Implausible and the Bagger stealing a barge load of fireworks from the Heropolis docks.

It was all fairly minor stuff as far as Hood crime goes, but there was a lot of it, and nothing obvious connecting the various heists. For example, why would Mempulse break into the Mask Hall of Fame and steal nothing but a box of old trading cards from the basement archives, when there were much more valuable and dangerous items there? Or, why would HeartBurn cut the cornerstone plaque off Washburn High School?

I didn't know what was going on, but I had a nasty feeling there was a bigger pattern to it all. Between Spartanicus and Backflash and the dark side of Deimos I was piling up too many mysteries. It made my bones itch. Especially Backflash's claim to have come from the future.

What happened between her and the Mark IX seemed so farfetched that I doubted Speedslick and the others would believe me even if I told them about it. I couldn't tell my parents—they'd never believe me, and if they *did* and found out I'd died twice . . . Well, I couldn't even imagine how badly that would go without breaking out in shivers.

I went back down to the range a couple of times. It's surprising how much better blowing things up can make you feel. Almost as good as punching out a bad guy. Thinking about that made me want to go out on patrol, Foxman or no, and I did climb into the Foxmobile and start the engine a couple of times. But I kept coming back to the things Backflash had said about me being a problem, and then I'd turn the car off again.

If I could have talked to Rand about it all, I might have felt better, but he still hadn't returned by the time I was supposed to head back to the AMO. I did a bunch of searching around on the Web for timeshifting and even had Denmother help me out, but we didn't come up with anything that wasn't either obvious fiction or totally crazy. And then my time was up and I had to go back to Mars.

I wish I didn't have to go back to Mars yet. Now, there's another thought I never expected to have.

Mike met me at the gate when I arrived.

"I hear you cut out of your afternoon classes on Friday," he said. "Why don't you come back to my office so we can have a little talk."

His voice was as gentle as ever, but it was one of those questions that didn't allow for any answer other than yes.

"Of course, Mike."

I pasted on a smile and fell in beside him, all the while racking my brain for what I ought to tell him about skipping class.

He led me along a different path than the one I normally used to get to his office, going up one of the steeper ramps that ran through the maintenance areas and avoiding most of the class-rooms. That took us along the hallway that held the demon-stration chambers—moderate-size soundproof rooms with one armor-glass wall. Mostly they were used by the upperclassmen to try out and show off new techniques for the teachers without hav-ing to go all the way down to the battle simulators. Students also signed them out as practice spaces.

At this time on Sunday, they were mostly empty, though we did see one room where a brute and a bouncer were trying out some team maneuvers. Brutes are your basic high-strength, high-durability sluggers, like Burnish in steel mode. Bouncers are a bit more unusual. In this case it was a kid from the class in front of ours. His handle was Rebounder, and he basically turned into a human tennis ball when he activated his powers.

As we passed, the brute, Ogre-X, or something like that, picked up Rebounder—grabbing on to one of the grips built into his battle suit for that express purpose—and threw him at one of the Hood targets along the back wall. *Whap!*

Then, when Rebounder bounced back, Ogre-X would smack him like a handball to send him down field again. And again, and once more. With each target down, they picked up speed, until, after the fifth bounce back, Ogre-X just got out of the way and let Rebounder ping-pong around the room. By the time he came to rest he'd taken out all the remaining back wall targets as well as half a dozen more that had popped up elsewhere. I had paused to watch, and I kind of wanted to see what they'd try next, but Mike raised an eyebrow at me and I moved on.

I still didn't know what to tell him about skipping out on Friday, and somehow I didn't think that the truth was a great idea in this case. *Yeah, so I died. Twice. And then I flipped out.* But, much to my surprise, the first thing out of Mike's mouth when we got back to his office had nothing to do with my missed classes.

Instead, he asked, "How did things go with Foxman this weekend?"

"I didn't mean to skip . . . Wait, what?"

"Foxman. How did things go?"

"Fine, it was all fine," I told him. "I thought you wanted to talk to me about skipping class?" I am never going to make sense of adults.

"Not really. I wanted to make you sweat a bit about skipping class. I'm pretty sure the walk up here managed that better than any lecture I could come up with. No, the main reason I wanted to have a talk with you was to see how the weekend went with Rand. So, what happened?"

I paused and tried to think of what I could say that wouldn't come back to bite me later. "I mostly just hung around the Den. Rand was pretty much checked out this weekend."

"But he didn't get drunk?"

"Not that I'm aware of, no. I can't tell you what he does when I'm not with him, but I've never seen him drink anything but MaskerAde."

Mike looked relieved. "I'm glad to hear that. I hoped it would go like that, but I didn't have a lot of faith. Not given how he gets about his birthday. Maybe he's finally starting to recover from whatever broke him back in the day."

"What do you mean, 'broke him'?"

"I don't think . . . no, he's your Mask, you deserve to know what I can tell you. I don't know why his birthday's such a hard day for him, but it is. But it's not actually his worst. That's Metamorphosis Day—which is only six weeks from now. This might be the first time in years he makes it from one to the other sober. I very much hope so. Rand was a great man once upon a time, and a friend of mine. I would love to see him get back on his feet for real."

"Do you know what—" I was still trying to figure out exactly what I wanted to ask, when Mike cut in.

"What turned him into a drunk? I'm not sure. Rand always drank pretty heavily. He was a work-hard, party-hard kind of guy. But it was never a problem for him till right after the M-Day memorial service here in '97."

"Memorial service?" I'd been meaning to learn more about that ever since I'd heard it mentioned in class. But other more important problems had been occupying my time and my mind.

"You know about the M-Day Mystery." It wasn't a question.

Everybody knew that meta activity went dark for a day on the anniversary of the Hero Bomb, and that both Masks and Hoods mostly vanished at that time, but I nodded anyway.

"Have you read the chapter on it in the AMO handbook?" I looked at my feet and Mike sighed. "No, of course you haven't. The school didn't get properly started until about five years after the Hero Bomb, but this facility opened on M-Day '89 with a memorial service for the fallen. It was the very first anniversary of our collective Metamorphosis, and all of us were invited, Mask and Hood alike."

I said something that had been bothering me ever since I first heard it. "Having the Hoods here seems wrong somehow."

"I was surprised myself. I wasn't much older than you are now at that point, and the idea of standing side by side with my enemies didn't sit well. But Backflash can be very convincing when she wants to be, and she insisted that we put aside our rivalries for one day."

"How did they get this place open that quickly? I mean, it's huge and . . . Mars."

"I honestly have no idea, but it must have involved the work of a number of the most powerful metas, including some of the Black Masks."

"Black Masks?" That was a new one on me.

"Government spooks, metas who work for OSIRIS and never revealed themselves to the world. I don't know how many of them there are, but I know they exist."

"Wait, I'm losing the thread here, what does all this have to do with Foxman?" I asked.

"I don't know for sure. All I know is that he missed most of the '97 ceremony, slipping into the back very late. I doubt many people noticed, but I'd arrived a little late myself. So I was tucked in right beside the door. Rand looked pretty shook up when he came in. Afterward, I saw Backflash back him into a corner, and she didn't look very happy about whatever she had to say to him. That was the last time I saw Rand fully sober before this year."

"I wonder what happened?"

Mike shrugged. "I don't know, Evan. I don't know."

It was obvious he didn't have anything more to say at that

point, so I pushed my chair back, and said, "Thanks for telling me."

"Least I could do."

As I headed for the door, he picked up a mandolin that had been lying on the desk. The last thing I heard on my way out into the hall was him beginning to sing a song that started out "Rocket ship, rocket ship, carry me away." There was something terribly mournful about it, or maybe that was just my current mood.

Burnish was leaning against the wall outside my dorm room when I got there. "Need to talk to you, Quick. Got a minute?"

"Sure, what's up?"

"Follow me." She led me to the nearest of the surface domes. "I'm pretty sure there's no surveillance here. Well, not beyond the tracers OSIRIS puts in our uniforms."

"Tracers in our uniforms?"

She nodded and gave me that thin-lipped you're-an-idiot-Quick look that I was coming to think of as her default expression where it came to me.

"So, I've been nosing around the entrance to Backflash's lab since we talked last. I tried to slip in through the wiring, but there's some kind of block or shielding at the interface where it goes past the door, and I haven't been able to find any other way into the far side of the base. I'm not sure what's going on over there, but I think I want to find out, and the only way to do that is opening the vault."

"Does that mean you're going to help us get in?"

"If I had any choice about it, no. But I can't do this alone, I need Blurshift and Emberdown, and probably NightHowl to actually crack the door—the security's an absolute bear. Blind-mark and Speedslick can play lookout."

"I notice a conspicuous absence on that list."

"Not my fault you're useless. But I know I can't get the others without putting up with you, so it looks like you get to come along for the ride."

I ignored the jibe. "When?"

Burnish looked thoughtful. "I need to talk with the others and get some more info. Tuesday maybe?"

"Wish we could do it sooner." If I was going to do this, I wanted to get it over with before my nerve broke.

"Get some real powers and maybe we can speed things up."

21

Safecrackers Inc.

"You ready for this, Quick?" The look Burnish gave me told me she was pretty sure the answer was no.

"Whenever you are," I replied.

"Then, let's get to it."

NightHowl, Emberdown, and Blurshift were already in place by the vault door. Blindmark waited at the fork where this section of tunnel met the rest of the system. Speedslick was at his side, ready to dash down and warn us if anyone headed our way. It was almost midnight Tuesday, well past the time students were supposed to be out in the halls.

"Everybody know what they're doing?" I asked.

Four nods said we were go for liftoff or whatever you wanted to call it. Burnish put a hand on the box housing the vault's biometric entry system. As she did so, her color slowly shifted from dull steel to bright copper.

"I'm going to slip into the wiring now, so that I can spoof the feeds," she said. Bright purple plasma danced along the surface of her skin as her arm sank into the box. "And . . . got it, I think. That should block the channel until we get the keys nailed down, though I do have to say it stings a bit."

Emberdown stepped forward then, holding her hand just above the retina scanner. "Flashing the system in three—two—one—" Bright lights shot from her fingertips to cascade across the reader, rapidly cycling through all the colors of visible light.

Burnish's face took on a look of intense concentration. "No. No. No. There! Back up."

"This one?" Emberdown's color show narrowed to a deep violet.

"That's the one. NightHowl, you're up."

The leather-jacketed girl leaned down over the voice recognition mic. Opening her mouth, she let out a high, warbling keen that slowly cycled lower and lower.

"That's the first one," said Burnish after a moment. "Feels like we need three more . . . and there's another. No. No." She grimaced and bit her lip in a way that suggested the contact hurt more than she was admitting. "Down a touch . . . there! Now, one more—got it! Can you do those four again without hitting the other notes?"

NightHowl rolled her eyes. "No, of course not. You're the only person in the whole school who has any real control over her powers. The rest of us are just second-raters who got lucky somehow."

Burnish's lips went extra thin, and I thought for a moment we were going to have a fight on our hands, but then she just nodded. "Okay, point taken. Maybe I even deserved that."

"D'yah think?" said NightHowl, but Emberdown put a hand on her shoulder and she subsided.

Meanwhile, Blurshift had stepped up to the hand reader. As they placed their palm against the plate, the constant steady shifting that normally rippled through their body slowed and became more deliberate. They became a she, with an appearance similar to, but not quite the same as, Backflash.

"It helps me get the hands right if I do the whole body," she said, answering the question I hadn't asked.

"That's really close," said Burnish. "I think the hand needs to be thinner and darker. Maybe longer fingers, too." No sooner had she said so than Blurshift changed to fit her request. "Yes, that's the right shape. We're really close."

"You do understand that I can't do the actual fingerprints without copies and time to practice, right?" asked Blurshift.

It was Burnish's turn to roll her eyes, though I could see sweat beading up at her hairline and rolling down her temples, which kind of undermined the effect. "Yeah, we discussed that. Several times. You just need to get the rough details and I'll take care of the rest. Just keep shifting and I'll tell you when—wait. I think that's good enough. Let's try it. Go!"

Emberdown and NightHowl leaned in on either side of Blurshift, addressing the iris scanner and microphone respectively. With a flash and a warble, and a grunt from Burnish, the system activated, "Handprint verified. Voice verified. Retina scan verified. Subject AAA111 verified. Bittersharp full-access status verified." That was followed by a clunk from the heavy door. A moment later, it began to swing open.

I leapt forward, ready to slip through as soon as the gap was wide enough. "We're in! Come on."

Burnish started to pull her arm free of the box, then swore and stopped. "Hang on! I feel something . . ." She pivoted in place and used her free arm to reach around behind her, feeling along the lip of the door. "That's not good."

"What?" I asked.

"I couldn't feel it through the shielding before, but the door's got a second layer of security. It's right . . . here." She touched a finger to a small black circle set into the steel vault's doorframe. "Let me . . . yeah. Only one of us can go through on a given biometric key without some sort of special authorization—which we don't have. Any more, and the door slams, alarms sound, and all kinds of mayhem breaks loose. Also, we're going to have to close it behind you, because things go boom if it stays open too long, too."

"Behind *me*?" I whispered.

"Got to," said Burnish. "It'll take all four of us to open the door again, and we need Blindmark and Speedslick on lookout. Time's wasting, get moving. We'll close up behind you to keep things from going pear-shaped, then crack it open every half hour on the dot until 5 a.m. to give you a way out. Make sure you get back by then, because the school will start to wake up not long after. Now, go! Or, are you too sidekick to handle this on your own?"

I wanted to argue, to tell her I really wasn't ready to go spying through the hidden underbelly of OSIRIS all by myself, but that would have wasted time we didn't have. To say nothing of confirming every bad thing she'd ever said or thought about me. So, I just nodded and ducked through the door. The heavy metallic sound of it closing behind me was the loneliest sound I'd ever heard. I quickly set the vibrating alarm on my uniform's built-in phone to silently buzz me at fifteen-minute intervals.

I hurried down the short hallway, stopping just shy of the big globe room, and creeping forward the last few feet. I couldn't see Backflash or anyone else in the main area around the freaky alien-looking equipment, so I peered down through the clear floor to check if she was in her cubicle. She wasn't, nor at the nearby lab bench where the Spartanicus-styled Mark IX was spread all over the place.

By chance, the head was turned my way. *Ugh.* Seeing those dead mechanical eyes looking up at me gave me the screaming creepies. I really wanted nothing more at that point than to turn tail and head back to the school side of things. But I'd come to unravel the mysteries of Deimos, and this was the heart of it all—probably the exact center of the moon.

Reluctantly, I crept down the ramp and started to make my way into the thicket of candy-colored weirdness that Backflash used to conduct her major experiments. It was only as I waded in that it occurred to me that this might all be technology Back-flash had brought back from the future. If so, who knew what it could do?

I froze then for about a dozen heartbeats, and I had to fight the urge to run back to the door and pound on it to have them let me out. I'd never been more aware that I was just a thirteen-year-old kid and not James Bond or some kind of superhacker. I mean sure, I had powers, but aside from my scabwebs, they were pretty minor and not even a little bit reliable. Burnish was right. I was just a freaking sidekick!

Only.

It was the "only" that saved me, because it was a pretty big "only." It was the one that started the sentence, "Only, I want to be more." And I did. So *very* much more. I wanted to be a hero someday, even if I did have to start out as a sidekick. I had always wanted that. That was why I'd cared so much about Captain Commanding and been so crushed when he turned out to be a giant jerk. Because being a hero mattered to me, because I wanted to be a Mask so that I could do some real good in the world. Maybe I wasn't there yet. But it had to start somewhere right? Maybe that somewhere was here.

I'd never know if I didn't try. Forcing my feet to carry me forward, I slid deeper into the maze of—possibly—futuristic technology. When I got to the console where I'd first seen Backflash, I took off my right gauntlet and hesitantly reached out a fingertip. The machine felt greasy slick and warm, but faintly prickly, like someone had rubbed olive oil on a piece of wedgwood. But I couldn't detect any residue on my fingertips when I pulled them away. It also gave off a faint, atonal hum that I could only hear through my fingers, if that made any sense.

The terrified voice in the back of my head was saying I should get the heck out of there and that this was the moment in the Mask horror movies where everything goes horribly, horribly wrong. Instead of bolting, I tucked my glove into my belt and climbed into the mesh seat. Predictably, that's when things went horribly, horribly wonky.

The spiky-bright blue-raspberry tentacle suddenly curled down and touched its starfish-shaped tip to my forehead, just as it had with Backflash. Word-tastes exploded into my mind like a sour-candy encyclopedia. My mouth filled with sharp/tart/meaning that had no relation to any human language, yet somehow made sense.

QUERY? USER-HUMAN, UNFAMILIAR TO THIS CANDY/KALEIDOSCOPE/MACHINE/INTELLIGENCE. IDENTIFY YOUR FLAVOR/NAME/SELF?

Evan, I thought. *I'm Evan Quick.*

HELLO, USER EVANQUICK/SWEET/SHORT/BURST. HOW MAY I ACCEDE TO YOUR THOUGHT DEMANDS?

What are you?

CONFUSED/BITTER/SHARP AM I. INTELLIGENCE CRYSTALLIZED IN SPIKE/CACTUS/COMPUTER. QUERY NOT SENSE MAKING. RELATED MACHINE INTELLIGENCE VAT GROWN/SOURSWEET.

It took me several long beats to figure that out. Whatever the thing was it used a lot of unusual words.

Did Backflash make you?

USER BACKFLASH FIRST ENTERED SYSTEM FOUR THOUSAND ORBITAL CYCLES OF THIS PLANET/MOON/SAVORY SOLIDS AFTER INITIALIZATION.

You're four thousand Mars years old? I guessed.

SWEET/BRIGHT/AFFIRMATIVE.

So, not from the future then.

Who built you? And why? And how did you end up as part of an OSIRIS facility?

CREATOR INTELLIGENCES HOT/BITTER/BRIGHT GREW
US FOR THE WAR WITH THE HATE/DARK/SOUR. THEY PUT
US IN THIS PLACE FOR YOUR PEOPLE TO USE IF/WHEN THE
HATE/DARK/SOUR ARRIVE. USER BACKFLASH FIRST AC-
CESSED THIS UNIT ONE HUNDRED AND FIFTY-FOUR EARTH
ORBITS FROM NOW, AFTER THE HATE/DARK/SOUR INVADED/
WILL INVADE/MAY HAVE INVADED—IRRESOLVABLE TEMPO-
RAL ERROR. USER BACKFLASH HAS RETURNED FROM THE/A/
POSSIBLE—IRRESOLVABLE TEMPORAL ERROR—FUTURE TO
PREVENT HER TIMELINE FROM COMING INTO EXISTENCE.

Wait, what? I don't understand. Can you explain?

PERHAPS IT WOULD BE BETTER TO LET SAVORY-
SWEET/BACKFLASH TELL YOU IN HER OWN THOUGHT/MEM-
ORY/FLAVORS.

The bizarre interface vanished and I found myself plunged
into Backflash's memories. Two hundred years flashed by in an
instant. History that followed our own up to the point of the Hero
Bomb—a device Backflash had brought back through time to split
our timeline off from her own.

In the other timeline, armadillo-like aliens, the hate/dark/
sour—Kith'ara to Backflash—invaded Earth in the 2050s, wiping
out most of humanity. A few survivors lived on in the asteroid
mining colonies, where habitats had been built in tunnels humanity had found when they arrived. The hot/bitter/bright had bored
and shielded them against Kith'ara technology, though the hu-
mans didn't learn that until much later.

The surviving asteroid miners weren't able to really fight the
Kith'ara until the accidental discovery of the Hero Bomb

technology. Originally much more physically destructive, the bomb had been devised as a mining tool. But even with the bomb the human population was simply too small to create enough metasoldiers to defeat the Kith'ara.

Humanity had nearly been wiped out by the time they found the facilities on Deimos. So, when Backflash got her powers, they made a hard decision. She would bring the Hero Bomb back in time to before the invasion and detonate it, erasing her own time-line's present to give humanity a chance at a future.

I wondered then why the machine was giving me such thorough access to a system that ought to have the highest level of classified protection of anything in the solar system.

IT IS MY PRIMARY/BRIGHT/SHARPSWEET PURPOSE TO PROVIDE INFORMATION TO ALLOW YOUR SPECIES TO FIGHT THE HATE/DARK/SOUR. INFORMATION MUST NOT BE RE-STRICTED/HIDDEN/SMOKY. YOUR QUERY IS NOT SENSE MAKING.

*I didn't actually mean it as a query, but—*I shook my head. *Never mind. Can you tell me anything about why Backflash runs the AMO the way she does?*

AMO CREATED TO BUILD/NURTURE/SMOKY-SHARP META-WARRIORS TO FIGHT THE HATE/DARK/SOUR.

How? Our powers are so much weaker than the Hero Bomb generation. And the school seems to create as many Hoods as it does Masks. That can't be right.

HOODS AND MASKS ARE TWO SIDES OF THE SAME SMOKY-SWEET/GAME.

What is smoky-sweet/game? I asked.

Hoods and Masks competing against each other to the death/ending/sour. Only the strongest will survive to fight the hate/dark/sour.

So, we were gladiators. That made a horrible sort of sense, forcing us to fight each other to become stronger.

But what about the weakness of our powers? The hero beam doesn't give us the same level of powers as those created by the Hero Bomb.

Weak powers force smoky-sweet/game players to work as teams. It teaches thinking in past/present/future optimization patterns over brute force. Power increases theoretically possible for later implementation—acceptable risk when weighed against extinction/dark/sour.

Argh!

Invalid query. Repeat/rephrase/sweet?

This was so much more frustrating than working with Denmother or any of Foxman's other systems. It made me want to bang my head on something.

Again bitter/sharp picked the thoughts out of my mind.

Query. You are familiar with user Foxman?

Yes, he's my . . . teacher. Does that matter?

User Foxman has interfaced/spicy/bonded with this unit. User Foxman had very similar questions. Do you wish to review user Foxman's interactions with this unit? Alternatively, user Backflash has just entered the globe. Do you wish to ask her directly about her—

I don't know what else the machine was going to say. I was already batting the interface tentacle away from my forehead. I had to get out of there! I rolled off the couch, touched the floor briefly with my feet . . . and landed flat on my face with an audible crack as my legs gave out and my nose took the brunt of my fall.

Reflexes trained in my various combat courses brought my arms forward to press my palms against the floor and launch me back to my feet. At least, that's what I intended. But none of my limbs seemed interested in doing exactly what they were supposed to. I realized then that I could more than half taste the nerve impulses running between my brain and the rest of my body. Apparently, interfacing with bitter/sharp had some less-than-happy side effects.

I could hear footsteps approaching. With no alternative, I dragged myself under the edge of the console. The space was small, not much bigger than I was really. I wedged myself as deep in as I could, and quietly wished I'd drawn invisibility from the powers deck instead of scabwebs. A pair of black Armex boots walked up to the console and paused for a moment before pivoting. The chair creaked and the boots vanished.

Now what? I'd barely thought of the question when I felt my skin catch fire. It hurt so much that I actually checked my hand for flames.

My fingers weren't even pink, and I had to conclude that the burning sensation was a side effect of my interface with bitter/sharp, or possibly, of the way I'd broken it off. It went on for a long, long time and I actually bit through my lip to keep from screaming—for the record, fresh scabweb tastes like condensed essence of armpit. Eventually the burning faded and I found that I could move normally again.

Of course, I was still only two feet away from the scariest woman in the solar system. In her lab. Which I had broken into. Hiding under her computer. Which I had also broken into. After she'd warned me that she wouldn't hesitate to make very bad things happen to me if I continued to be a problem. Other than that, everything was great. Yeah, about that . . .

I edged my face forward a couple of inches and looked up. I could see the side of Backflash's face. All she would have to do to spot me if I moved so much as an inch forward was to turn her head. I didn't think she could see me if I stayed where I was, but I honestly wasn't sure. Which meant I had to get out of there, and the sooner the better. That's when I noticed the smear of blood on the floor where I'd broken my nose. So yeah, I needed to clean that up, too.

About the only thing I had going for me was that bitter/sharp's interface was pretty all-consuming. Or, at least, it had been for me—a kid—when I tried it for the very first time. Reassuring thoughts, those. Still, I had no choice.

Moving as quietly as I could, I turned my glove inside out and used the padding on the inside to mop up as much of the blood as I could. Not perfect, but not awful. Also, the easiest part of the operation by far.

Next, I reached above my head to find the end of the console. Grabbing on to the greasy-slick alien material there, I slowly dragged myself along the floor until my head and shoulders emerged into the open. If Backflash so much as glanced downward out of the side of her eye right now, I was dead. I couldn't bear to look and see if she was looking at me. I just shifted my grip and pushed myself the rest of the way out from under the console.

Backflash shifted on her chair.

I froze. This was it. I was a goner. But seconds ticked past and nothing happened. Maybe she hadn't seen me. Or maybe she was playing with me. She could always step back in time after she'd seen exactly what I was up to. I choked back bile as fear churned my stomach like a swirling acid smoothie. Finally, I couldn't bear the suspense any longer and I started moving again. Staying on my belly, I dragged myself around to the back of the console.

I was covered in sweat and sick to my stomach, but I was also out of the direct line of sight from Backflash's chair. Victory! Well, a small one anyway. I still had to cover half the length of a football field on hands and knees without getting caught by someone who could always timeshift back a few minutes and change the rules. Then I had to climb the ramp, get down the hallway, and catch the vault door timing exactly right. Oh, and did I mention that part about the floor being transparent? If anyone happened to wander into Backflash's office for any reason, and look up, I was cooked.

Whee.

I'll spare the details, which mostly consist of fear, sweat, and moving really, really slowly, and skip to the part where Speedslick pulled me through the open vault door about three million years later.

"So, did you learn anything?" he asked as the door quietly closed behind me.

"Uh, yeah, I did. But none of you are going to believe it. Let's go someplace where we can talk about it."

"You know," said Burnish, "I'm kind of digging the big patch of beige goo where your nose used to be. That's a good look for you, Quick. Remind me to punch you if it starts to go back to normal."

"Oh, just get over yourself, Burnish." NightHowl scowled at the older girl. "You're not half as cool as you think you are."

Burnish's lips went thin and tight. "And you, remind me to push your face in when this is all over."

"Whatever," said NightHowl.

Emberdown stepped between the two of them, but they both dropped it at that point and we headed out.

It wasn't until that moment that I realized I'd actually done it. I might not have real Mask-level powers, and I sure wasn't some kind of superspy guy, but maybe I didn't have to be. I hadn't even really used what powers I had.

Maybe sometimes plain old Evan Quick was enough.

22

OutFoxed

It took a lot of explaining to bring the others up to speed on everything I'd seen and learned in the vault. Even then I didn't think most of them completely believed me. It *was* all pretty farfetched—time travel and aliens and metas as gladiators—and some of the looks I got reminded me of the way people had treated me after I broke the weight machine at Camp Commanding. Emberdown and Blindmark seemed especially skeptical, and even Speedslick sounded doubtful on a couple of points.

By the time I finally crawled into bed around five, my earlier sense of triumph had faded into a sort of dull gray fog. My dreams were lurid and crazy, full of taste-words and alien imagery, and when my alarm went off at eight, I felt like I hadn't gotten any sleep at all.

I spent the whole day in a weird sort of buzzing trance. Whether that was due to my experience with bittersharp or simply because of all the things I had to think about, was anybody's guess. The hours seemed to pass in a weird series of jumps with only bits and scraps of all that I saw and heard really sticking in memory:

Try reversing the polarity!

Right. Because comics and movies teach us that it's as easy as flipping a switch, and that it will transform electricity and magnetism into death rays and anti-vampire shields.

Wait, let me get this right, you shoot banana peels from your fingertips?

Completely frictionless banana peels. Very handy for stopping getaways. Explosive oranges and knockout cantaloupes as well.

The proper procedure for disposing of bio-agents and radiation devices is to call in a code thirty-eight to the OSIRIS hood-mat emergency line at . . .

Estimate Boy?

Yep, I can show you. Do you want a rough count of the number of days before she breaks up with you?

Then this tiny little tornado comes through and everything goes black and white.

But nothing else changes?

Nope, weirdest bad guy ever.

Armex allergy?

Yeah, and it activates my powers in the weirdest way—I've melted three uniforms . . .

Don't touch that.

Why not?

It activates the transform beam and—there, now you've done it. Someone take Winslow to the infirmary.

Explanation Lad?

It started on an ordinary Thursday, much like this one. A boy—me—was minding his own business when . . .

I'm an eeeevil geeeeeeenius!

Of course you are, dear. Now turn in your homework.

While artificial wings appear to act as a psychological aid in controlling flight powers for some metas, there is no evidence that any of them actually provide significant lift or thrust. You're much better off not becoming dependent on them.

Almost before I realized it, classes were over, and I knew exactly what I had to do next. I had to confront Foxman.

~~ ~~

"Denmother, where's Rand, we need to talk, now!" I was calling out before I even finished sliding down the ramp from the *Flying*

Fox. And this time I'd checked ahead of time, so I knew he was back from wherever he'd been.

"In the kitchen, Master Quick."

I bounced to my feet and went straight on through the door into the dome, dropping my bag on the first couch I passed. Rand was sitting at the counter in his pajamas, eating a sandwich, and taking giant gulps off a huge can of MaskerAde.

"Helloooo, Evan. Is it Thursday already? Because if it is, then I lost a day somewhere." His voice came out fast and slick, like he was vibrating at a really high frequency, and he looked at the MaskerAde dubiously. "I *was* up for ninety-seven hours straight, but I don't think I've slept more than thirty hours since I sugar crashed. If I did, then I need to think about . . . Wait, it's easily solved." He glanced up. "Denmother, what day is it?"

"It's Wednesday, sir."

"Oh, good. That explains a lot." He suddenly whipped his head back down to stare at me. "Well, except you. It doesn't explain you—I was pretty sure that you didn't come in on Wednesdays— unless you're a hallucination. You aren't a hallucination, are you? Because, I haven't had one of those in ages, and I'd prefer to avoid having them start up again. Especially since I'm not drinking any-more, so I don't have a good excuse for a hallucination. For that matter, hallucinations are usually way more blurry than you are, with these shimmery things off to the sides. You aren't actually blurry, are you? Because you don't look blurry. Or is that just me?"

"Rand!" I said angrily. "Shut up. We need to talk."

"Are you sure? Because I hate the words 'we need to talk.' I've never been involved in a single conversation that begins with 'we need to talk' that didn't go horribly wrong."

"I've been inside the vault on Deimos! I talked to bittersharp!"

Rand blinked rapidly and somewhat confusedly. "Bittersharp? I think I missed a step there."

"Don't lie to me!" I yelled at him—he knew all this stuff and he'd never said a word to me. "I interfaced with the alien computer on Deimos, and it told me that you had, too. It even offered to play your memories back for me."

"Oh. Well. That. Yeah, see, I *told* you that no conversation that starts with 'we need to talk' goes well. And this is just another example of . . . Bittersharp, really? When I linked with it, the name tasted more like smokystrong to me, but I guess I can see bittersharp, too. I don't . . . Wait, it offered to play you my memories?"

"Yes. It said you asked a lot of the same questions I did."

"Did you? Go into my memories, that is." His voice came out very small.

Something about the way he said that burned a lot of my anger away, and the idea of looking into Foxman's mind, even at one remove, suddenly seemed like the worst kind of violation. "No. I didn't." And then, because I felt strangely ashamed of myself, "I didn't have time, but I probably would have if I had. I'm, uh, sorry."

He took a deep breath. "Don't be. I went into Backflash's memories without a second thought—I haven't got a lot of room to judge. So, you know about the aliens coming to kill us then."

"Yes, a bit. But I had to get out before bittersharp finished explaining things, and a lot of what the computer showed me didn't really make sense. There's still so much that I need to know."

"Tell me what you've got and I'll see what details I can fill in."

When I finished relating what had happened to me, Rand sighed, got up from the table and began to pace. "I didn't actually get much further than you did before Backflash caught me."

"Caught you? I thought—"

"What? That my session with bittersharp was official?" He laughed, and not in a pleasant way. "No, Backflash doesn't want anyone else getting near her magic alien oracle. I used one of the M-Day celebrations as cover to break into bittersharp's vault. I'd have gotten away with it, too, if Backflash hadn't spotted me sneaking into the back of the memorial and then checked the logs to see when I arrived on Deimos."

"Wait, I thought you said she caught you *during* your interface?"

"She travels in time, Evan. She found out what I'd done and jumped back as far as she dared. That kept me from getting more than an hour with bittersharp."

"I'm confused. If she can jump back in time nearly two hundred years to deliver the Hero Bomb, why couldn't she jump back far enough to stop you completely?"

"It's *very* dangerous for her to go more than about half an hour. I didn't know it then, but I hacked the daylights out of OSIRIS's computers to find out more later. She's a fixed time-space wave-function and"—he paused—"no, forget that. Understanding it involves a lot of math you haven't learned. Suffice to say that jumping back far enough to block me completely would have posed significant risks to timeline stability."

"All right." I was actually a little relieved when he didn't go into the details. Despite what my parents do for a living, math isn't my best subject. "If you didn't have that long—"

"Do I really know much more than you? Probably. I already had a lot of information I'd pried loose from OSIRIS's secure servers, so I knew what questions to ask. I've also learned more since."

"And?"

"And we aren't alone in the universe. There are quite a few aliens out there. Most don't care about us, but the Kith'ara don't like competition. They destroyed the home world of bittersharp's people and nearly wiped out the entire species. After that, bittersharp's people dedicated themselves to fighting the Kith'ara. But they are few in number and not powerful militarily, so they've spent their resources building bases like the one on Deimos in as many developing solar systems as possible. They want to give people like us a fighting chance."

"Aliens . . . wow!" I mean, bittersharp was an alien creation, but somehow the idea didn't seem real until I heard it from a real person. It was awesome and scary and almost too big to get my head around. "What else do we know about them?"

"Not a lot. Backflash has been careful not to let information get out of OSIRIS's backrooms. She doesn't trust the Web, possibly because the Kith'ara will use it against us, or *did* use it, or . . . I hate time travel."

"Is Backflash a hero or a villain?" I asked, suddenly. "I mean, she set off the Hero Bomb, but—"

"I don't know, Evan." He closed his eyes and clenched his fists hard enough to turn the knuckles white. "I really don't. I'm not sure those terms mean anything where she's concerned. She is directly responsible for more than half a million deaths, including my father's. But she did it to save the planet."

"Bittersharp said that we were like gladiators . . ."

"Yeah, they've set things up in a way that pushes nearly as many young metas into turning Hood as becoming Masks because they want us at one another's throats. Backflash believes—and the government agrees—that we need to have as many powerful metas as possible when the Kith'ara arrive, or *if* they arrive. Backflash coming back through time destabilizes the timeline in a way that means those sorts of *ifs* and *whens* aren't really clear anymore. Did I mention how much I hate time travel?"

He shook his head. "Never mind. The important bit is combat. OSIRIS believes we need lots of practice with our powers or the Kith'ara will walk right over us. They set up the entire system to give us live combat practice against the toughest enemies around—each other. That's why metamax cells practically come with a revolving door. Hoods in prison aren't putting a fighting edge on us or them."

"Oh." It made a horrible sort of sense. "What about the hero beam?" I asked. "Why are we so much weaker than your generation?"

"You know about the beam, too? Did you get it out of bittersharp?"

"No, I figured it out on my own."

"You're one smart kid. I'll say that for you." He took a deep breath. "That's my fault, actually."

"Your fault?" I asked "How?"

"I built the hero beam. Backflash recruited me for the effort very early on, long before I accessed bittersharp and we had our falling-out. She told me OSIRIS had uncovered some of the secrets of the Hero Bomb, but not everything. The government needed some way to harness the technology without killing ninety-eight percent of the people it touched."

Rand closed his eyes and I could see that talking about this hurt him. "She lied and told me we didn't know who had detonated the bomb but that we didn't dare let someone else have a monopoly on that kind of power. She said my powers made me perfect for the job." He snorted bitterly. "Too bad she was wrong."

"Wrong? How? I mean, you did build the hero beam, right?"

"Sort of. It doesn't work the way it's supposed to, and that's my fault. Well, and Backflash's for not anticipating all the new powers people would develop. You see, she thought I was a technopath—which I am—but that's not all. I'm technokinetic as well, and that's a power that didn't exist in her future."

"Could you back up a couple of steps?" I asked. "Technopath? Technokinetic?"

"Sure. Denmother, bring up my armor on a test rack."

A moment later, the Foxman suit rolled into the kitchen on a little platform.

Rand tapped the chest plate. "Being able to build this is what makes me a technopath. I can *hear* machines, all machines, in my mind. When I pick up a blender, say, or a pistol, I can instantly see

everything about how it works and how it . . . wants to be better."
He angrily waved a hand in the air. "That's not quite right. Machines don't *actually* want anything, but for me, they feel like they do, like they *want* to be perfected. Combine that with a natural aptitude for design and it makes me one of the best inventors in the world."

"So, why don't you sound happy about it? And what's technokinesis?"

"My curse. Or my real power. Depends on how you look at it. The technology in this suit doesn't make me a Mask, though I thought it did once upon a time. I was going to show all those metahuman masters of the universe what a normal human with a little bit of good old American know-how could do. I would fight crime by night and build a company on the tech I used to do it by day. Billionaire, genius, Mask, entrepreneur. That was my plan. There was only one tiny little problem.

"*That* was the real reason I lost Foxhammer Industries." The words were just spilling out of him, like a dam had broken and he couldn't stop himself. "I thought I was a technological genius and not just another silly meta—well, actually I am a technological genius, just not as much of one as I thought. Or, in the way I thought, because . . . technokinesis. You see, every bit of tech in this armor works anywhere, but it only works together *on* me, and it only performs at optimum capability *for* me.

"My supercapacitors are the best in the world under normal circumstances, but when *I* run the tests they operate at seven hundred and fifty percent the efficiency of what anyone else gets. The electrokinetic artificial muscles operate at over two thousand percent efficiency if I'm wearing them. The rockets will propel an article the size of this suit with no problem, but no one else can get them to fly in a straight line. The computer controls, the stopping power of the armor, even the reflectivity of the paint—it all comes together for me but not for anyone else. And that's because genius is only thirty-two point five-seven-two-eight percent of the equation—I calculated it once."

Now I saw it. "So when you built the hero beam for Backflash—"

"Exactly." He smashed a fist into the chest piece of his battle suit. "When I wasn't the one operating it, the beam was only thirty-two point five-seven-two-eight percent as efficient as it was supposed to be. And that means that unless I'm sitting at the controls, you only get about a third of the powers you might otherwise. Which, has its pluses actually. The machine kills one in four test subjects when I operate it. More, if they've fully completed puberty—don't ask me why. When it operates without me the fatality rate drops to less than one in a hundred."

"But won't that leave us too weak to fight the Kith'ara? Why didn't Backflash try to make it better?"

"Because she wants you weak, at least to start with. It makes you easier to control and train, and it forces you to learn to work together. Look at how you got into the vault. None of you could have broken in alone like I did—well, except maybe Burnish if she didn't mind making a lot of noise. You were forced to work together, to form a team, like an army unit. Backflash and OSIRIS want you all doing things that way. Not like the mavericks of my generation. She felt we were 'too individualistic and too emotionally scarred by the half-million deaths that gave us birth.'"

Rand's entire body stiffened when he quoted Backflash, and something like hate flashed in his eyes.

"There's more though," I said. "Isn't there? Something else about us being weaker." Then I remembered Mike telling me why they never used the memory ray on metas, how it could amp up our powers, or, kill us. "Oh, the memory ray."

"Exactly. A very brief application will usually increase powers. Longer exposure grants more powers, or changes them."

"Or blows us up like human bombs."

"Possibly, yes. Even a short dose isn't safe. The death rate climbs back up. One in eight, or higher." He rubbed his temples. "God, I wish I could have a real drink."

I had another flash of understanding. "It was bittersharp."

"What?" he asked.

"When you learned about the aliens, and what Backflash was doing. *That's* why you started drinking."

"No. Learning that the woman I was working for had murdered my father really hurt me. But that wasn't what turned me into an alcoholic. That was Captain Commanding. You see, our beloved *Captain* knew about the Hero Bomb all along. Backflash let him in on the secret almost from day one. He knew it all and he never told me. He thought it was worth it. Not because Backflash was here to save the world, mind you. No, he thought it was worth it to create him.

"I found out when Backflash caught me in the vault—she

brought him along as back up. I confronted him later. When he explained how he felt about the bomb I wanted to kill him. I wanted to kill him sooooo bad. I could have, too. I've got a special gun I built just for that."

"Why didn't you?" I asked. "Kill him, I mean?" I was horrified and fascinated.

"Because he wasn't wrong. Neither was Backflash. The aliens are out there, and they're probably coming to Earth. Even if we win, they're going to kill millions. And Captain-freaking-Commanding is one of the best weapons we have. If I kill him, I'm killing every single person he might otherwise have saved. Likewise, Backflash. I can't do anything to stop her, not unless I want to build an annex to the trophy room to give me enough wall space for all those extra names."

Rand hid his face in his hands then. I put one hand on his shoulder because I thought he might be crying and I didn't know what else to do. I had been so angry when I came in, and now . . . now I didn't even know what I felt.

23

M-Day

There's something about school lunch. No matter how horribly your week is going, a trayful of gray glop can bring you down even further.

"What is this stuff?" I spooned up a glob and let it fall back onto my plate.

"Kith'aran goulash maybe?" replied Speedslick.

"Good one," said NightHowl.

Blurshift chuckled. Emberdown rolled her eyes. Blindmark pretended like he didn't know why he was sitting with us, which is to say, he acted like he always did. The odd one out was Burnish. She looked like she had a rash and she didn't know how to get rid of it.

"I can't believe I'm sitting with you losers," she said finally.

"So, don't," snapped NightHowl. "Go find yourself a place at the borderline-psychos table."

Burnish clenched one copper-colored fist. "I am so going to enjoy beating the living daylights out of you at some point, 'Howl."

I found myself rubbing my forehead. "Could we save all the posturing for some other time? We've got much more important things to worry about."

"Like what?" demanded Blurshift. "Foxman was right. There's nothing we can do with all the stuff we learned that won't make things worse. It's too much for us."

"Don't you think people should know about the aliens and the Hero Bomb? Or why it's so easy for Hoods to bust out of jail?" I asked.

"No." Blindmark spoke for the first time, his voice flat and angry. "Are you any happier for knowing all that stuff, Evan? Knowing it, and knowing that there's nothing you can do about it? Because I'm sure not any happier. "

I looked down at my plate. He had a point. I *wasn't* any happier. Things were all screwed up and I had no idea what to do about any of it. I shook my head. "I guess not."

Blindmark picked up his tray—he hadn't touched the main dish. "See you around." He walked away.

"I'm out of here, too," said Blurshift. "It's been fun, but not really worth it."

Emberdown followed. "Next time you have a smart idea about breaking into a top-secret OSIRIS facility, leave me out of it, Quick. One pointless, potential black mark on my record is more than enough."

Burnish shook her head, but she got up, too. "Later, losers. I'm glad we did it, and I'm glad I know. I've always known my dad was a rat, and it's nice to know just how big of one, but, well, I don't actually like any of you. Look me up if you learn anything new or if you want to try cracking more of the system. Otherwise, expect me to push your face in if you get in my space."

I looked at NightHowl and Speedslick. "You two gonna bail on me as well?"

'Howl shrugged. "Nah. Interesting stuff seems to happen around you. I like interesting."

Speedslick leaned over and punched my shoulder companionably, but didn't say anything. I looked down at my plate again, but for a different reason this time. I'd never really had friends before, and I was actually a little choked up about having them now.

It was weird, considering that I knew the answers to some of the biggest mysteries in the Mask world, but things kind of settled into a routine over the next couple of weeks. You can only worry about invading aliens and possibly villainous time-traveling Masks from the future for so long before it becomes just another thing you know and have to deal with.

In the short term, it didn't matter nearly as much as doing well in my classes and internship, or hanging with my newfound friends, or trying to repair my relationship with my parents—I was now spending Sunday and Monday nights at home.

I didn't tell my parents about the aliens or Backflash and the Hero Bomb either. It would only have made them worry about me and my future even more. It was weird having such a big secret from my parents, but after the huge blowup when I became a Mask I didn't want to put any more strain on them.

Things *definitely* weren't back to normal there. My mother

kept looking at me worriedly whenever I turned away, and my dad . . . Well, it was like someone had flipped a switch. Before our dinner with Foxman, he'd been angry with OSIRIS and with me. After? Well, he never said it where my mom could hear him, but I think he was secretly proud to have a Mask in the family.

Things with Foxman continued pretty much the same way as they had from day one. He drank tons of MaskerAde, stayed awake, and ran around like a maniac for days at a time, then sugar crashed and slept the clock around. On the days he was awake we snuck out and busted ordinary criminals and the occasional minor Hood. In addition to the Fromagier, we took down the Rugsucker, Master Mosquito, Chinchilla, and the Haberdasher. Rand actually felt pretty bad about that last one, since he'd gone to private school with the guy. He told me the Haberdasher's real name was Michael Damian, or something like that, and he insisted we offer him a running start.

I spent hours and hours learning all the Foxgear because Rand wanted me to be able to operate every last bit of equipment, or at least all of it that would work for anyone that wasn't him. Even at 32 percent efficiency, things like the Foxblaster packed a heck of a wallop, and he didn't want me caught off guard if I had to use them. He also made me a set of cybernetically augmented Meerkat armor.

I was no technokinetic, so it couldn't do nearly as much as his did. No flying, no built-in sonic blaster, no cutting lasers. But it did give me about six hundred pounds of hyper-dense poly-ceramic armor, and enough of a strength boost to move around with it on when my own superstrength–lite happened to be working properly.

I wasn't nearly as agile as I was in my normal suit, and that didn't thrill me. Also, if my metamuscles cut out on me while I had the armor on, it pretty much turned me into the world's fanciest turtle. That wasn't any fun at all and it happened more than once. But I kept at it. After catching a direct blast in the face from Spartanicus without any protection and spending the next week in a cocoon, the idea of armor that could soak up the worst of that kind of damage had real appeal.

I actually spent a lot of time thinking about Spartanicus. Mostly because reports about him and his little band of Hoods kept popping up on the Foxsnooper—both on regular law enforcement bands and the secret OSIRIS scrambled channels. The latter were especially tantalizing, as they included the occasional eyes-on report.

It was clear Spartanicus was planning something big, but nobody seemed to know what. Sometimes, though, I felt like I was the only one who cared. When I mentioned it to Minute Man, he shrugged and said, "Spartanicus is always planning something big. It's what he does." Foxman actually seemed to semi-admire his old adversary and told me, "It's probably another plot to kill Captain Commanding. The man's obsessed. And, frankly, more power to him. I won't kill Captain Commanding, but I'll sure pay for an open bar and a dance band at the funeral."

I couldn't let it go that easily. Spartanicus scared me. There's something about having someone kill you that really leaves an impression. So I paid special attention to those reports, and I started putting together an electronic chart with all the sightings and news linked together by little lines of light and hypertexted to summaries of the reports. I kept it on the new secure laptop Foxman built for me. It had a secret second drive and operating system that tied directly into Denmother and the Foxservers.

That's pretty much where things sat as the days ticked slowly by. Well, right up until the morning of Metamorphosis Day, when everything went kablooie.

M-Day started like most school mornings, with all of us kids slouching off to the cafeteria for breakfast. That's where the normal ended though, because we weren't alone. The Masks and Hoods had already started to arrive. We'd known to expect them, of course. But being told that every Mask and most Hoods were coming your way was entirely different from seeing Sprintcess Speed having a quiet cup of coffee in your lunchroom with Minute Man and the Haberdasher.

"I thought you said that you and Foxman caught him," Speedslick whispered to me, as I pointed out the Haberdasher.

"We did, I don't know what he's doing here."

NightHowl joined us then. "I asked Mike about that, because the Manchurian Mambo's right over there," she pointed. "He was arrested two days ago in my hometown. Even knowing what we do, I didn't think metamaxes were quite that easy to get out of."

"What did Mike say?" I asked.

"Any Hood who asks for an M-Day release in order to come up for the ceremony will probably get one. The main exceptions are the genuine psychopaths—Hoods like Cannibal Carnie who can't be trusted outside of a padded cell without a muzzle and leash."

"Isn't he the guy who tried to bite off Captain Commanding's ear a couple years ago?" asked Speedslick.

"That's him," said 'Howl.

"I wonder who all will be here?" I said as my inner Mask nerd realized it had died and gone to heaven.

"Everybody," said Burnish, who had slipped up behind us without any of us noticing. "That's the point, mushbrain."

I barely noticed the insult, as I was too busy mentally ticking names off my big list of Masks and Hoods. I felt like a bird watcher who realizes they're about to knock off most of their life list in a single morning. I insisted we move to one of the tables along a wall facing the door so I could see everyone come in.

After breakfast, the others got bored, but I wasn't going anywhere for anything. Not even when we had the whole day off to do whatever we liked. Nope. I settled in for the *long* haul. The memorial happened at four, and I wasn't planning on moving one minute before I had to.

At least, that was my initial plan, but when the lunch crowd came in, I realized something. There were a *lot* of missing Hoods. Hoods that I knew were in prison, either from my hours with the Foxsnooper, or from the time I spent noodling around on Mask sites on the Web. At first, that didn't seem too odd even with the release day. Prison, after all. But I couldn't help but notice that it was disproportionately the smarter and more powerful Hoods who were missing. Something about that bothered me.

I decided I'd better go see what I could find out. There were a ton of strangers in the halls of the AMO. Well, strangers in the sense of being people I didn't personally know, though I recognized most of the uniforms. The more I wandered the school, the more certain I became that a lot of important Hoods were missing. High on that list were Spartanicus and his crew.

I would have liked to talk with Mike about it, but he'd left the lunchroom before I had and he wasn't in his office or anywhere else I could find him. I eventually headed back to my dorm to see if Denmother might be able to help out. The room was empty when I arrived, so I grabbed my laptop and hopped onto my bunk where I typed in a quick query about meta traffic through OSIRIS headquarters.

Denmother told me that the information I wanted was restricted and that it would take several minutes for her to attempt to retrieve it for me. As I was waiting, Speedslick came in swearing.

"What's up?" I asked.

"Spilled soda all over my best uniform," he said disgustedly. "I need to change back into civvies while I clean it up." He started yanking on his shoulder tabs.

He was about half peeled out of his shirt when the holographic projector on my laptop blinked on, putting a glowing, translucent Foxman in the center of the room.

"Evan, I noticed that subroutine you had Denmother running and took a look myself. There's something hinky about the footage I'm getting out of OSIRIS's security camera system. That worries me. I wonder if you'd be willing to nab a ride down on one of the returning transport shells and walk around in front of a couple of the cameras for me. I'd do it myself, but I can make adjustments to the tap line program much better from this end where I have direct access to Denmother. Besides, if I go in and don't get directly on the first available shell, people are likely to take notice—given my ambiguous security clearance status."

"Uh, sure, I guess. Won't anybody notice me shuttling down?"

"Not today. There are only a half-dozen shells for the gravito-metric accelerator transport system. With all the traffic going up, they're going to be cycling as fast as the system will let them fire the empties back to Earth. Just hop into one as it unloads a pile of metas. You won't even need to use your ring for travel authoriza-tion. And as long as you don't go beyond the transport depot, nobody will pay any attention to one more uniform going up for the M-Day memorial either when you come back."

"*Two* more uniforms." Speedslick blurred out of his good uniform and into a ratty-looking older one. "That sounds way more interesting than hanging around here with all the geeze-roids complaining about how we don't measure up to the old standards."

Foxman's projected figure turned its head. "You must be Speedslick. I do wish Evan had mentioned he wasn't alone *before* I blabbed about illegal taps into OSIRIS's systems. Bad form, Meer-kat. However, since he didn't, I might as well get the best use out of you. With two of you and your speed powers, I should be able to calibrate off multiple cameras simultaneously. That'll give me a much better read on the data. Now, get moving, I don't like that I can't trust what I'm seeing out of OSIRIS."

A few minutes later, Jeda and I were slipping quietly along one of the utility access halls on our way to the transport station. One big benefit of our efforts to map the station was that we knew more about its back ways than probably anybody but Backflash and the aliens who built it. The plan was to hide out on the utility side of the ventilation grill just across from the transport arrival platform. We could wait there until a likely shell came along. We were about to round the last corner before climbing into the ductwork when I heard a couple of girls' voices ahead.

The first sounded angry and maybe a little scared. "I have well and truly had it with you, Burnish. Let's settle this."

"If that's really the way you want it, 'Howl, I'm not going to keep saying no." Burnish seemed more resigned than pissed off, though, which struck me as really strange. "But remember when you're in traction that it was your idea to meet me here for a callout."

"We'd better stop them," Jeda whispered. " 'Howl's my friend and way tough, but Burnish will tear her to pieces."

I nodded. NightHowl might have vocal chords that could shatter steel—when they worked perfectly, which wasn't all that often—but she simply wasn't in Burnish's league. The question was how best to shut this down. Then I had an idea.

"Come on," I said loudly as I rounded the corner. "Foxman wanted us to get down to Earth as quickly as possible. This is important, so we shouldn't keep him . . ." I trailed off when I looked up and met Burnish's eyes.

"What are you up to now, Quick?" she asked me, and I swear I saw relief in her expression—like she really didn't want to beat the daylights out of NightHowl for some reason. "More breaking and entering at OSIRIS high-security facilities? Because, I could be up for that."

"Uh, no. Nothing like that. We're just out for a walk, right, Jeda?"

"Wha—I mean, sure." Speedslick looked very confused, but he went with it. "Whatever you say, Evan."

"You two are the worst liars I've ever seen," said NightHowl. "You might as well tell us what's up now and get it over with. Otherwise, I'll have to beat it out of you." She still sounded angry, but like she was getting it under control.

Burnish very visibly clenched her fists. "I'll help."

"All right, all right." I held up my hands. "There's something funny going on with the cameras down at OSIRIS headquarters in Heropolis. Foxman asked us to take a look."

"Us?" Burnish looked skeptical. "That seems a bit unlikely."

"He thought it would be better if Evan didn't try to handle it alone," said Speedslick. "He seemed worried."

"Then we're going with you," said Burnish.

NightHowl nodded, then looked angrily at Burnish. "But don't think you and I are done."

Burnish shrugged. "It's your funeral, honey."

A few minutes later we were looking out through the grill at the incoming transport gate. The arrival well was a perfect mirror of the facility at OSIRIS headquarters, complete with black floor and that same eerie inertial damping effect. The first two shells that came in were absolutely packed, which made the platform way too busy to sneak across. By the time it cleared out the shells had already been picked up and loaded onto the conveyers above.

"We might have a problem," NightHowl whispered to me.

I shrugged. "Let's wait and see. If they're all this full, maybe

Burnish can do her sliding-through-wires thing, and hold one up for us."

"Or," said Speedslick, "if we get one with less of a crowd on board, I might be able to zip across and hit the hold button without being spotted. The alarm doesn't sound for a couple of minutes."

"How likely is that?" asked Burnish. "It's M-Day. They're all going to be packed."

That's when the next shell opened, and we could all see the lone individual standing in the exact center of the transport.

"Of course." Burnish's voice came out like pure acid. "Who proves me wrong? My dad. Coming in all by his lonesome. And why? Because there isn't enough room in one of those things for him, his ego, and another single human being."

Captain Commanding slowly sauntered out of the transport shell.

"Whatever the reason, this is our chance," I hissed as the Captain stepped away from the closing door. "Speedslick, go!"

The ventilation grill flipped up as soon as the Captain turned toward the exit and Speedslick blurred across the platform. He nipped between the closing doors of the shell and hit the back with an audible thud. The Captain looked over his shoulder, but by then the shell doors had all but finished closing, and there was nothing to see. He glanced around suspiciously, but I had eased the grill into place before it could bang shut.

He frowned, but finally just shook his head and went on through the outer doors. They had barely closed before I slipped out onto the platform followed by Burnish and 'Howl. Burnish was first to the transport, placing a palm against the dull steel of the doors and shifting color to match. She slid her fingertips into the tiny gap left open when Speedslick had hit the hold button and slowly forced it wider.

It froze at around eight inches and she couldn't get it any farther, which made for a bit of a squeeze, but we all managed it. Speedslick released the hold button as soon as NightHowl followed me through. The lights went out when the door closed behind Burnish, because no one was supposed to be in the shell when the conveyers moved it over to the launch cannon. Now, as long as no one had picked this particular shell to catch a ride back to Earth in, we were home free.

Given the way traffic was flowing, I wasn't all that worried, but I do admit to breathing easier once I felt the gravitic accelerator cannon take hold of our darkened shell to fling us back toward Earth.

24

Blackout

"Now what?" Burnish asked me as we stepped out into the arrival well.

"Now we get in front of a couple of security cameras and wave nicely for Foxman so that he can calibrate the system."

"That's it?" She raised both her eyebrows.

"That's it." I walked to the nearest camera and waved both my arms.

"So what do you need us for?" she demanded. "I mean, I'm plenty happy to skip the inevitable fight my parents are going to have whenever HeartBurn gets to the memorial, but this seems kind of anticlimactic. What was Foxman so worried about?"

I didn't have a good response for her question—Speedslick had just made up the bit about him being worried on the spot. And I *really* didn't know what to say about the sudden revelation of her mother's identity. I was still trying to think of an answer ten seconds later when the lights went out.

"What the heck?" asked Speedslick.

"I don't know, but . . ." I trailed off suddenly because I had just taken a step, and my foot came down with a distinct clunk. "Uh-oh."

"What?" NightHowl asked.

"I think the inertial damping field just cut out," I whispered.

"What does that mean?" asked Speedslick.

"Run!" I yelled as several pieces of the science Foxman had been pounding into my head came together to form a really ugly picture. I activated the Foxlight at my waist as I started running. "If another shell comes in now, there's nothing to slow it down. It's going to hit like a freaking meteor strike!"

"We can't outrun that," squeaked NightHowl.

"No," I agreed. "But, if we're very lucky, whoever built this place thought of that, and put in some really heavy-duty blast containment. If so, getting out of the well might save our lives. If not, thanks for being my friends, all of you." Then I was all out of breath for anything but running.

Now I know what Armageddon sounds like. As we ran into the hallway that led away from the landing well, we had to duck under a slowly descending slab of Indestructabilium that was over three feet thick. There was still no power, so the system was probably a simple gravity-driven emergency measure triggered by the blackout. Two really, since a second slab was closing off the other end of the short hallway.

For that one we had to throw ourselves flat and slide. Night-Howl couldn't have had more than three inches to spare when she came through at the back of the pack. As soon as Burnish and I yanked her back to her feet, we started running again. We made it maybe another thirty feet before the world came to an end.

BOOOOOOOOOOOOOOOOOOOOOOOOOOOOM!

I can't even begin to describe the noise as it really was: unimaginably big and loud and long, like being inside a tree that's just been struck by chain lightning—thunder, and the sky falling—and a wave of sound that hit like someone breaking a board across your face. The ground leapt and twisted. I fell, bouncing and sliding like a stone skipping across the surface of a lake.

I stopped when I ran into a portion of the ceiling that had collapsed, and I had a vague awareness of NightHowl or Burnish piling into me from behind. I'd lost track of Speedslick by then. He kept running ahead and then coming back to try to hurry us along and I had no idea which side of the cave-in he was on.

Then the world went away.

When it came back, I was lying on my back and staring up into a pair of deep green eyes from a distance of about six inches. The light was very dim and full of concrete dust.

"B-burnish," I coughed—my throat was dry, packed with that same dust and worse.

The eyes blinked, and I saw more filth caked on her lids. "Yeah." Her voice sounded terribly distant, and I reached up to touch my right ear.

I wanted to check both, but my left arm didn't seem to work right. When I touched my ear, a big chunk of scabweb fell out. "Are we dead?"

"Not yet, Quick. Not quite." I could hear her better now, and reached across to my other ear, removing another big chunk of scab-stuff.

"Good."

"Can you do me a favor?" There was strain in her voice.

"Probably. What do you want?"

"I need you to see if you can slide out past my knees."

It was only then that I realized that Burnish was more or less crouched atop me, with one arm on either side of my head, and her knees straddling my waist just below where the light shone up between us. There was a chunk of I-beam across her shoulders and what looked like a slab of concrete on top of that.

"Did you save my life?" I asked.

"Maybe. A lot depends on whether there's a way out down by my feet. Speaking of which, could you get moving? Because this rubble is really astonishingly heavy, and when I dived on top of you I didn't have time to get set properly."

"Oh. Thanks. I, uh, thanks." I tried moving my foot, and was pleased when it seemed to work. I started to slide myself downward, but paused after a couple of inches.

"Is something wrong?" she asked, and I could definitely hear the strain this time.

"No, I guess I . . . You don't even like me!"

"Not really, no."

"Then, why?" I asked.

"Do we really have to have this conversation right now?" she demanded.

"I want to know, in case we don't make it out of this."

"Fine, but if we get squashed I'm going to blame you."

"Fair enough."

"It's because of what you said after 'Run!' Are you happy now? Can we go?"

"About the meteor?"

"No. After that."

"I don't . . ."

Burnish closed her eyes, and I could see her practically counting to ten. "You thanked us all for being your friends, and you did it with what you thought might be your last breath."

"Well, yeah. In my old school I didn't really have anyone I cared about, but I still can't see what—"

"Quick!"

"Yes?"

"Shut it for five seconds. I don't have a lot of friends—well, any really. You're not my favorite person in the world, and you piss me off a lot, but you called me your friend when it really mattered. So, when I saw the ceiling about to fall on you, I decided that I should maybe keep you from getting squashed. Now, will you *please* quit talking and move?"

"All right." And then, because I'd never done it before and I didn't know if I'd ever get another chance, I lifted my head and kissed my first girl.

It was awkward, and she only barely kissed me back, and when we were done she shook her head and muttered, "Idiot." But it didn't sound nearly so angry as I'd expected.

I started inching my way downward at that point, turning on my side to get past her knees. As my head slid past her ankle I felt someone grab on to my feet and start pulling. A half second later I was lying on my back in an open section of the hallway with NightHowl and Speedslick each holding on to one of my legs. A sudden crunching behind my head made me look back in time to see the rubble mound settle abruptly, filling the hole I'd just come out of.

"Burnish!"

Before I could get too panicked, a purplish ball of plasma emerged from a broken conduit end, shaping itself into a copper-skinned girl. She stepped closer and glared down at me.

"Quick."

"Yes."

"I'm going to forgive you this once. But if you ever kiss me again without me asking you to first, I'm going to pull your lips off and feed them to you. Seriously, not cool. Is that perfectly clear?"

"Yes." And not just the threat part. She was right. It wasn't cool. It was pure impulse, and bad manners at the very least. "Crystal clear. I'm sorry."

"Good."

I raised a finger. "One question?"

"Now what?"

"Is there any chance you're going to ask me?"

"What do you think?"

"No."

"Good answer. Now, let's see if we can get out of here somehow."

NightHowl dropped my leg. "You kissed Burnish?"

"Uh, yeah. Moment of madness."

"Ewwww!"

I looked at Speedslick, who simply shook his head.

At that point, I was saved from further embarrassment by the sound of the Foxphone ringing.

"Meerkat here." I rolled my eyes as I said it, but Foxman had insisted I use that phrase when he keyed in the voice recognition prompt.

"Are you all right?" said the voice from my earbud—I switched it over to external speakers so the others could hear. "I'm on my way."

"Yeah, I think so. Nothing feels broken anyway. My left arm doesn't like me much, but it's cocooned and it'll be back to normal in a few minutes."

"Where have you been? Your phone's been registering as blocked or destroyed ever since the blast hit."

"That'd be my fault," said Burnish. "In steel form I tend to block transmission."

"Is that Burnish?" asked Foxman. "Why is she with you?"

"Long story. Do you have any idea what's going on? Why did everything go black?"

"Another long story. Short version, Spartanicus is making his move. Step one was taking out the only way for the metas on Deimos to get back to Earth in anything less than six months. It was supposed to happen during the memorial. But when you waved for the camera, he must have realized someone else had noticed the security system was compromised, so he hit the go button. I was able to trace that back and hack his system, but it was already too late to do anything more than grab his plans and trip into his communications."

"Spartanicus is here somewhere?" I asked, and my voice squeaked embarrassingly when I said his name.

"Not yet. HeartBurn is the one who killed the lights. But he's on his way there now. There aren't many Masks still on Earth, but nearly all of them are either at OSIRIS headquarters or en route, and hitting them while they're still dazed from that orbital strike is Spartanicus's best chance at taking over Heropolis."

"How bad is the damage?" asked Speedslick.

"Bad," replied Foxman, "but it could have been a lot worse. The impact-protection system focused much of the force back up into the sky—that's why the landing well is shaped the way it is, to channel blasts upward. But the city still got hit with something like a magnitude-six earthquake and it's not built for that. A lot of people died today."

I felt my throat clench. "My parents?" I couldn't help but ask.

"Are fine, I checked."

"Good." I didn't ask for the others. Neither NightHowl nor Speedslick were local to Heropolis, and we already knew where Burnish's dad was, to say nothing of her mother—OMG!

My speaker made a strange crackling noise followed by Foxman's voice saying, "Uh-oh."

"What is it?" I asked.

"The OSIRIS air defense systems just locked a phalanx of surface-to-air missiles on the *Flying Fox*, and my computer tap is detecting multiple launch orders."

"Can you dodge them?"

"Not a chance. I'll be bailing out with my suit cold to avoid retargeting in about seventeen seconds here."

"What should *I* do?"

"Hold there, I'm going to launch your armor pod on ballistic with a homing beacon when I bail out. You are not to move from the spot or do anything at all until you are fully suited up. That's a direct order."

"You're not going to tell me to sit this out?"

"Of course not, you're my sidekick. You belong at my si—"

Denmother's voice cut in, "Pod launched, eject, eject, eject!"

Then the line went dead.

"Now what?" asked Speedslick, who had started bouncing off the walls—literally.

"We get in the game," I said.

Someone had shot down my hero, and they were going to pay. My childhood Mask dreams had never put me in the role of sidekick, and I'd been horribly disappointed when Speedslick first explained the situation at the AMO. Even more so when I was assigned to Foxman. But over the past few months I'd come to like and respect the man. If he needed me, I owed it to him to be there.

"I'll see if I can't find us a way out," said Burnish. "And hope I don't run into my mother."

"About that—" I said.

"Don't ask." Burnish's shoulders slumped. "She was very young, my dad is a jerk, and she never wanted anything to do with me because of him. She dropped me off at the doorway to OSIRIS about ten hours after she gave birth to me. We don't talk. We don't write. We simply don't." Then she flashed into plasma and slid into another conduit end.

I tapped the phone key on my cowl. "Denmother, can you tell me anything about Foxman?"

"He went into the river suit cold and then went to stealth mode. I have no further information."

"What about my armor pod?"

"Initial launch was ballistic and it avoided all missiles before engaging rocket and activating nap-of-Earth flight mode. It should be at your location"—a tremendous *whung* noise from somewhere above cut Denmother off for a moment—"now, Master Quick."

One corner of the fractured ceiling bulged downward and fell in as a coffin-size steel lozenge dropped into the other end of the hall with a metallic *clang*. Burnish was riding it like a bucking bronco, and she jumped free as it rolled to a stop a few yards away from me.

She grinned at all of us through the fresh wave of dust. "Saw this coming in fast, and figured it'd make the perfect door knocker if I gave it a little boost."

NightHowl shook her head. "I'm sure glad my sonic powers come with major ear protection."

I'd wondered about that, and Speedslick as well—Burnish in steel form was practically indestructible. But I didn't have time to indulge my curiosity. I had to get into my armor so I could get to where I needed to be—backing up Foxman, because he was my hero and that's what sidekicks do. I reached over and put my thumb on the locking panel of the armor pod.

It split open like a clamshell, with the front half of my armor in the top and the back in the bottom. The armor itself was likewise blown open, rather like an unfurled flower. I quickly laid down in the pod and let the servo motors close me up. Ten seconds later, I had six hundred pounds of protection wrapped around me and it was time to move.

Burnish was first out of our little slice of tunnel, since she was by far the toughest. Speedslick bolted after her. I'd planned on going second, but it's hard to outmaneuver a speedster. But just as I started up through the passage opened by the armor pod, Speedslick came tumbling right back down again and I barely caught him. He was unconscious, with blood streaming from his nose and ears. Shaking him didn't wake him, but he seemed otherwise unhurt and we had to move on. So, I set him on the ground and headed up to see what the heck had happened to Burnish.

Things got a little blurry after that as I plunged into the maelstrom of a full-on metawar. There were dozens of Hoods and about a third as many Masks, all blasting away at each other with every kind of bioweapon you could imagine, and quite a few that you probably can't, to say nothing of the various guns, lasers, swords, and other more conventional weapons.

I wish I could describe it in any detail, but it was so loud and crazy and bright that I couldn't force the scene to make any sense at all. All I can say is that it was like the opening minutes of a really complex, new first-person Mask game, where you get flashes and bits, but you know that you're not going to stay alive for long if you try to do anything besides keep your head down.

I'd have been KO'd quick if Denmother hadn't started

313

feeding me tactical info as soon as I hit the surface. And this wasn't a game where I'd get a respawn; this was real. She started with the fact that some of the Hoods I'd missed at the M-Day festivities up on Deimos had arrived on the scene—mostly the ones from the nearest metamax.

Despite the danger, I knew we had to head for the thickest fighting. That was where we'd find Spartanicus and, with him, Foxman. We started moving immediately, though we did take the circuitous route Denmother recommended. That meant backing away from the central building and circling behind three towers that might once have been grain elevators.

Somewhere along the way NightHowl ended up with a twenty-inch spike of synthetic ivory driven through her thigh and went down with a bone-shattering shriek. Literally. She pulverized the bones in her attacker's legs with her scream.

"'Howl!" I yelled, kneeling beside my fallen friend.

"I'll get her clear," said Burnish. "You go find Foxman." Then she picked up NightHowl and started running back the way we'd come.

I was alone.

And getting very close to the center of the fighting. I slowed down and activated Foxameleon mode on my armor once I saw the open campus that centered the OSIRIS compound. The supercapacitors in my suit couldn't sustain active Foxouflage for long, or I'd have done it sooner. The armor-glass roof over the sunken plaza of the central building had mostly caved in. It was a surreal view. The remaining shards maintained their camouflage, making a sharp contrast to the view down into the plaza below.

Flareup came roaring in over the featureless black cube that anchored the northern edge of the campus just then, surfing an incandescent wave of plasma. She slowed down as she soared over the open well of the plaza and fired off a series of energy blasts, then started to accelerate away again. Before she could clear the edge of the giant hole, three precisely placed bolts of green lightning hit her in the chest and face.

The plasma wave died and Flareup tumbled through the air, spiking herself on a long spear of armor glass at the lip of the pit. She didn't even scream. She simply stopped moving, and I had to look away.

I crept toward the nearest edge of the fallen-in roof, moving as quietly as I ever had. The green lightning told me all I needed to know about where Spartanicus was and the danger I was about to face. I was shaking inside my armor, but I didn't let that stop me. I didn't want to die again, but Foxman would be somewhere around here. I was his sidekick, and together we could do this.

When I reached the lip, I turned sideways and cautiously edged one eye out over a long crack between two jagged pieces of glass. Spartanicus stood in the exact center of the plaza below. Dozens of dead or unconscious Masks and Hoods lay scattered around him, including his henchmen Bagger and Mempulse, the former almost certainly dead. There was no sign of HeartBurn, the Fluffinator, or Mr. Implausible. I figured they were off implementing other elements of his plan, though there was more than enough rubble to hide any number of bodies.

Spartanicus was the only figure still upright, though he had a long bloody gash running from his right collarbone down to his left hip, and the Armex on the back of his cowl was visibly smoking. His head was whipping from side to side, as though he were looking for more enemies. I hadn't decided what to do next when a hand caught me by the ankle and yanked me back from the edge.

"Careful there, Meerkat," Foxman's voice whispered into my earpiece. "Your armor won't stand up to a direct hit from Spartanicus. Even with your Foxouflage that was a risky move. That armor glass is clear from below. Or, had you forgotten that?"

I felt my face flush and admitted, "Actually, I had."

I rolled over onto my back and looked up at Foxman. Well, looked for him, might be closer to the truth. He'd activated Foxameleon mode, too, so he mostly registered as a human-shaped blurry patch.

"Do we have a plan?" I asked.

"Not as such, no. And we have a serious problem. I had to fight my way here and that's burned off a big chunk of my suit's charge. With the whole compound powered down, and the *Flying Fox* a thin smear of flaming wreckage scattered across the river side of downtown, I can't recharge either. So I figure I've got about three minutes and change to take down Spartanicus once I actually engage him."

That was ugly. "Can you pull the remaining power from my armor?"

"I could, but that would leave you completely out of the fight, and only add eleven seconds of operational time to my suit. I think you're more valuable as you than playing battery for me. Also, I'd prefer it if you stayed in Foxameleon mode. Regardless of what Backflash knows or figures out, if there's any chance of you getting out of here without OSIRIS having to officially notice that you've been sidekicking without a permit, that'd be optimum."

"I'm not afraid of the consequences," I said defiantly.

"I am, and you should be, but I appreciate the sentiment. Look, we're running on draining batteries right now, so we don't have time to talk this out. I want you to stay up here. I'm going to give you the Foxblaster, but your capacitors will only sustain two, maybe three, shots at max power, so you have to make them count. Spartanicus is going to pound the living daylights out of me once I get in close, but I want you to hold fire until you get a clean shot at the back of his head. The Armex back there looks like it's sustained a lot of damage, and a head shot is the only way I know to be sure to take him down."

"Will it kill him?" My voice came out very small and squeaky, and I mentally kicked myself.

Foxman didn't seem to notice. "I wish. But, no, he's even tougher than Captain Commanding, if not as strong. It should knock him out though. I don't know if that will win us the fight, but taking down the general will sure as heck help. You ready?"

"Anytime you are, boss!" I chirruped.

Chirruped? Oh no, my overconfident banter superpowers seemed to be kicking in again. Wait, was that really a thing? Had becoming meta given my vocal cords a sort of suicidal life of their own? It would explain so very much. Or was it just narrative expectation built up by reading too many Mask comics?

"You hit him low, and I'll hit him high, Foxman! *Bam, pow,* and he's down!" No, my vocal cords were *definitely* out to get me.

"That's the spirit, Meerkat!" Foxman sounded more than a little like a man touched with superbanter himself. Maybe it was a thing. "Now, I'm on my way. Don't poke your head over the edge until he starts beating the stuffing out of me, and make sure that you hit him hard when you fire."

Then he was gone, and it was too late to do anything except wait for the fight below to start, and line up my shot.

Foxman went in smart and silent, taking a running jump, and then simply falling straight down toward Spartanicus. But somehow, despite his Foxouflage, the big Hood detected Foxman's presence. He stepped out of the way at the last minute and swung his sword around to bat Foxman halfway across the plaza. The blade bit into the armor over Foxman's hip. By luck or design-forethought the broken edges of the armor clamped down on the sword, wrenching it free of Spartanicus's grip.

Foxman landed hard and bounced, the Foxouflage flickering and shutting down as he smashed into a huge concrete planter. He staggered to his feet, pausing only long enough to snap the hilt off the sword embedded in his hip before charging back toward Spartanicus. I slid forward on my belly, carefully bringing the Foxblaster into position. But they moved so fast and hit each other with such force that I had real trouble following things, both in terms of what was going on and with the scope of the Foxblaster.

Then, almost as fast as it had begun, the fight seemed to be over. Spartanicus caught Foxman by thigh and shoulder, lifted him high over his head, and smashed him into the pavement hard enough to create a shallow Foxman-shaped crater. As Spartanicus raised his right foot high over Foxman's helmet I finally got my sights lined up and took my shot.

A beam of ropey red fire as thick around as my wrist sizzled out of the end of the blaster and smashed into the base of Spartanicus's skull, driving him to his knees. I dropped the barrel a fraction of an inch and fired again when the crosshairs touched the top of Spartanicus's head. This time, the blast actually tumbled him forward, rolling him across Foxman's fallen form and a dozen feet beyond.

As I tried to line up a third shot, Denmother's voice spoke in my ear: "Armor power at eight percent and falling, Master Quick. Cutting feed to all external units."

Below me, Spartanicus had dragged himself back onto hands and knees and was slowly turning to face Foxman.

"Wait, I need one more shot!" I yelled.

"Not possible, Master Quick. Apologies. Armor shut down in three—two—"

Spartanicus had finished his turn, and now he began to crawl back toward Foxman, drawing a dagger and tucking it between his teeth as he went.

"One," finished Denmother. "Armor shutdown initiated."

No! It couldn't end this way. Fear and fury raced along my nerves like an acid slurry—a burning concoction that seemed to kick my meager powers up to a higher gear. Somehow, despite the lack of servo assist, I forced myself upright and started slow-walking my way along the edge of the sunken plaza. I tried to gauge Spartanicus's progress with one eye, while focusing the other on the big support beams that crisscrossed the space above the plaza.

There!

I turned and started to edge out along one of the beams. It had been bent and twisted by the forces that had shattered the armor glass, but that actually put it in a better position. Now, if I could just manage not to fall off until I got to the right spot.

As I reached the point closest to directly above Spartanicus, I found myself thinking, *This is the dumbest idea you've ever had, Quick.*

Yes, brain voice, it is. I just hope armor-plus-healing factor is enough.

You and me both, Quick.

Then I was there. I took one last look and . . . jumped. It was a long fall, and I had plenty of time to second-guess myself on the way down. This time, Spartanicus didn't see it coming. I landed feet first on the back of his head, driving his face into the pavement. There was a huge green blast, and that was the last thing I remembered for a very long time.

25

Scenes From a Recovery

This time, I recognized the crinkling candy-wrapper sound of my healing cocoon coming apart.

"Hey, it's about time you came around." It was Foxman, or Rand, since I saw that he was out of costume as soon as my head broke through the cocoon.

"Where are we?" I asked.

Foxman used the arm that wasn't in traction to gesture around the room. "OSIRIS hospital, Heropolis. Why, what does it look like?"

"I would have expected you to get a private room," I said muzzily.

"And leave my sidekick? Never."

"That makes sense, I guess. But, you know what, I think I'm going to take a little nap now . . ."

⚡⚡

The next time I woke up, someone had removed all of the cocoon bits, and my mother was sitting beside the bed. There was a lot of hugging and crying and a little bit of yelling after that, but I don't think I'll share the details.

I woke to see Speedslick wheeling NightHowl into my room ahead of him. Her leg was raised up on one of those wheelchair brace thingies. Well, Jeda and Melody, given their civvies, but never mind.

"Glad to see you awake, amigo," said Speedslick.

"Glad to see you, too. *Both* of you, alive. You had me worried there, especially you, 'Howl."

"Ah, it wasn't as bad as it looked."

"How's Burnish?" I asked.

'Howl blushed. "Good. She's good."

"Why the red face?" I asked.

She turned an even deeper shade of red. "Well, I was little delirious there toward the end of things—not so sure I was going to make it."

I raised an eyebrow. "And?"

"I figured if it was a good idea for you to kiss her when you thought you were dying, it couldn't hurt for me to try."

"Really?"

"Yeah."

"How'd it work out?"

"Pretty much like yours did."

I blinked blearily as a small team of orderlies and nurses came into the room and started rigging Rand's bed for travel.

"What's up?" he asked.

"More tests," said the lead nurse.

"Needles?" He sighed.

"Lots."

"Stinking vampires."

"You know it," she said as they rolled him out.

I'd just started to drift back into sleep when the door opened again.

"Who is i . . ." I trailed off as another orderly wheeled a monitor up beside my bed. I recognized Backflash's face on the screen. "Oh, hi."

"Hello, Evan. You've given me quite a lot to think about these last few weeks. I've been keeping a close eye on you and your friends ever since that day you broke into my lab. That showed initiative and talent. Bravery, too, hiding under the console and then crawling away like that, never knowing whether I was about to turn and catch you. That was the moment I decided you were more of an opportunity than a problem. You haven't disappointed me yet."

I felt my chest sink in on itself. "You knew about that?"

"Please, child. Bittersharp keeps a record of everyone who comes in and it refuses to censor information in any way. Of course, I knew. In fact, I even traveled back in time a little way to see how you performed when dealing with the machine. Add in your insane attack on Spartanicus, and I expect great things from you."

"Does this mean I'm out of the AMO?" I asked quietly.

"Not at all."

"But I broke into your lab and I've been sidekicking without a license. Doesn't that kind of make me a"—my voice dropped—"Hood?"

"Well, yes, technically. I will certainly hold that option in reserve, though I frankly don't see how that would prevent you from doing great things. After all, Spartanicus is one of my proudest creations."

"He's a mass murderer!"

"So am I. It doesn't change things, and, honestly, our motives aren't that far apart. Special Agent Sanders wants to prepare for the aliens every bit as badly as I do. We just differ in opinion on how best to do that. We always have."

"Sanders?" I was getting more confused by the moment. "Who's that?"

"Spartanicus, of course. He was the OSIRIS agent assigned to oversee my project when I first arrived from the future. He disagreed with both me and his superiors about the morality and necessity of the Hero Bomb. He even tried to defuse it at the last minute—the blast tore him in half. If it hadn't also given him his powers, he'd have died then. But he heals better than anyone."

"I don't know what to think about that," I said. "Isn't he a villain?"

"To you and most of the rest of the world, certainly. In an absolute sense? Only time will tell. He hated the 'system of gladiatorial combat' I cooked up. That's why he took the Hood name that he did—as a direct challenge to me. He thinks we'd be better off announcing the coming invasion to the world and trying to unite all the metas under one banner, and that's what he keeps trying to do. He might even be right, but I don't think so."

She paused then, and checked something out of the picture. "But the monitors say that you're fading again, so I should let you sleep."

"Wait! I want to know why."

"Why what?"

"Why everything?"

"That's a big question, Evan. But the answer is simple. Because I have to. Because failure means the extermination of the human race. Because, in this case, results are all that matters if there's going to be a tomorrow for Earth. Now, good night, Evan."

I didn't say good night and I didn't think I'd be able to sleep anytime soon, but somehow I managed to doze off. Or, at least, that's what I had to assume from the way I jerked awake when I heard a very familiar voice say my name.

"Captain Commanding?" I said blearily. "Sir?"

In my dreams I'd wandered back to a simpler time in my life, before I got my powers and learned how much darker and stranger the world was than I'd ever believed. That's where the "sir" came from, the boy who'd once thought that the Captain was the best and greatest Mask the world had ever known.

"You're a durable little creep," the Captain said from the same monitor Backflash had used. "I'll give you that."

"And you're a monster!" I snapped back without thinking. "A horrible man with no moral core and no right to call yourself a Mask."

I was shocked at myself for saying it, and momentarily wondered if my banter reflex had kicked in again. But, no, this felt different. This was me all the way down, and it felt good to have a chance to tell the man who'd tried to have me blacklisted exactly what I thought about him.

The Captain's perfect smile twisted into something petty and vicious. "How dare you! I'm Captain Commanding, and you're a wretched little snot with nothing powers. You aren't fit to be my toilet paper."

"Why? Because I know that you're a coward who's more concerned that his precious reputation will get dented than he is about what the aliens might do to us if we don't have every available meta ready to face them? Is that why you think you're better than me?"

The Captain literally reared back at that, as though I'd slapped him. "You watch yourself, boy. You're not made of the kind of stuff that'll stand up to a single punch from one of these mighty fists." He held one hand up to the camera so that it filled the screen. "If you're not extra careful, you might find yourself as collateral damage in one of my future battles with evil."

Somehow, after facing Spartanicus three times and dying twice, being threatened by Captain Commanding just didn't have the same impact. He just didn't feel as dangerous as Spartanicus, or even Backflash. He was a cartoon, while they were the real thing. Oh, he could certainly kill me if he tried. There was no doubt about that, but I'd faced worse. Somehow I knew that if Captain Commanding came after me, I'd come out all right.

There was no remote to turn the monitor off, so I picked

up the heavy vase my mom's flowers had come in and pitched it right through the screen. There was a satisfying burst of sparks and that was the end of today's episode of the Captain Commanding show.

I was asleep before the orderlies arrived to clean up the mess.

It felt good to be up and around. The new and improved *Flying Fox* was waiting in my parents' backyard—it had squashed the rhododendrons—and I had just finished putting on my uniform. My mother was waiting for me by the back door with her usual lunch bag and a frown.

"I still don't like you going out there every night, honey."

"I know, Mom. And you're right."

"I am?" She looked surprised.

"You are. Thirteen is too young to make someone into a hero, or even a sidekick." I thought of my most recent screen conversation with Backflash. "It's not fair to you or to Dad or me." It would still be a couple of months before the bulk of Earth's Masks could return, and Backflash had called to let me know she was authorizing my sidekick's permit two years early.

"But, Mom, sometimes things aren't fair. Sometimes the world needs saving and the only one who can do it is someone who shouldn't have to." I still hadn't told them about the aliens— I didn't think they were ready for it. "Today, that's me." I leaned down and kissed her on the cheek. "I love you, Mom, and I promise I'll be careful, but I have to go now. Foxman's waiting."

Then I ducked out the door and climbed up into the cockpit.

As I settled into my seat, I looked over at Foxman and I decided that this whole sidekick thing was a pretty good gig.

Foxman reached for the liftoff button. "You ready to save the world, Meerkat?"

"Always."

It was, after all, my dream come true.

ACKNOWLEDGMENTS

Extra-special thanks are owed to Laura McCullough, Jack Byrne, Holly West, Jean Feiwel, and to Neil Gaiman for giving me the run of one of the larger comics libraries around.

Many thanks also to the Wyrdsmiths: Lyda, Doug, Naomi, Bill, Eleanor, Sean, and Adam. My Web guru, Ben. Kyle Cassidy for the barking cheese. Beta readers: Mike, Matt, Mandy, Sean, Hans, Carol, Kevin, Benjamin, Becky, Sari, Dave, Jason, Tom, Todd, Steph, Ben, other Ben. My family: Carol, Paul & Jane, Lockwood & Darlene, Judy, Kat, Jean, and all the rest. My extended support structure . . . and so many more. Thanks also to Kevin and Marilyn Matheny for agreeing to let me memorialize my dear friend Michael in the pages of this novel.

And finally, the Feiwel and Friends folks: Anna Booth, Rich Deas, Dave Barrett, Anne Heausler, Nicole Moulaison, and the rest of the group.

GOFISH

KELLY McCULLOUGH

Evan has always dreamed of being a hero. What did you want to be when you grew up?

All sorts of marvelous and ridiculous things when I was very young—a knight, a wizard, a mercenary on Tau Ceti. . . . Once I got to a place where I was seriously considering careers, what I wanted most was to be an actor. I went to a school with a really good arts program from about the middle of second grade to graduation, and from the age of eleven through college, I was very focused on theater, and that's what I ultimately got for my degree.

When did you realize you wanted to be a writer?

In my last year of college. I'd always gotten a lot of praise from teachers for my writing, probably even more than I got for my acting. By the time I was finishing up my degree, I'd had quite a lot of experience in theater, and while I was good, I knew that I'd probably never be good enough to make it in the movies or in a serious way on TV. Also, I'd burned out on the lifestyle, which involves a lot of working nights and weekends and endless travel. So, when I was trying to figure out what to do with my life, I tried writing a novel . . . and I fell in love with writing books.

What's your favorite childhood memory?

Probably having my mother and grandmother read to me. It's not one memory, but a whole series of them going back to my earliest awareness of being a person—a sort of never-ending story that ran from *Barney Beagle* through *Charlotte's Web* to *A Midsummer Night's Dream* and the Lord of the Rings.

When the book starts, Evan's favorite hero is Captain Commanding. As a young person, who did you look up to most?

My grandmother, Phyllis Neese. I had kind of a crazy child-hood. My mom and dad divorced when I was quite young, so I lived with my mother and my grandmother through a lot of moves, several schools, and a variety of other things that didn't make for a lot of security. Through all of that, my grandmother was the rock that sheltered and supported my family. She was wise and kind and tough as nails—she was one of the first women to go through her local technical college and get an electronics degree, and she ended up as a radio engineer and then a computer test equipment technician at a time when those jobs were unheard of for women.

What were your hobbies as a kid? What are your hobbies now?

I was an avid reader and a gamer, both role-playing stuff like Dungeons and Dragons and video games. That and I did a lot of roaming on foot and on my bike, just seeing what there was to be seen. These days, I still read and play video games, but I also do a bunch of physical stuff: hiking, biking, running, weightlifting, some martial arts. . . . I also travel as much and often as I can—so, still roaming around and seeing what there is to see.

Sadly, most schools don't yet have classes like Combat with Dinnerware. What was your favorite thing about the school you attended?

I went to the Saint Paul Open School, which was this amazing hippie-run place that encouraged us to be whatever we wanted and gave us enormous freedom to pursue our dreams. Attending formal classes was much less important than demonstrating that you were learning, and we usually had at least one free period per day built into our schedules to do whatever we wanted—within reason. The freedom was amazing and it came with an expectation of responsibility. It didn't work for every student, but it was perfect for me.

What book is on your nightstand now?

I've got around a dozen novels, two graphic novels, and a collection of cartoons from the Oatmeal. What I'm actively reading at the moment is one of the graphic novels in the Birds of Prey series and a pair of novels, Henry Beam Piper's *Uller Uprising* and Terry Pratchett's *The Shepherd's Crown*.

Where do you write your books?

I work on a chaise lounge these days in a beautiful, custom-built second-floor studio space that has windows on three sides so I can look out at the world while I work. I've always worked on a laptop with my feet up and as good a view of nature as I can manage. Desks drive me crazy.

What challenges do you face in the writing process, and how do you overcome them?

My biggest problem is usually distraction. I've always got a ton of stuff to do that isn't the current book. There's housework and e-mail and a social media presence to maintain, and a thousand other bits and bobs, and it's really easy to let those things eat into my writing time. The basic answer to how I overcome that is discipline. I make myself work even when I don't feel like it, usually by having a daily word quota. Of course, once I actually start writing, I generally lose myself in the process, because I love the job, but getting started is a pretty big hurdle some days.

Evan believes it is his job as a Mask and a sidekick to fight crime. What was your first job, and what was your "worst" job?
The first thing I did that was like a job was an internship at the Science Museum of Minnesota. I ran lights and sound for the educational skits, took tickets, answered questions about exhibits, etc. I did some other technical theater work as I got older, more lights and sound, opening and closing the theater. My first "job" job was installing communications systems—mostly running cable through ceilings and floors and then hooking it up. I've never really had an awful job, though delivering flyers wasn't much fun, and I did some pretty heavy physical labor while working as a temp that left me wiped out at the end of the day.

What is your favorite word?
Most days, it's *wombat*. But *rutabaga, tintinnabulation, troglodyte,* and *serendipity* are all up there. Oh, and *scuffle* and *scurry.*

If you could live in any fictional world, what would it be?
That depends on who I get to be there. If I'm one of the family, then Amber from Zelazny's the Chronicles of Amber, sometime after the first five books. If I'm me, I would want to be in Niven's Known Space, living on Earth. For me, the problem

with living in most fictional worlds is that the bigger the adventures, the worse the living conditions. I mean, I love the Harry Potter stories, but fundamentally, getting anywhere near Voldemort strikes me as not much fun, and the kind of magical bullying that happens at Hogwarts is pretty appalling.

What's the best advice you have ever received about writing?

Simply to write. Everything else is more or less author-specific, by which I mean that it works for some and not for others. And none of it matters if you don't get the words on the page in the first place.

What do you want readers to remember about your books?

That they had fun reading them. I put a lot of things into my work that are important to me—bravery and honor and love and duty—and I hope that many of them will be important to my readers as well. But, more than anything, I want my readers to have fun with my work and my worlds. I want them to enjoy their time with my words and to want to come back to them.

If you were a superhero, what would your superpower be?

Either persuasion or regeneration. I've always been freakishly good at talking people into things—the classic silver tongue—and when I was younger, I bounced back from injuries so well that people started calling it my mutant healing factor. There are lots of other powers that I'd love to have, but if I'm going to be honest, I have to point to those two things as the closest I've got to a superpower. At least, so far. Hopefully, it continues to hold.